Adventures in Cartooning

James Sturm
Andrew Arnold
Alexis Frederick-Frost

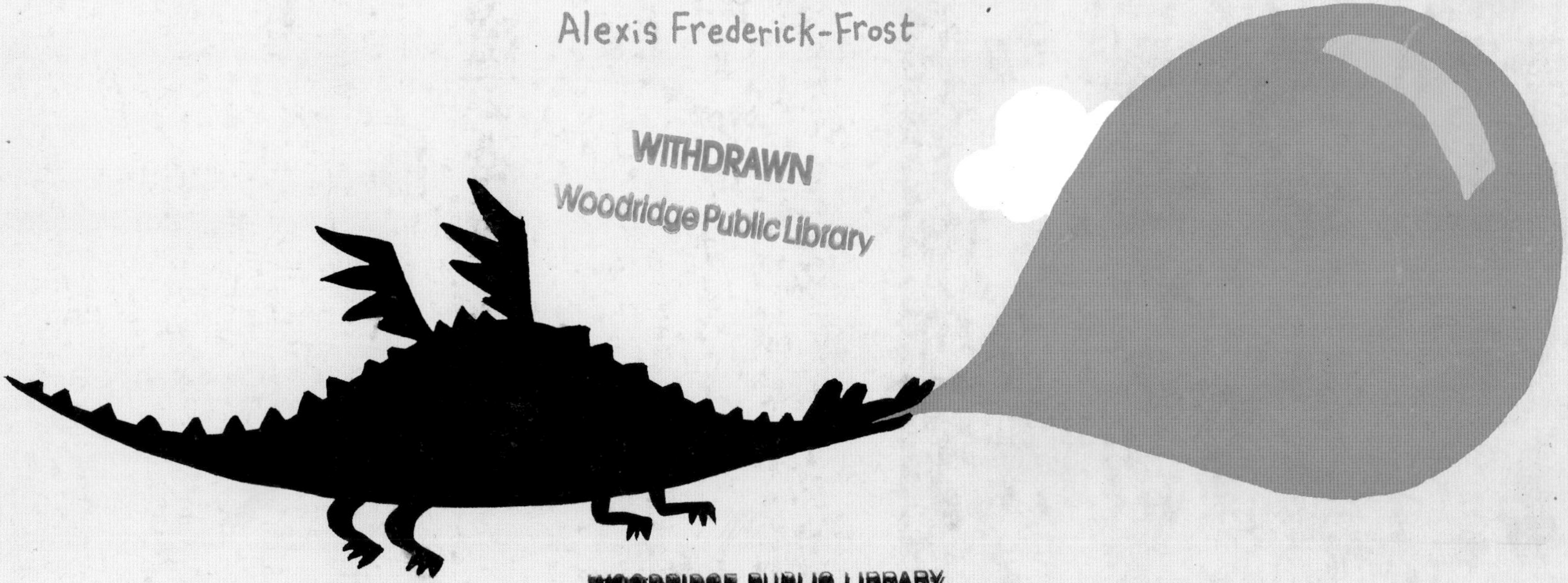

:01
First Second
New York & London

For Eva and Charlotte
-JS

For Mom and Dad
-AA

For Grandma, Leslie, Mom and Dad
-AFF

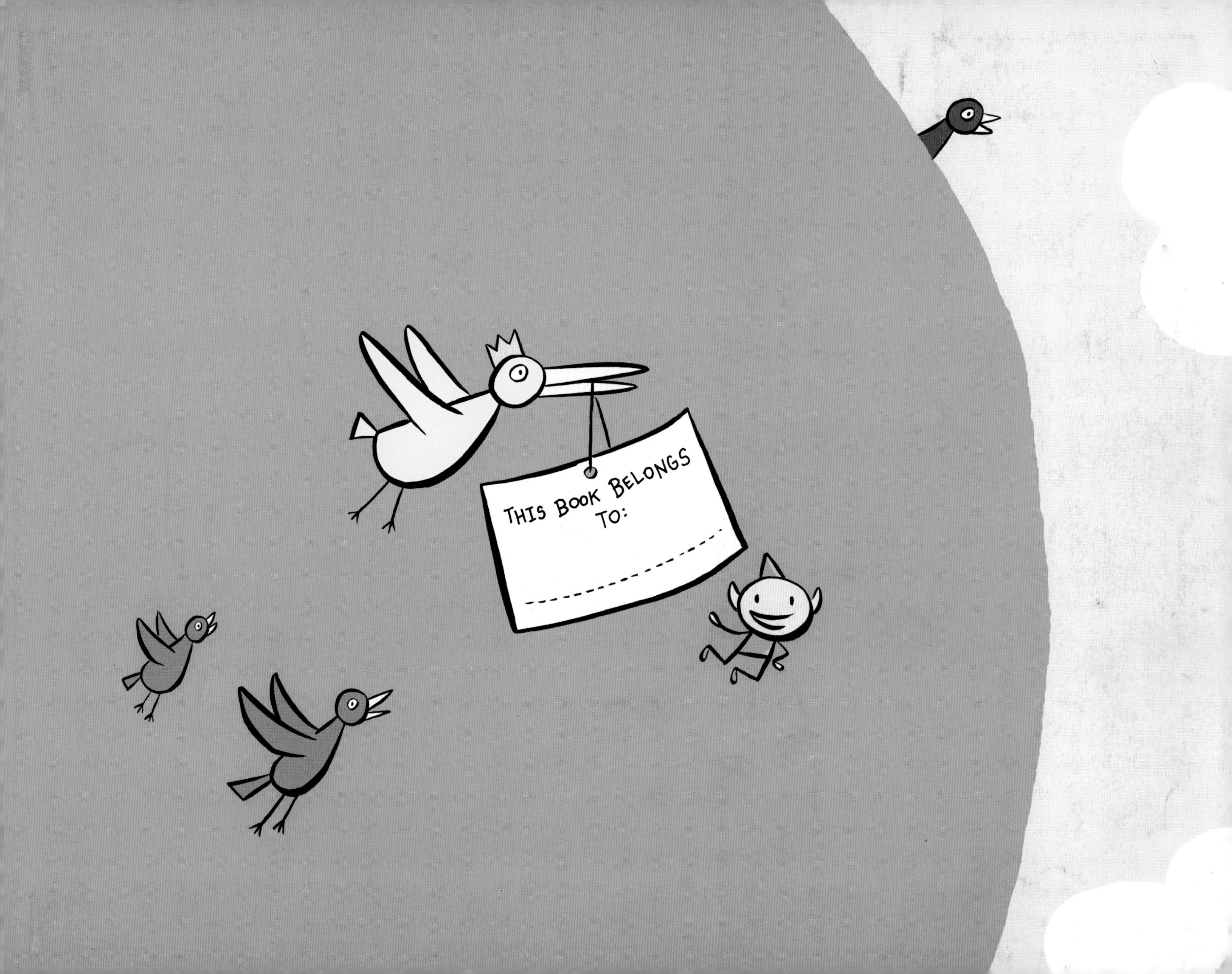
THIS BOOK BELONGS
TO:

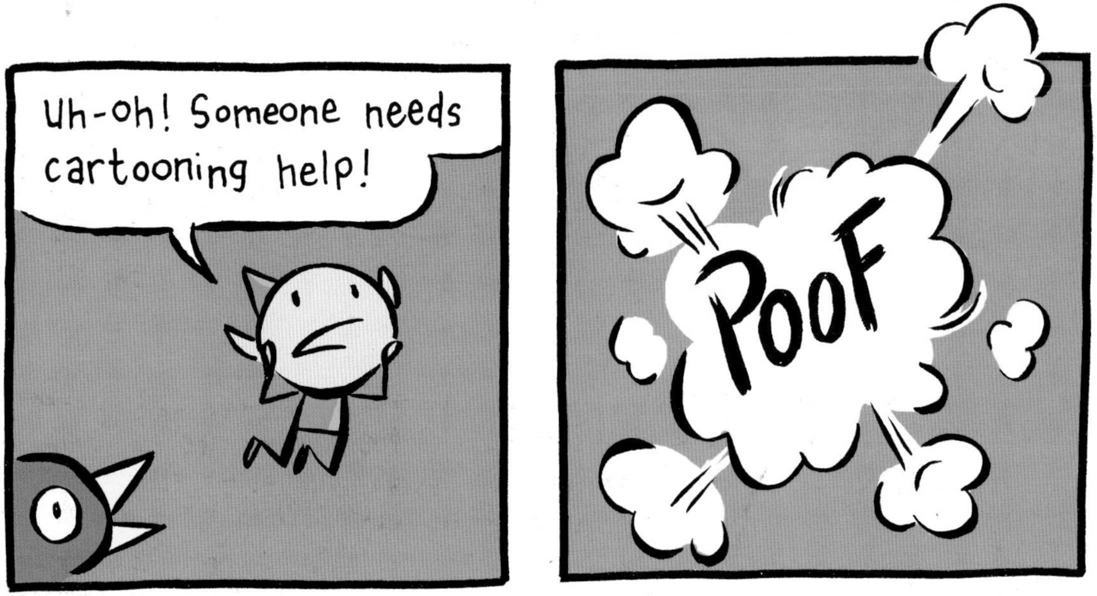
Uh-oh! Someone needs cartooning help!
POOF

Once upon a time... a princess tried to make a comic...

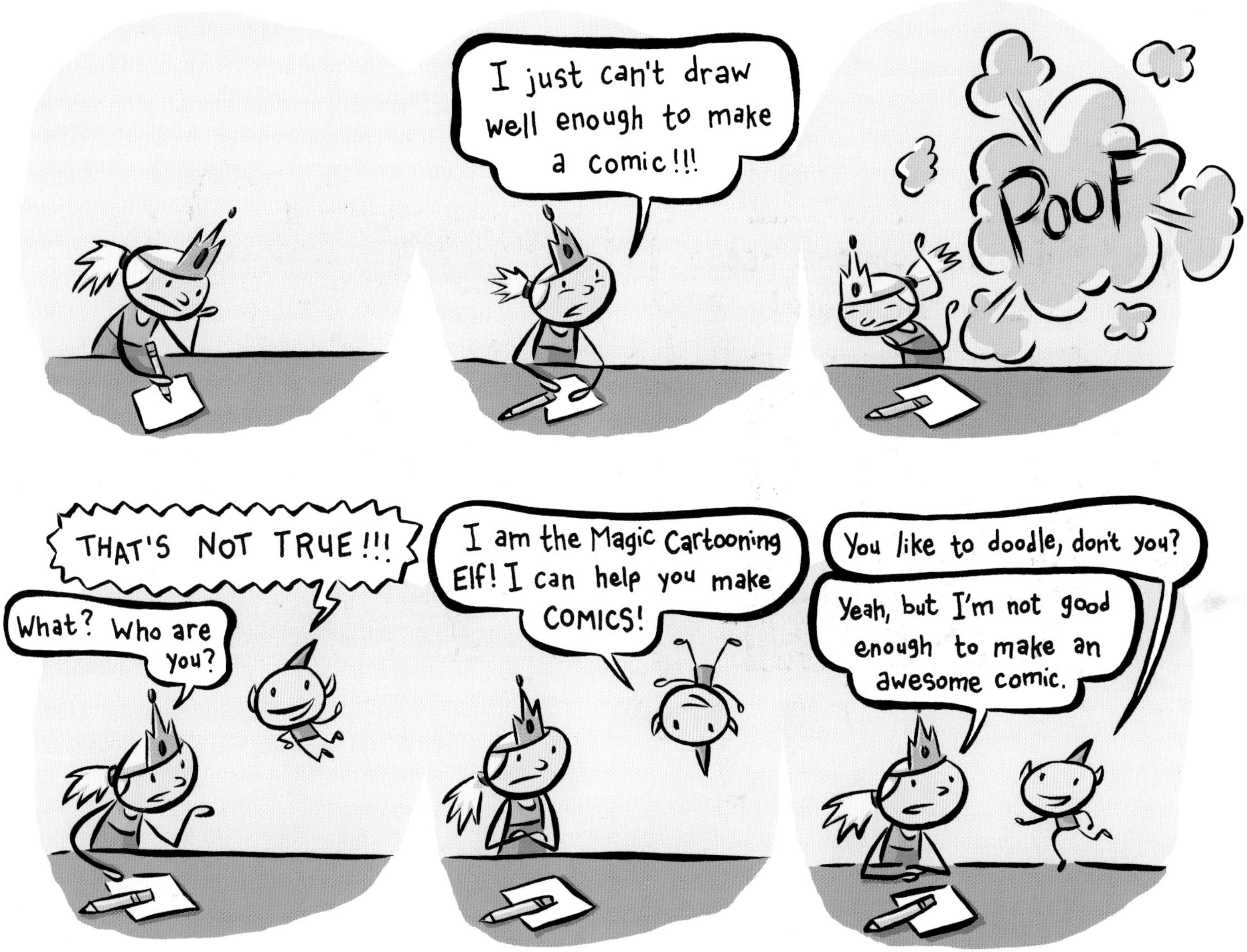
I just can't draw well enough to make a comic!!!
POOF
THAT'S NOT TRUE!!!
What? Who are you?
I am the Magic Cartooning Elf! I can help you make COMICS!
You like to doodle, don't you?
Yeah, but I'm not good enough to make an awesome comic.

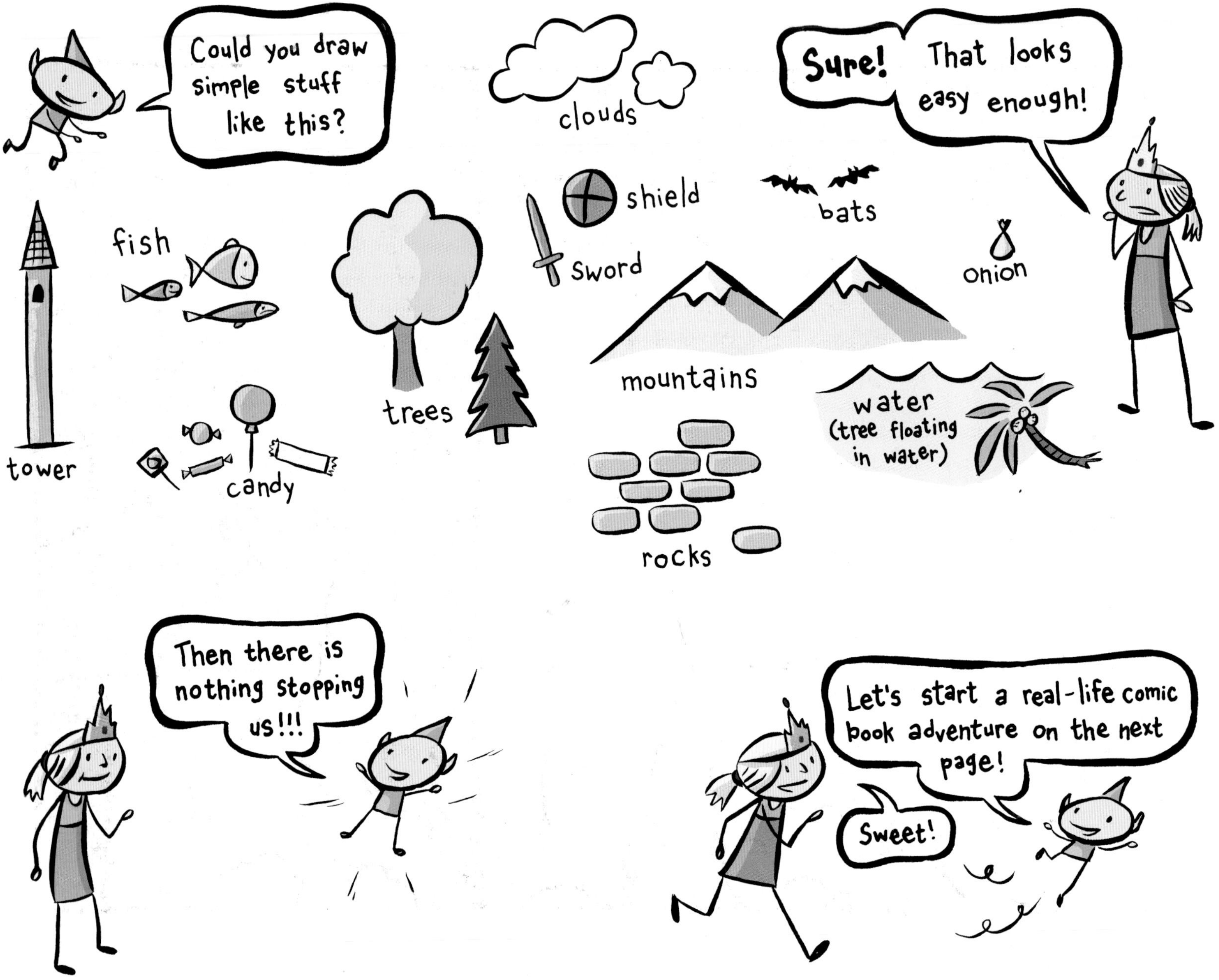

Could you draw simple stuff like this?
clouds
Sure! That looks easy enough!
shield
bats
sword
onion
fish
tower
trees
mountains
water (tree floating in water)
candy
rocks
Then there is nothing stopping us!!!
Let's start a real-life comic book adventure on the next page!
Sweet!

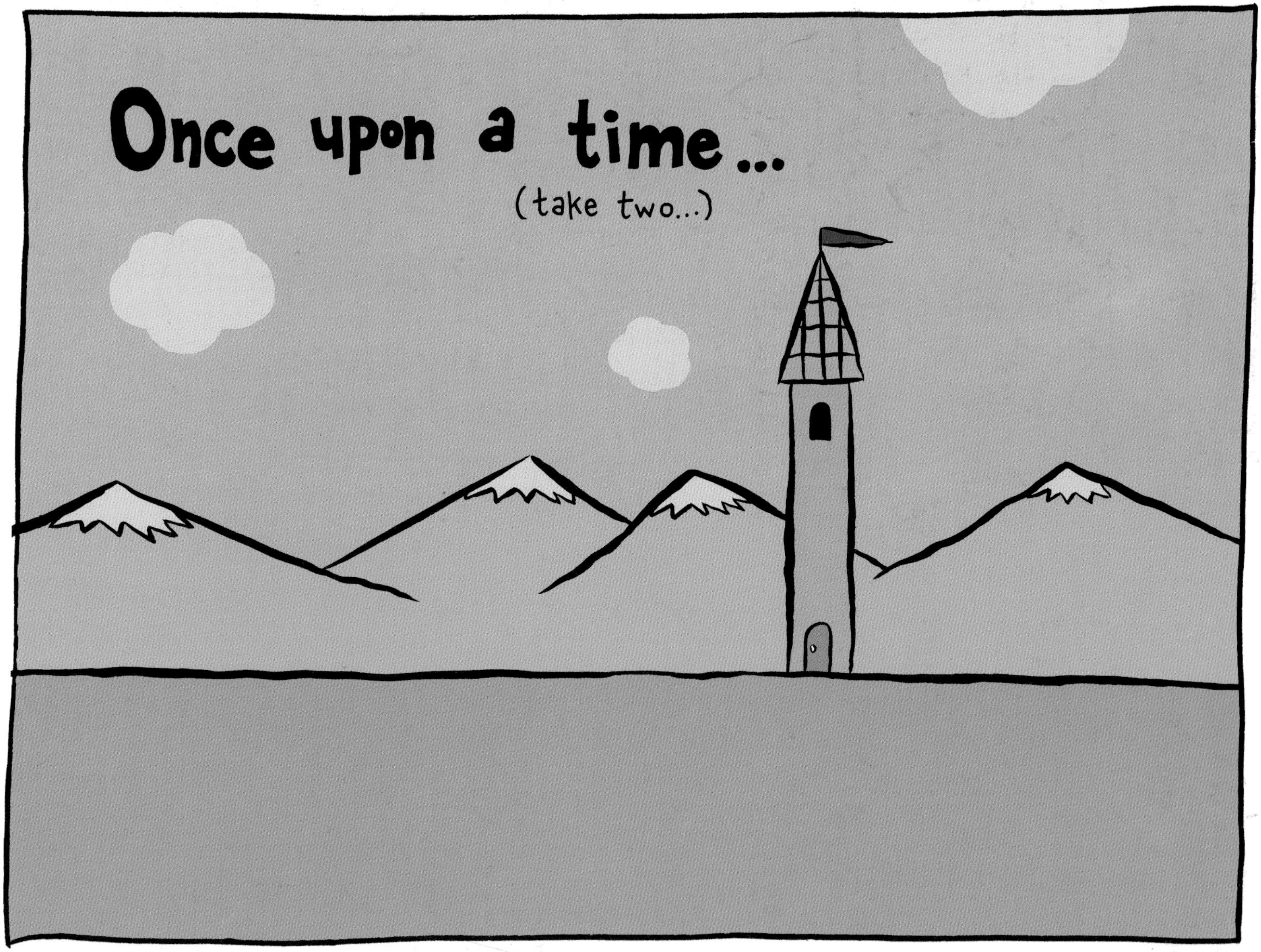
Once upon a time...
(take two...)

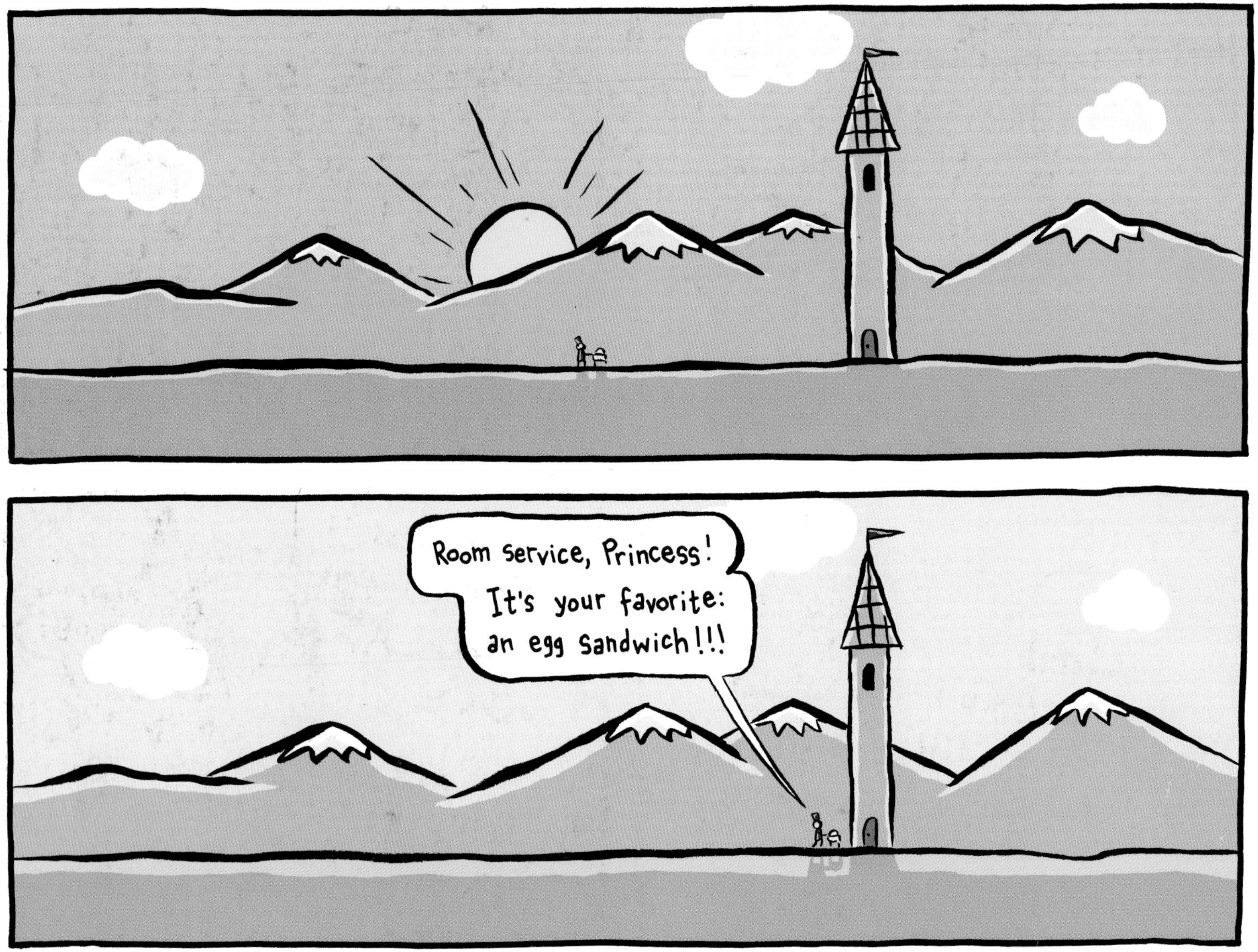
Room service, Princess! It's your favorite: an egg sandwich!!!

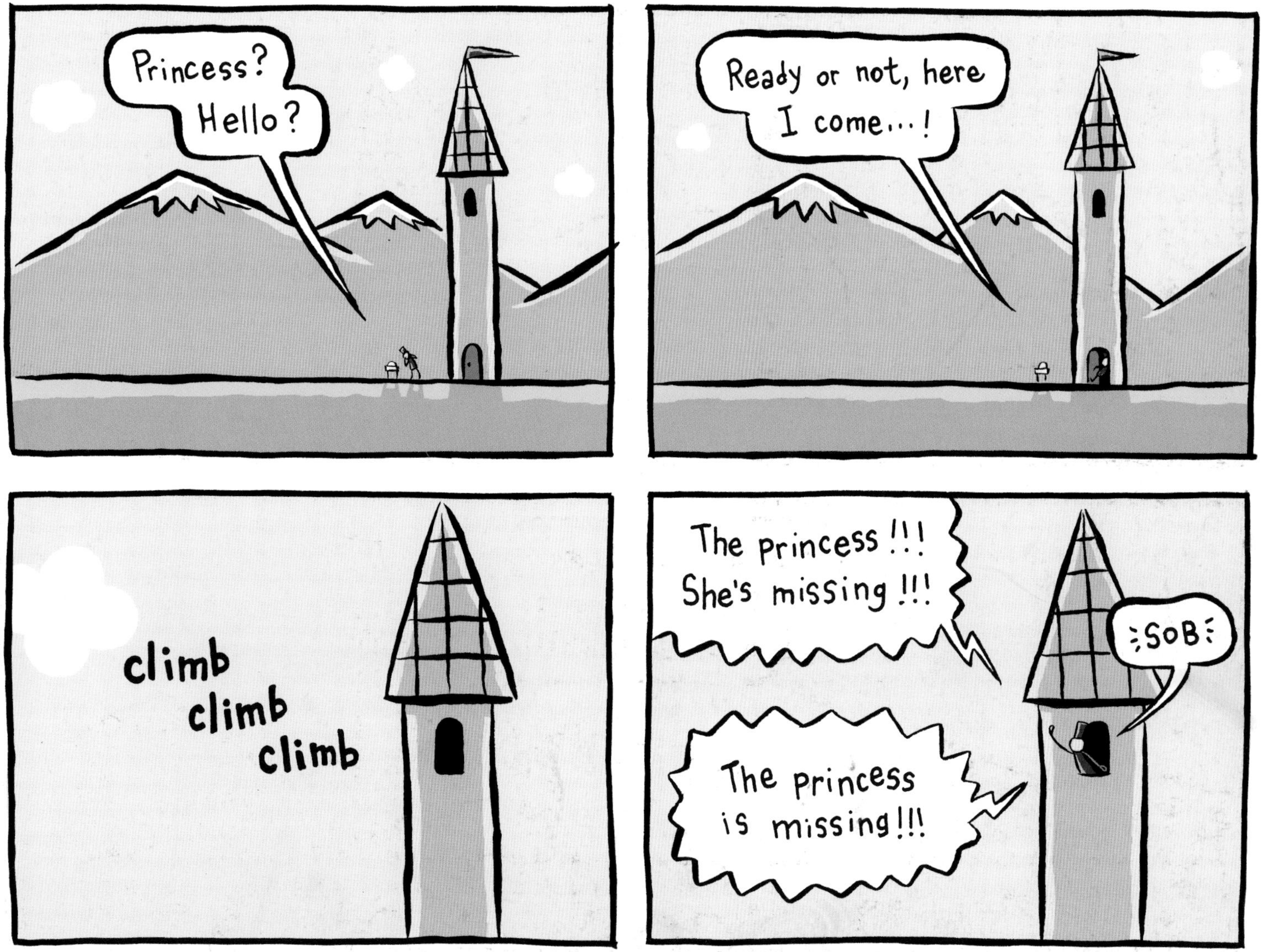
Princess? Hello?
Ready or not, here I come...!
climb climb climb
The princess!!! She's missing!!!
SOB
The princess is missing!!!

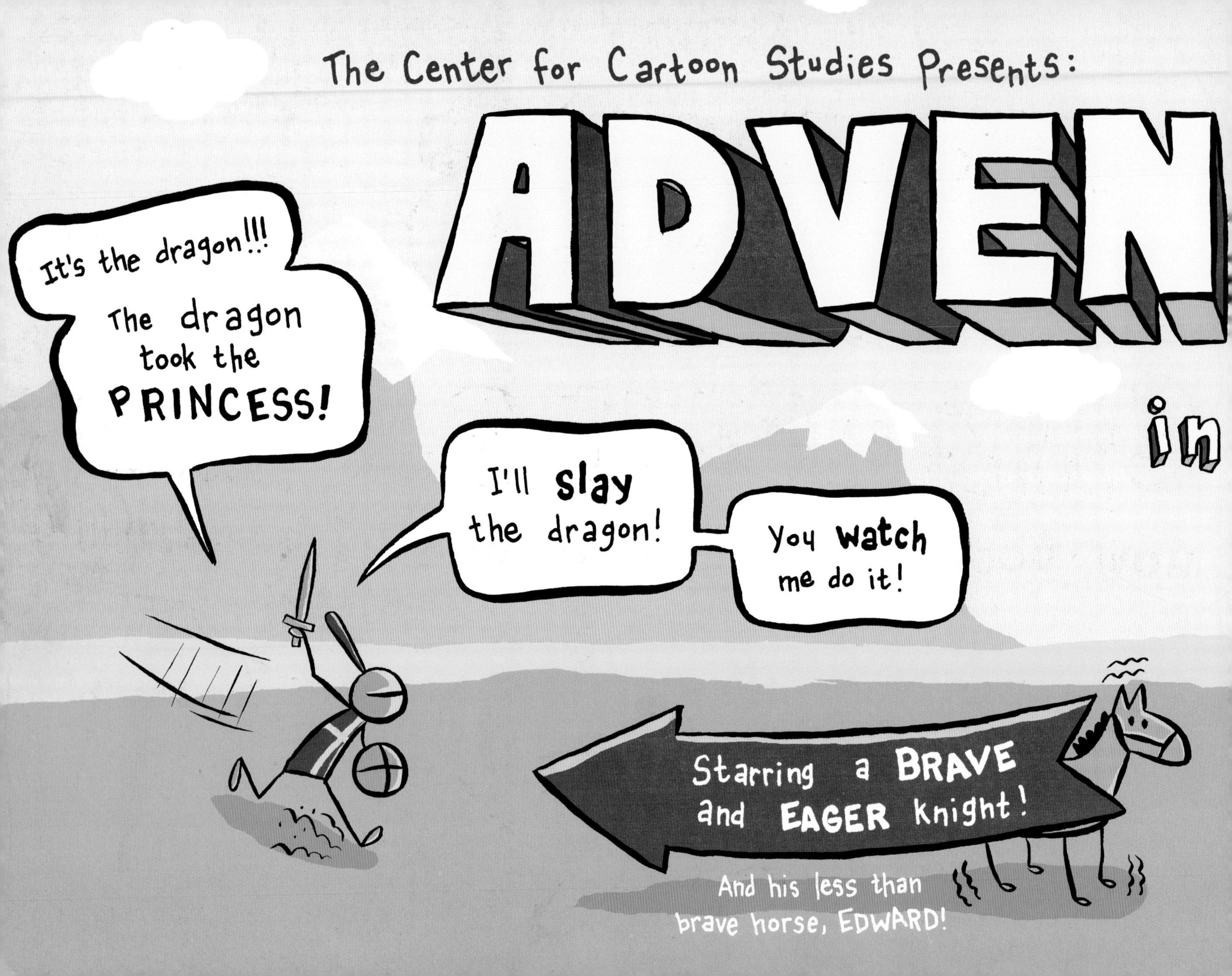
The Center for Cartoon Studies Presents:
ADVEN
in
It's the dragon!!!
The dragon took the PRINCESS!
I'll slay the dragon!
You watch me do it!
Starring a BRAVE and EAGER knight!
And his less than brave horse, EDWARD!

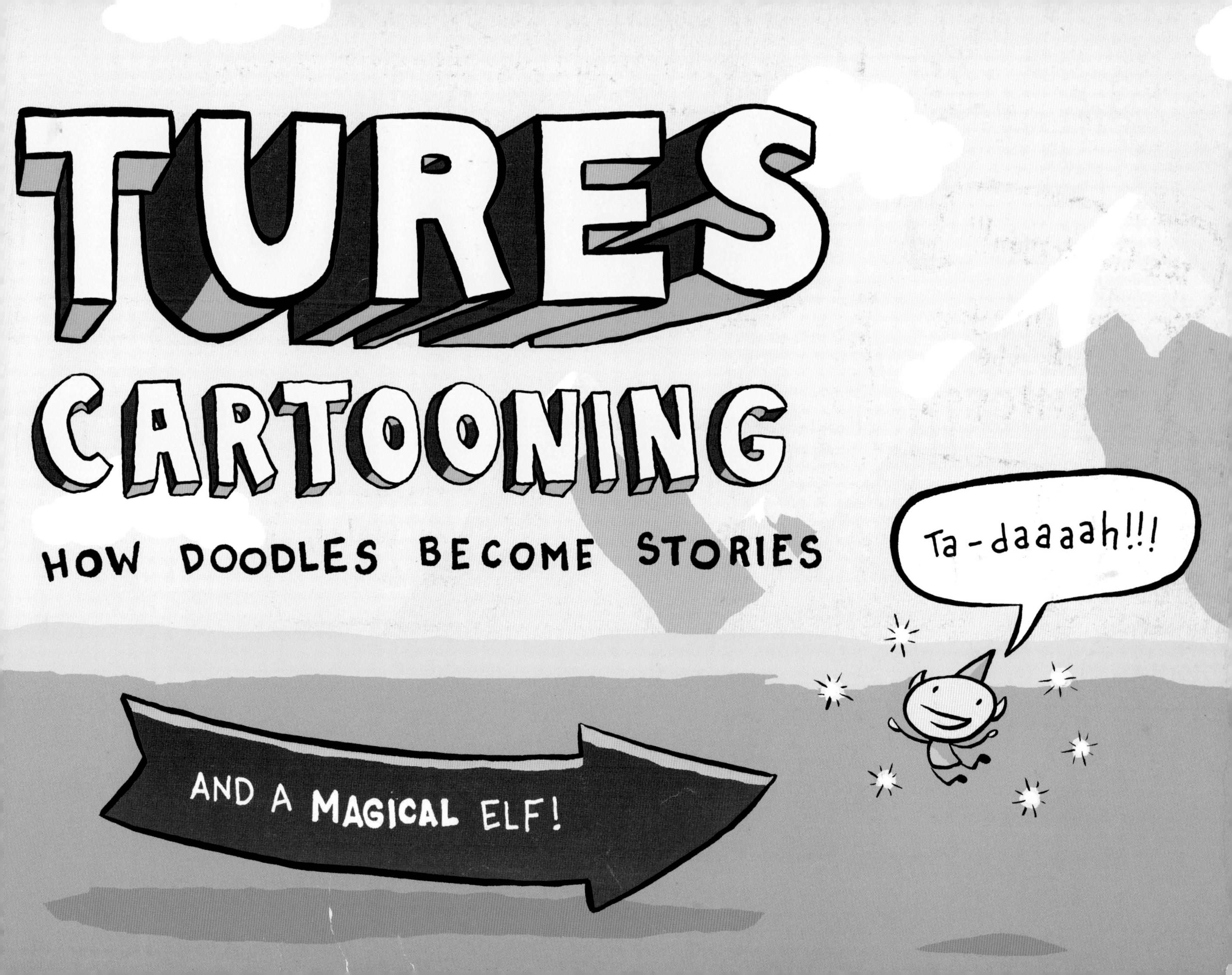
TURES
CARTOONING
HOW DOODLES BECOME STORIES
Ta-daaaaah!!!
AND A MAGICAL ELF!

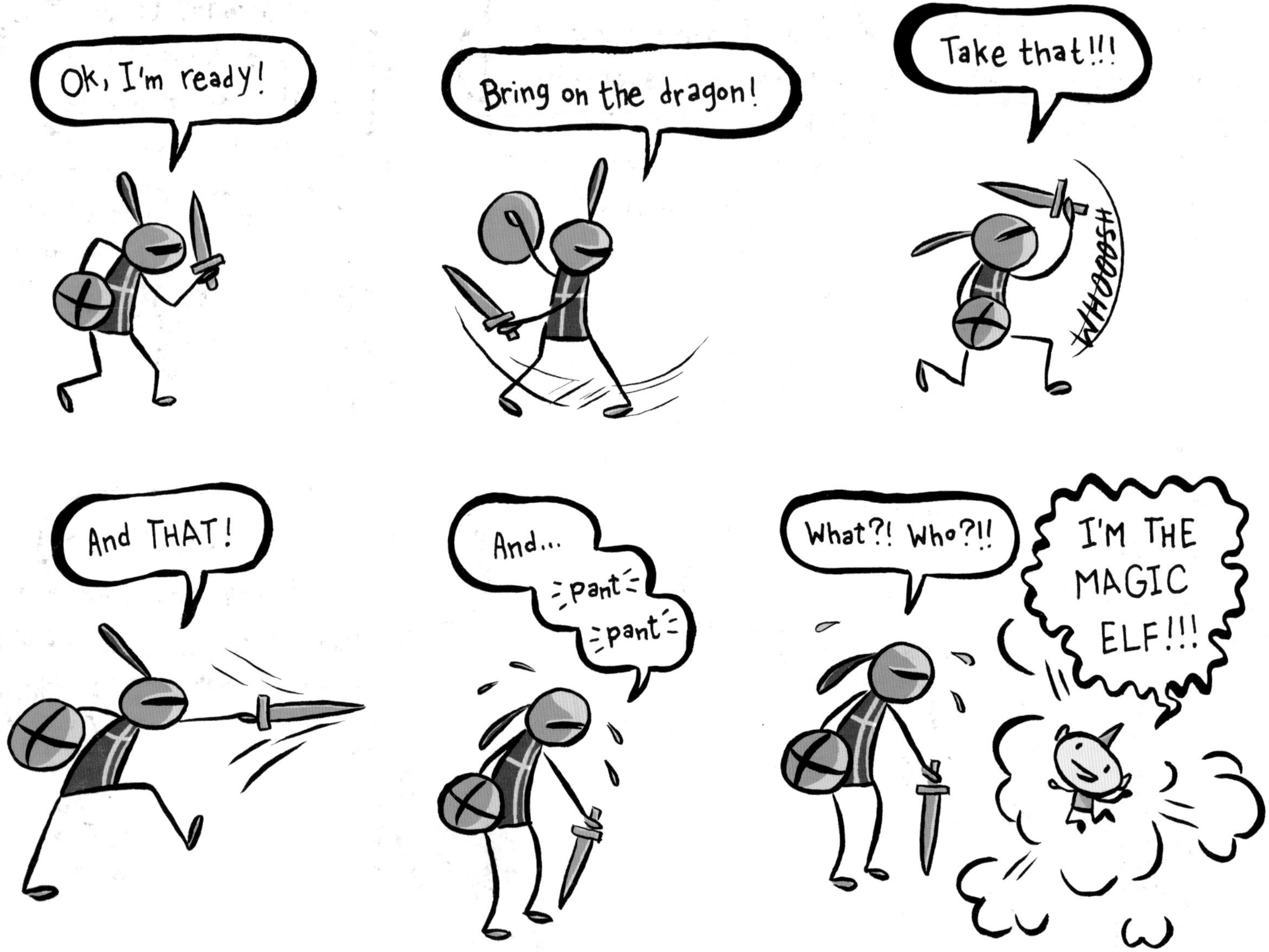
Ok, I'm ready!
Bring on the dragon!
Take that!!!
WHOOOOSH
And THAT!
And...
pant
pant
What?! Who?!!
I'M THE MAGIC ELF!!!

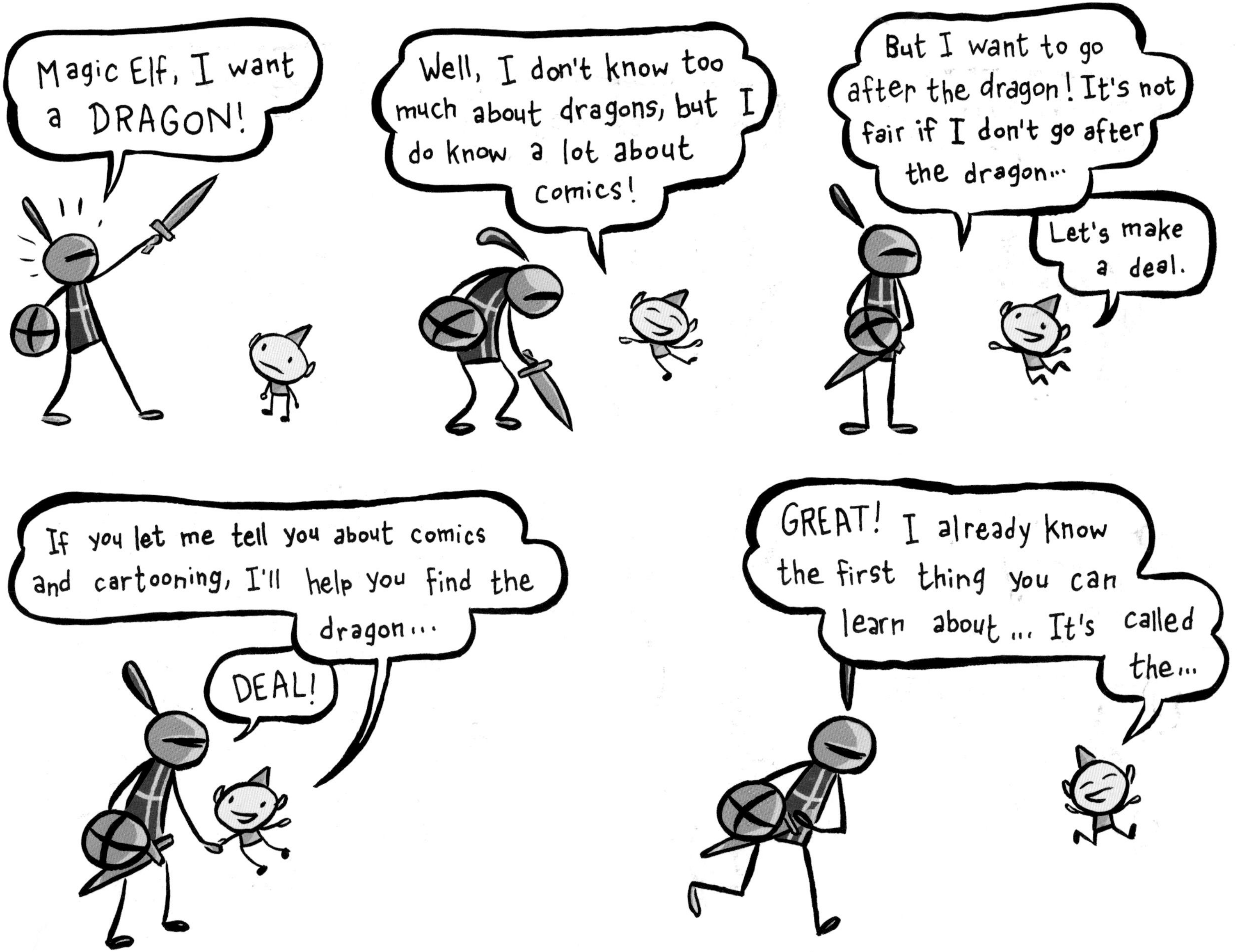
Magic Elf, I want a DRAGON!
Well, I don't know too much about dragons, but I do know a lot about comics!
But I want to go after the dragon! It's not fair if I don't go after the dragon...
Let's make a deal.
If you let me tell you about comics and cartooning, I'll help you find the dragon...
DEAL!
GREAT! I already know the first thing you can learn about... It's called the...

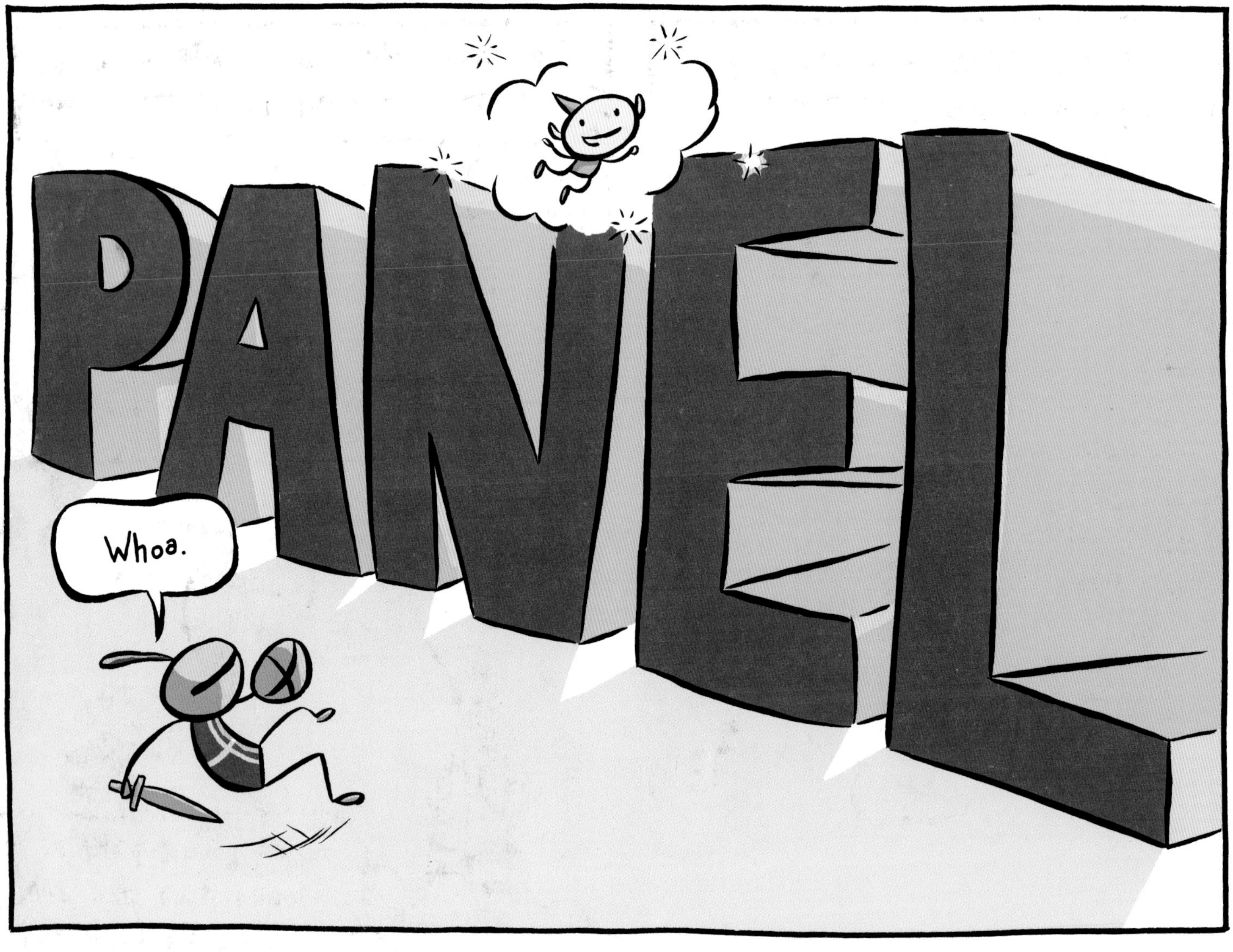
PANEL
Whoa.

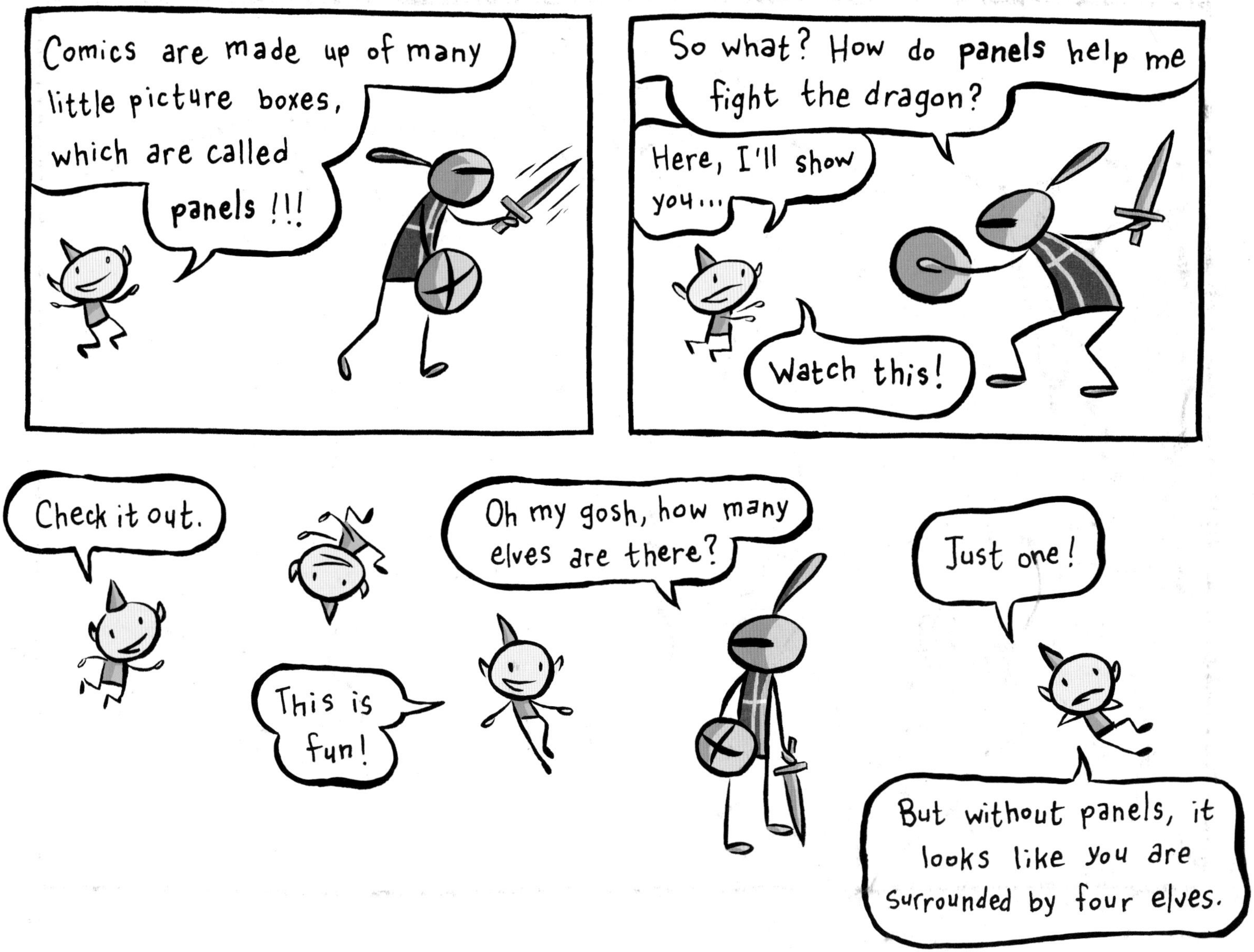

Comics are made up of many little picture boxes, which are called panels!!!
So what? How do **panels** help me fight the dragon?
Here, I'll show you...
Watch this!
Check it out.
Oh my gosh, how many elves are there?
This is fun!
Just one!
But without panels, it looks like you are surrounded by four elves.

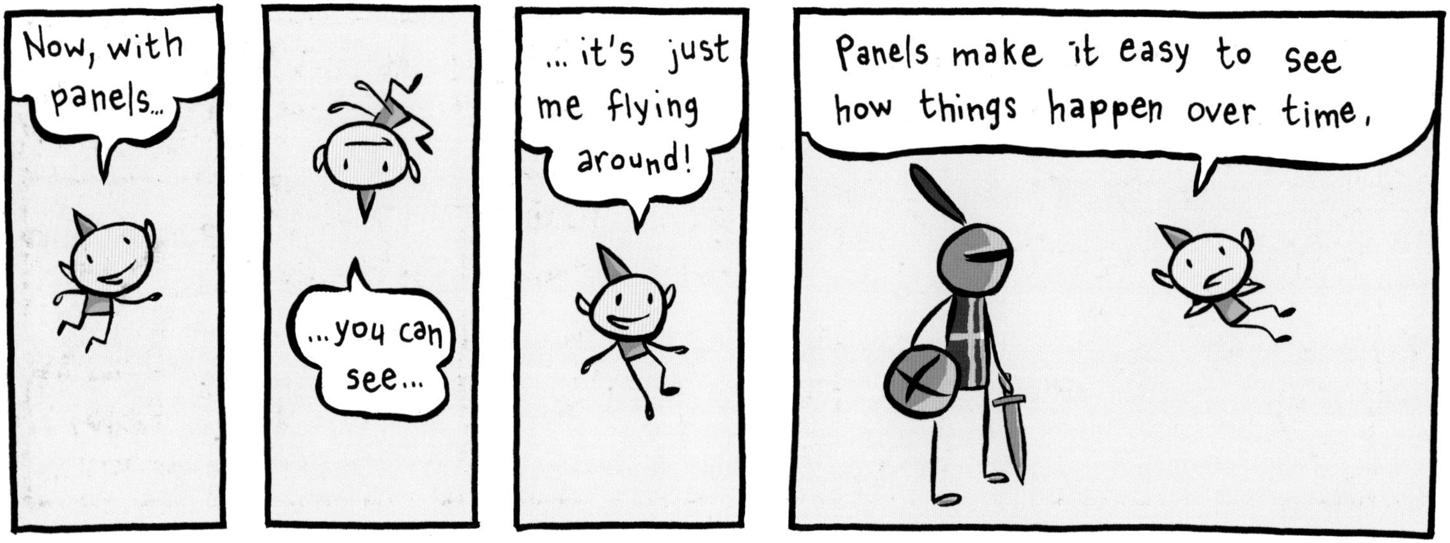
Now, with panels...
...you can see...
... it's just me flying around!
Panels make it easy to see how things happen over time.

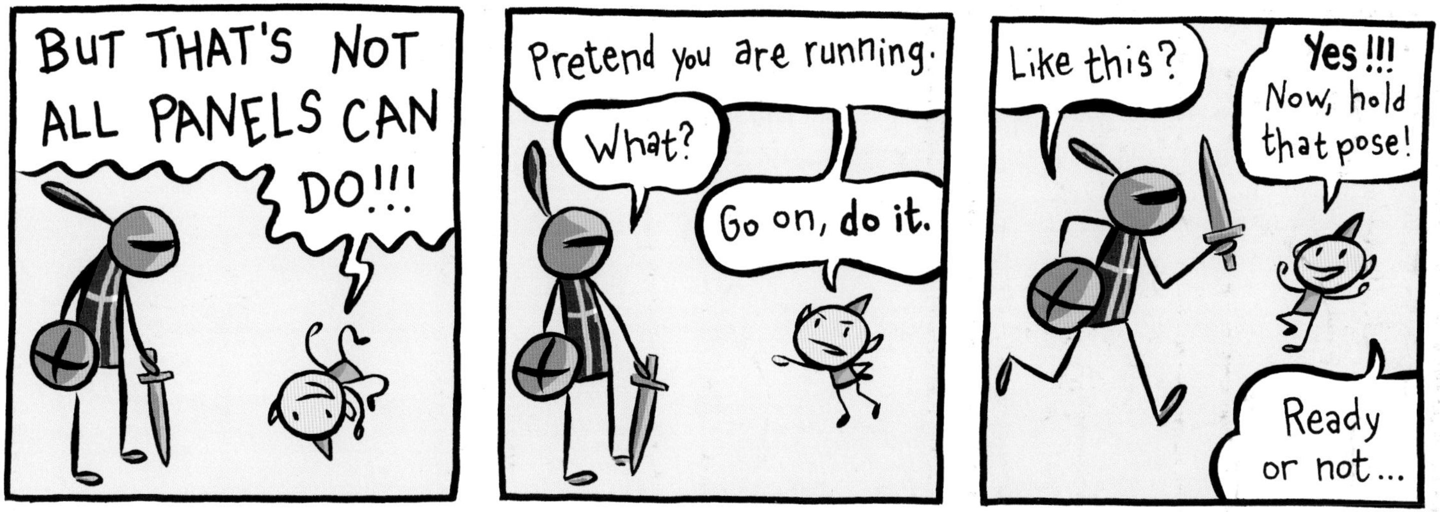
BUT THAT'S NOT ALL PANELS CAN DO!!!
Pretend you are running.
What?
Go on, **do it.**
Like this?
Yes!!! Now, hold that pose!
Ready or not...

Hey, a forest! But I haven't moved!
A meadow!
I'm passing the mountains!
And the desert!

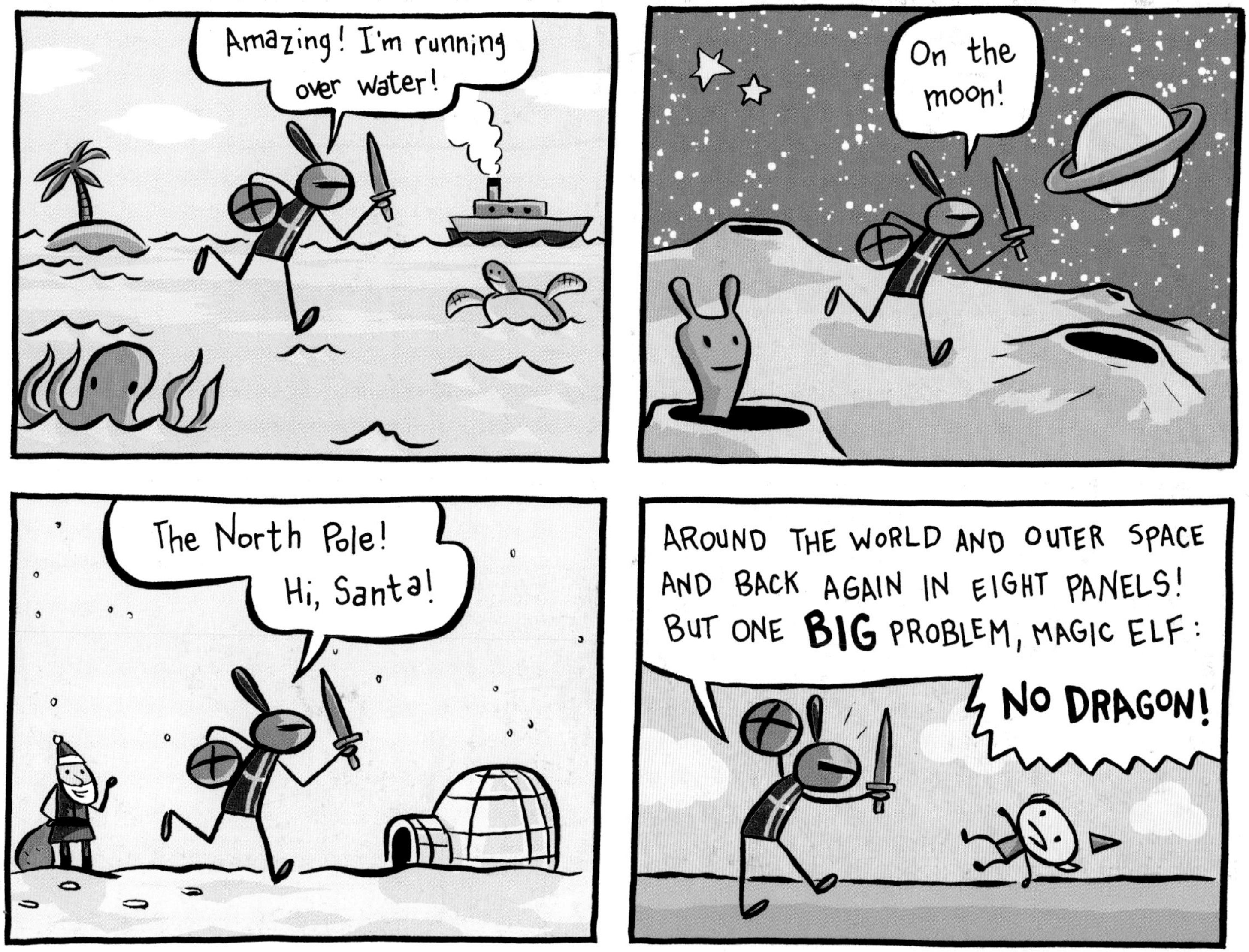
Amazing! I'm running over water!
On the moon!
The North Pole! Hi, Santa!
AROUND THE WORLD AND OUTER SPACE AND BACK AGAIN IN EIGHT PANELS! BUT ONE BIG PROBLEM, MAGIC ELF:
NO DRAGON!

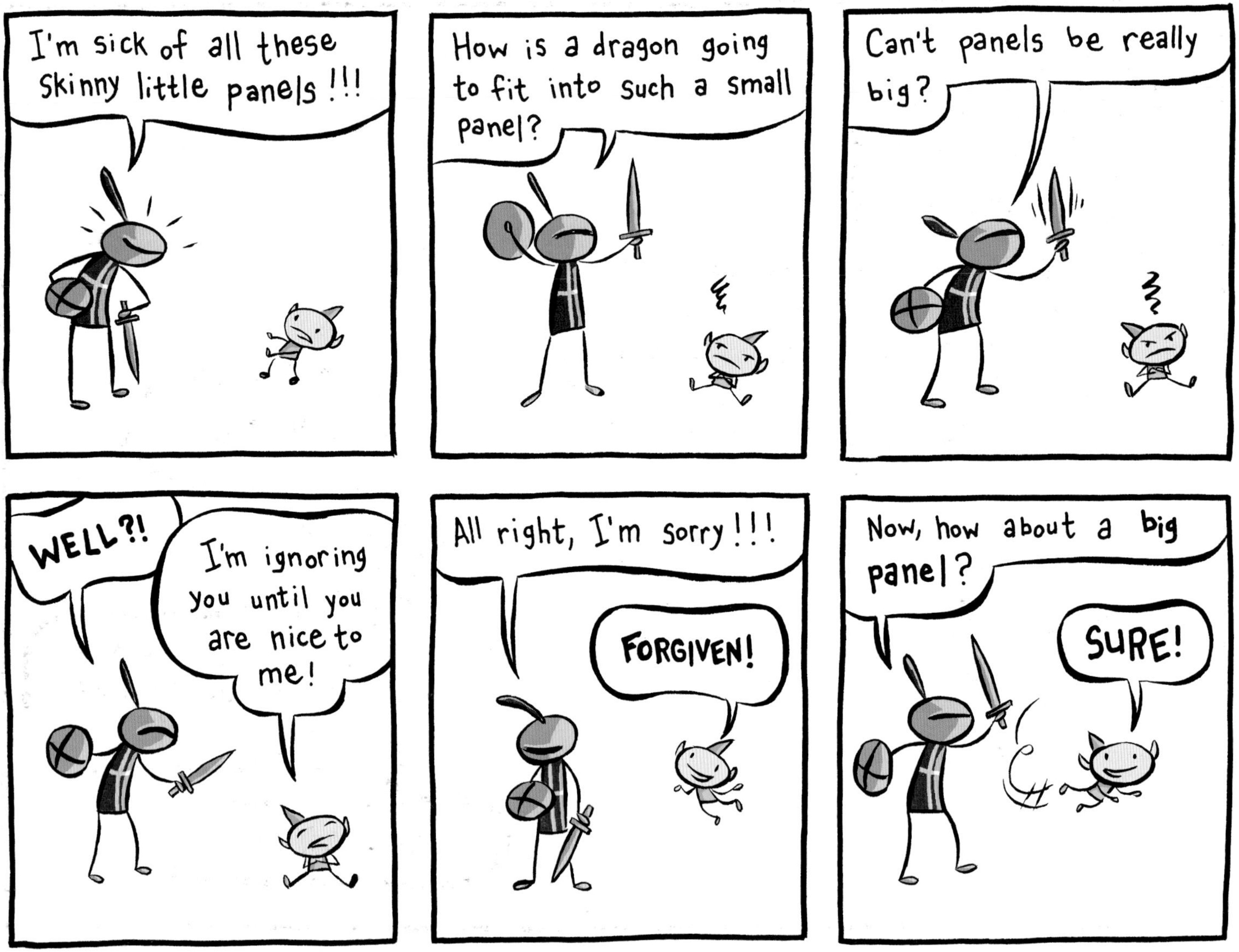

I'm sick of all these Skinny little panels!!!
How is a dragon going to fit into such a small panel?
Can't panels be really big?
WELL?!
I'm ignoring you until you are nice to me!
All right, I'm sorry!!!
FORGIVEN!
Now, how about a big panel?
SURE!

Cool!
But, um... sort of empty...
I mean, for a proper adventure, you need places to explore!
GOOD POINT.
More cartooning magic is on its way!!!
abracadabra!

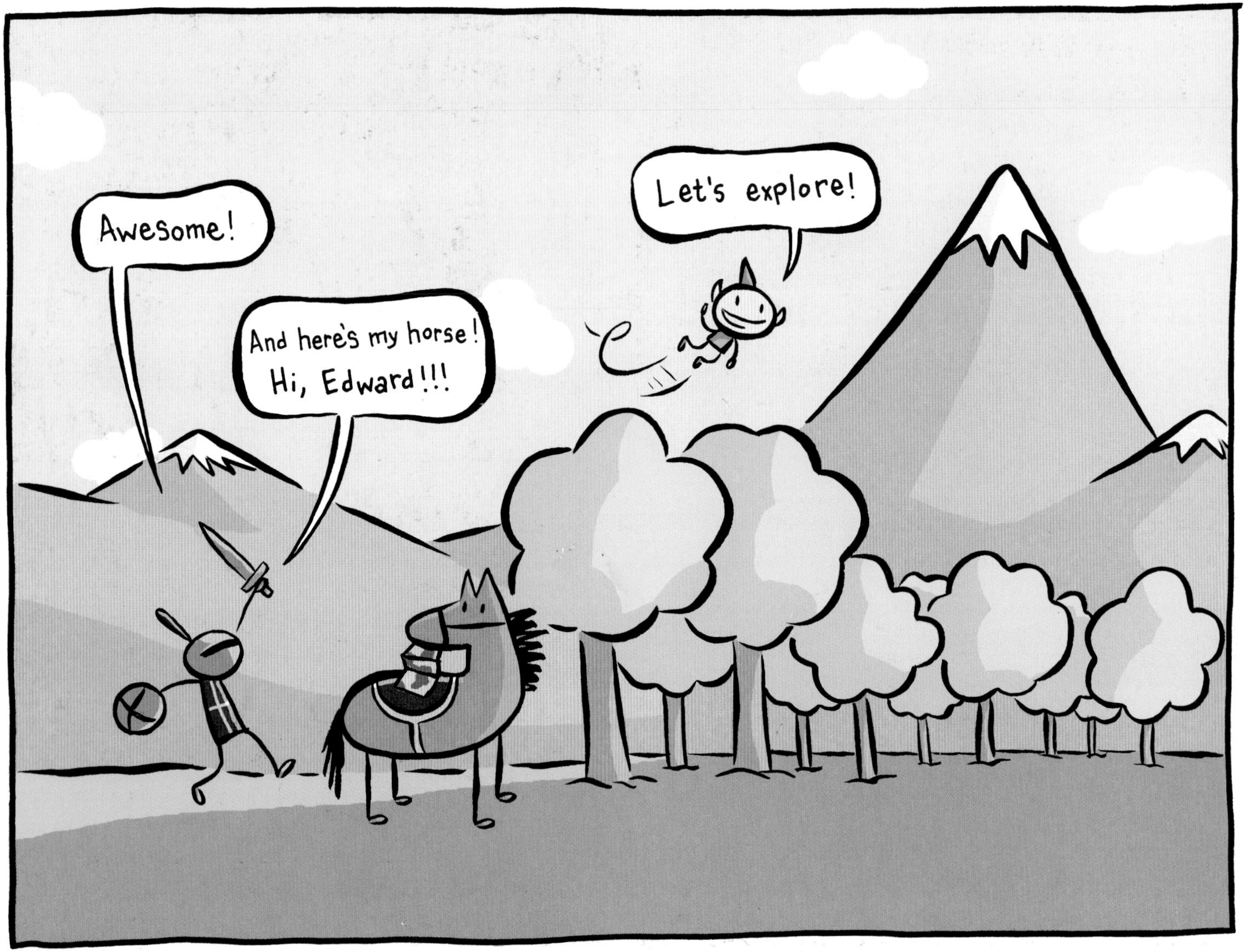
Awesome!
And here's my horse! Hi, Edward!!!
Let's explore!

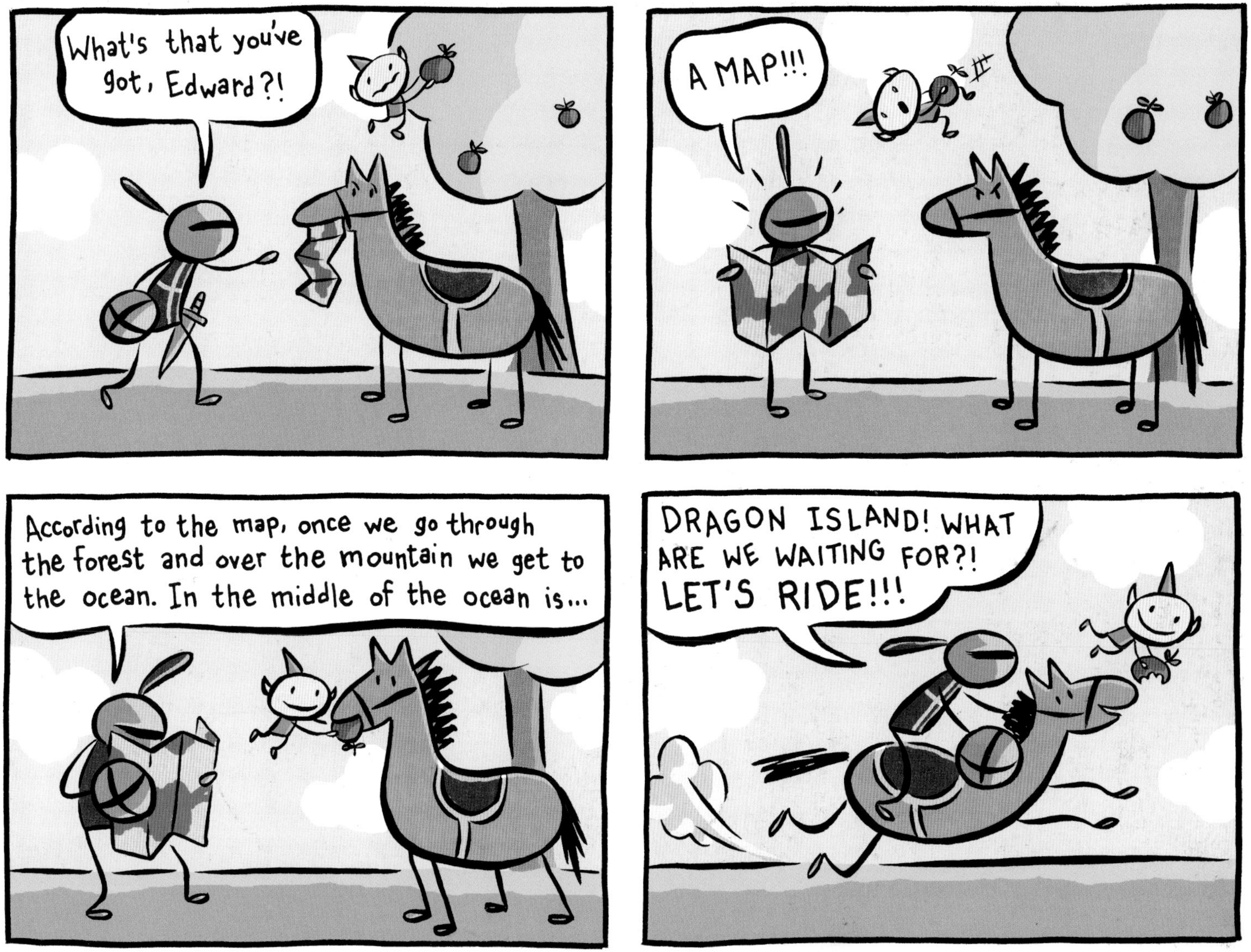
What's that you've got, Edward?!
A MAP!!!
According to the map, once we go through the forest and over the mountain we get to the ocean. In the middle of the ocean is...
DRAGON ISLAND! WHAT ARE WE WAITING FOR?! LET'S RIDE!!!

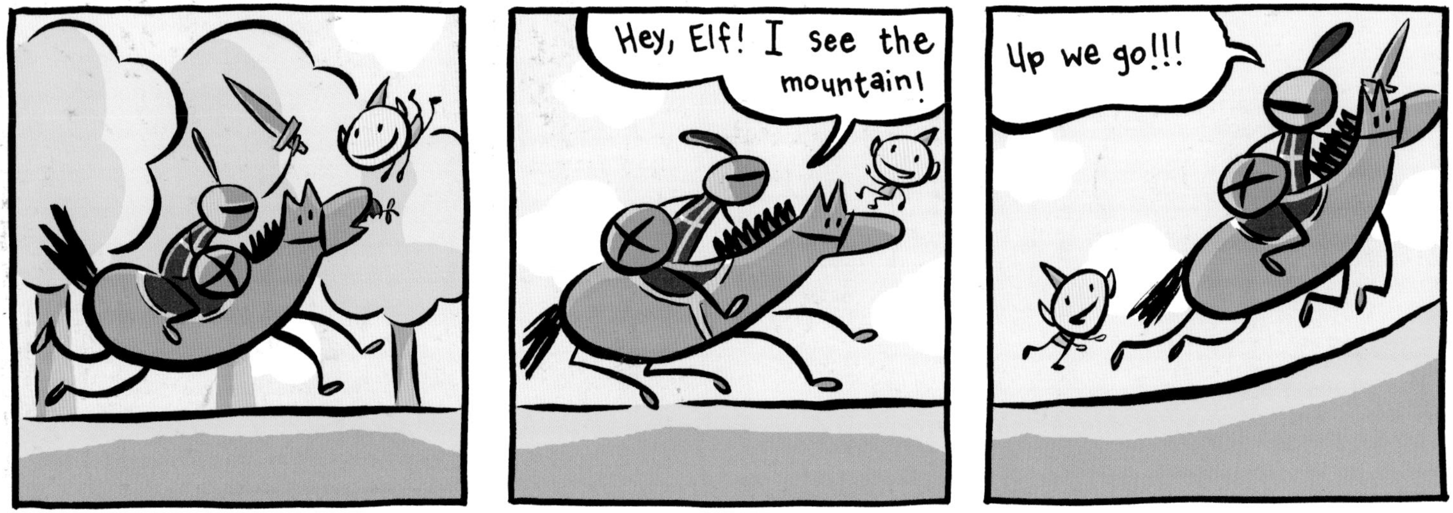
Hey, Elf! I see the mountain!
Up we go!!!

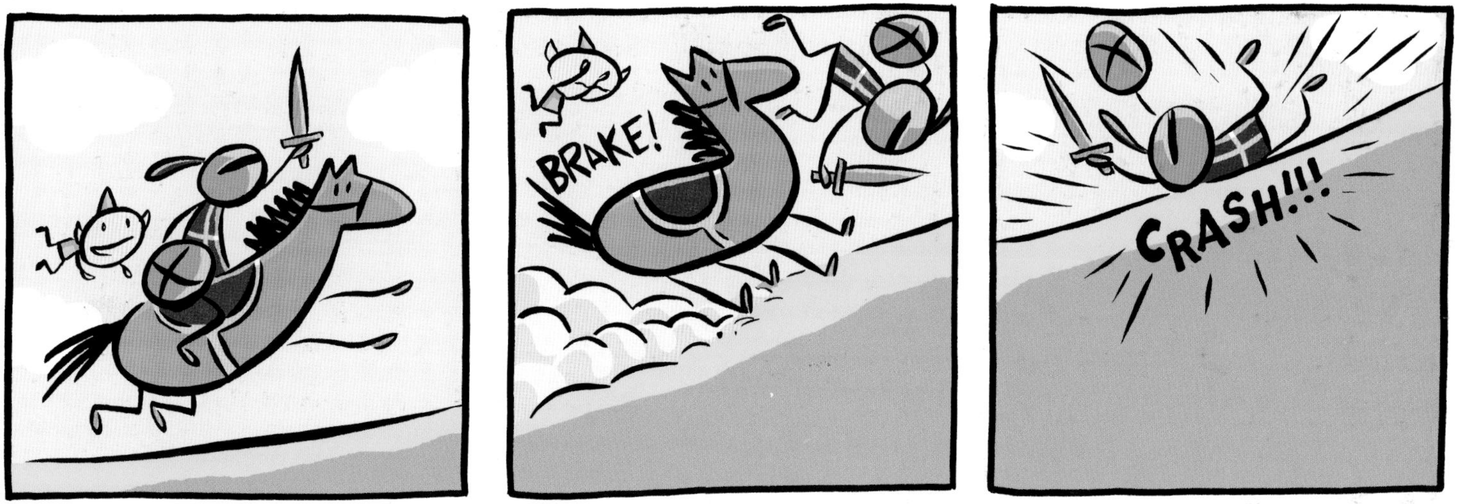
BRAKE!
CRASH!!!

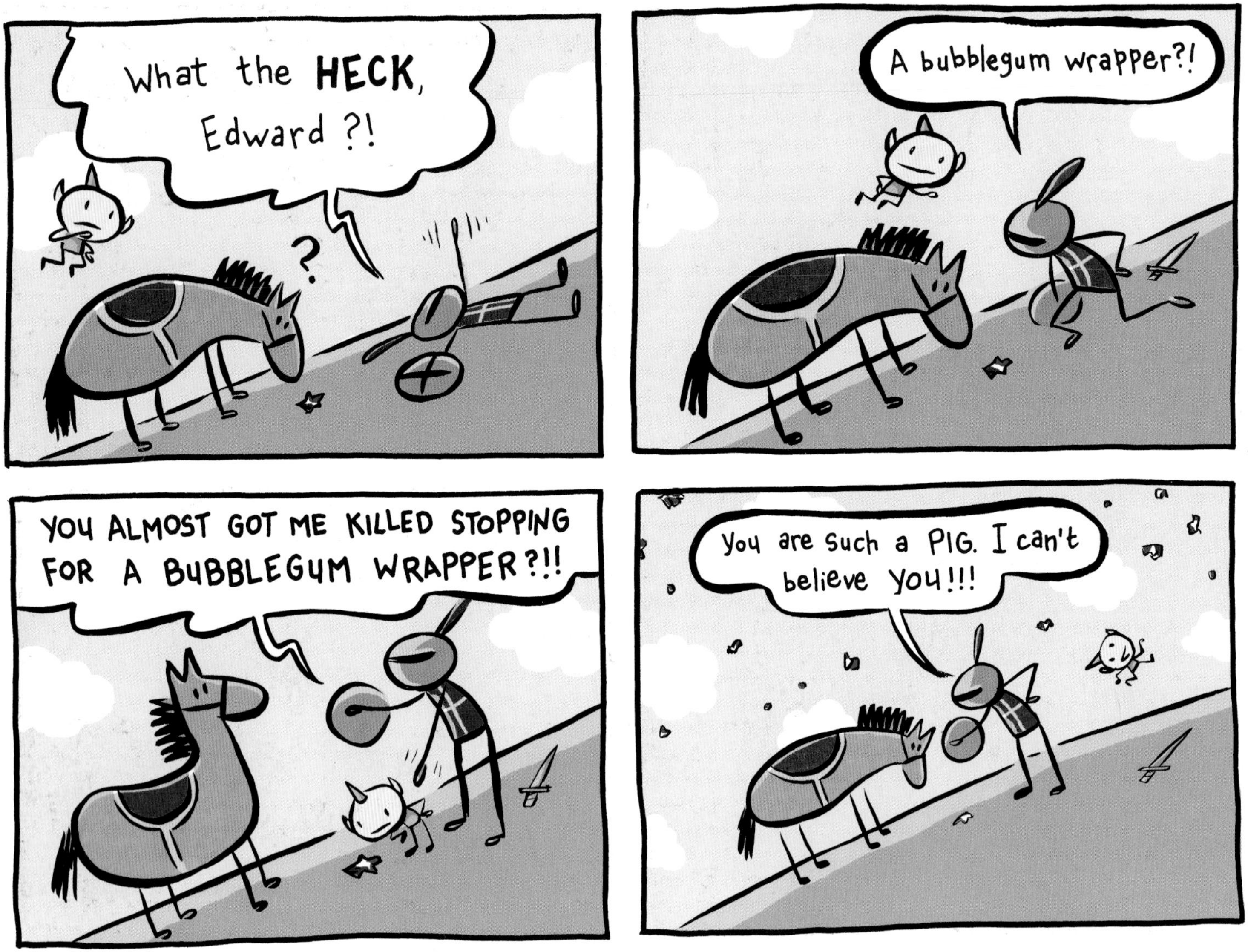
What the HECK, Edward?!
A bubblegum wrapper?!
YOU ALMOST GOT ME KILLED STOPPING FOR A BUBBLEGUM WRAPPER?!!
You are such a PIG. I can't believe YOU!!!

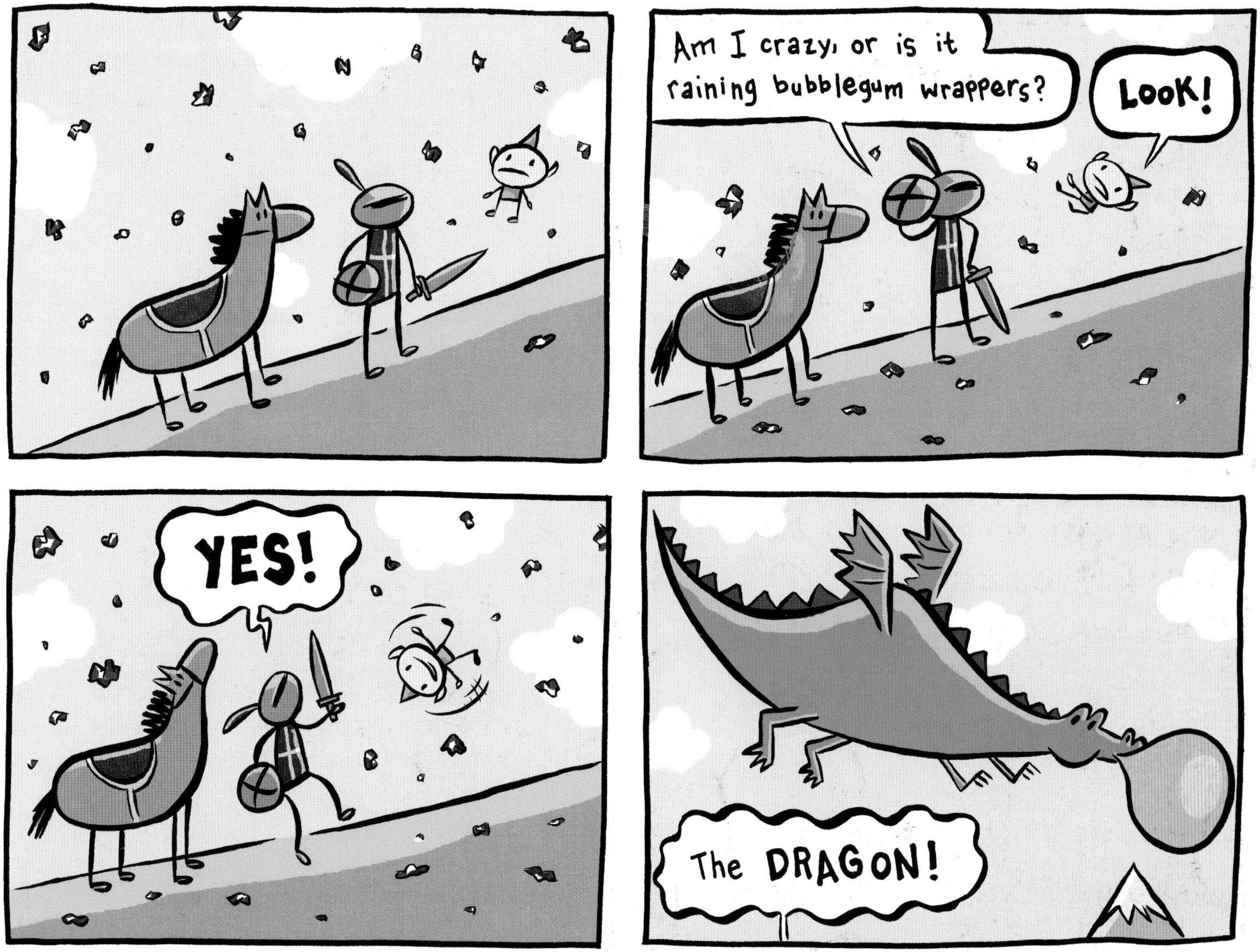
Am I crazy, or is it raining bubblegum wrappers?
LOOK!
YES!
The DRAGON!

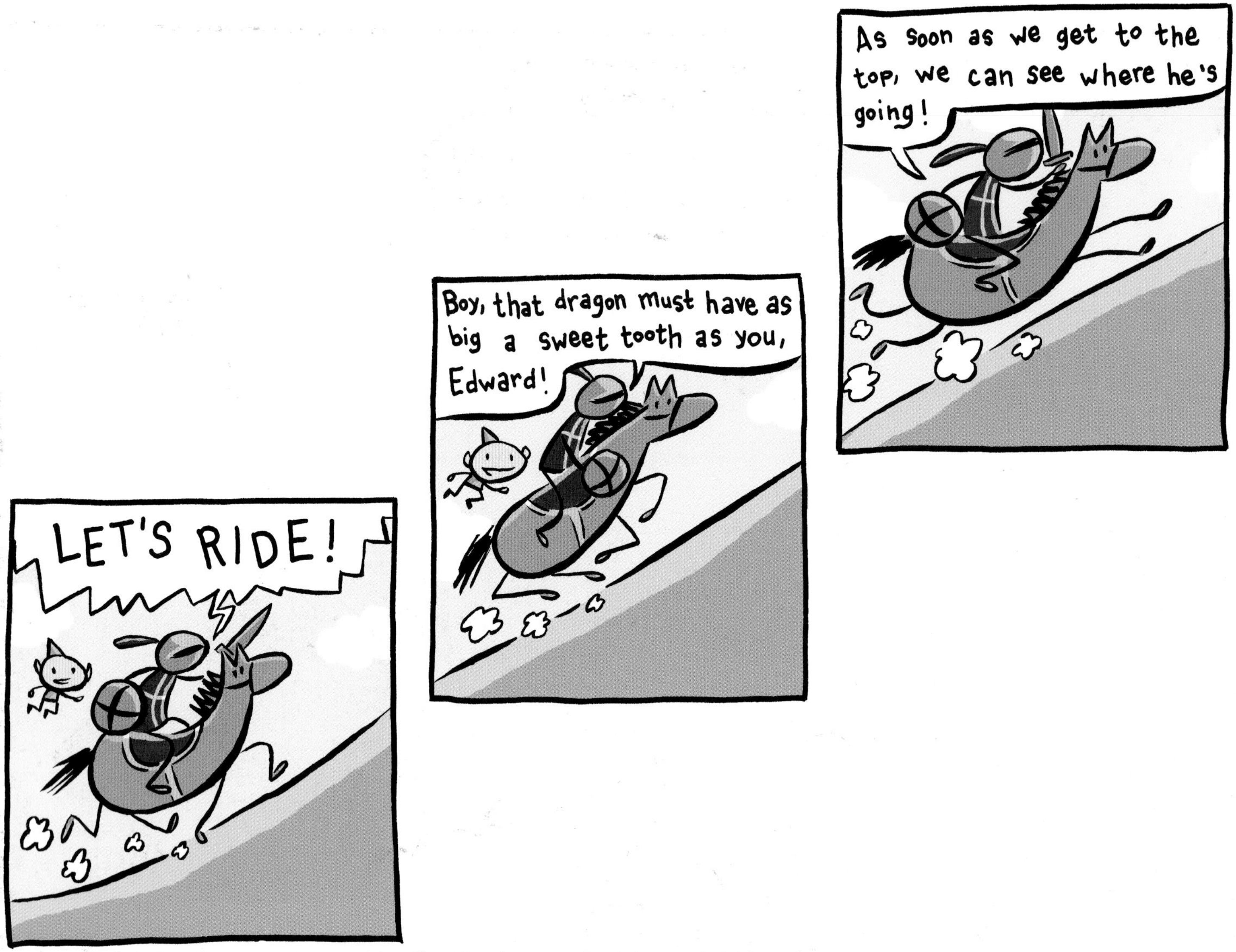
LET'S RIDE!
Boy, that dragon must have as big a sweet tooth as you, Edward!
As soon as we get to the top, we can see where he's going!

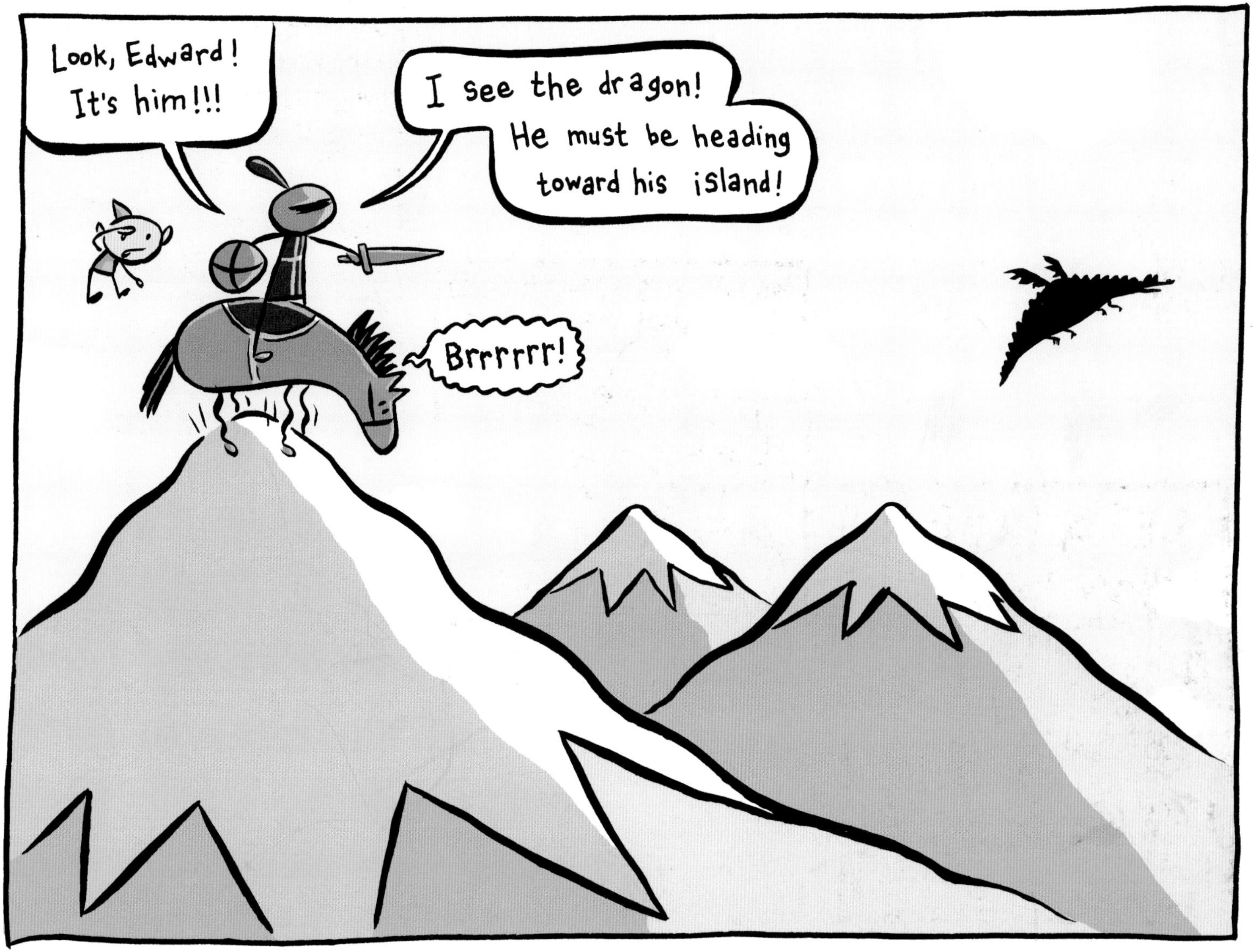
Look, Edward! It's him!!!
I see the dragon! He must be heading toward his island!
Brrrrrr!

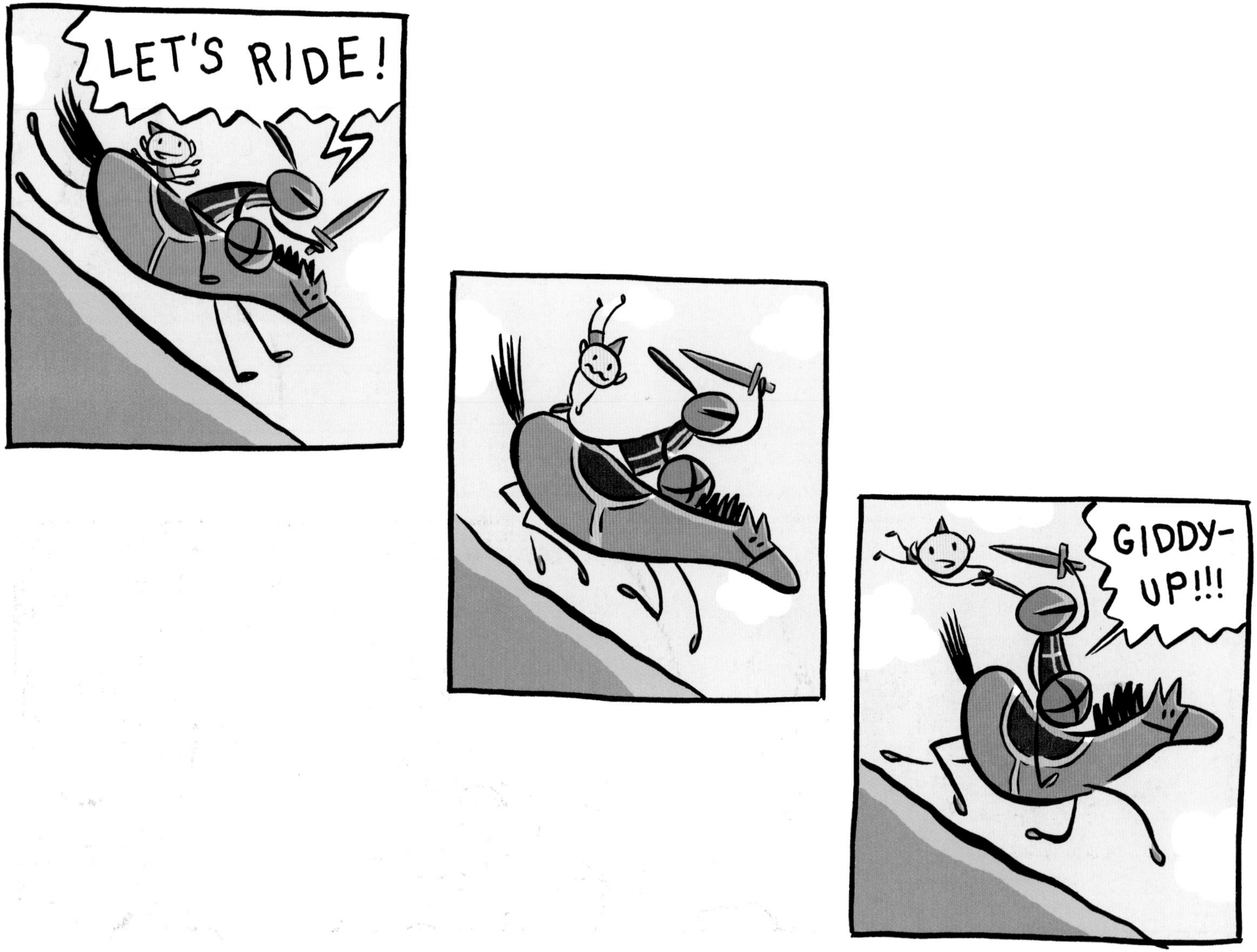
LET'S RIDE!
GIDDY-UP!!!

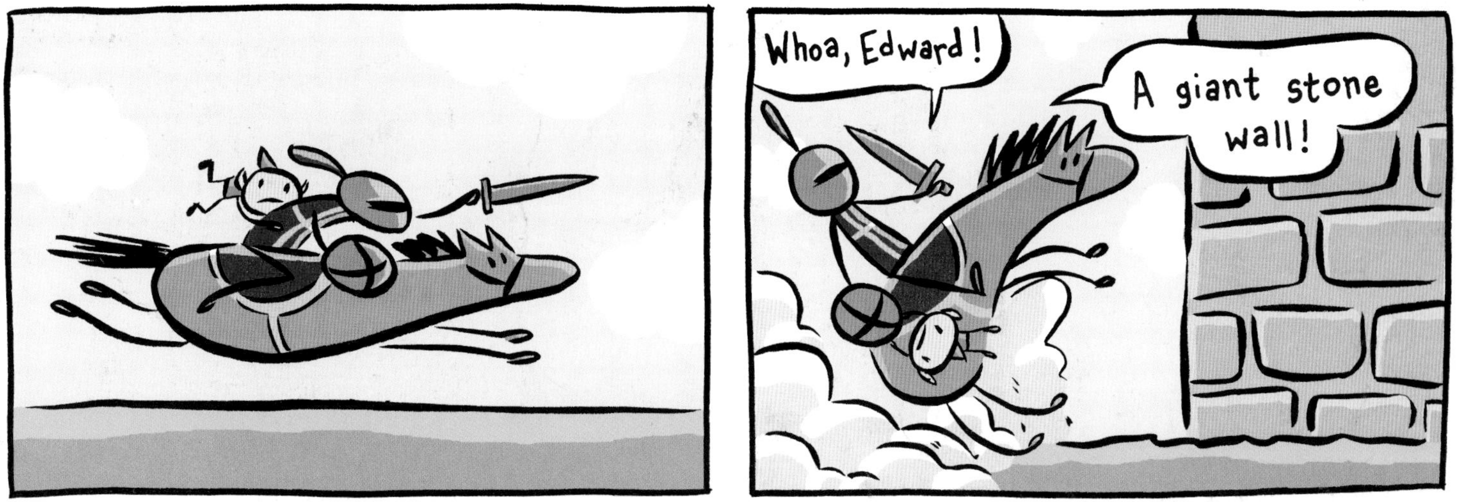
Whoa, Edward!
A giant stone wall!

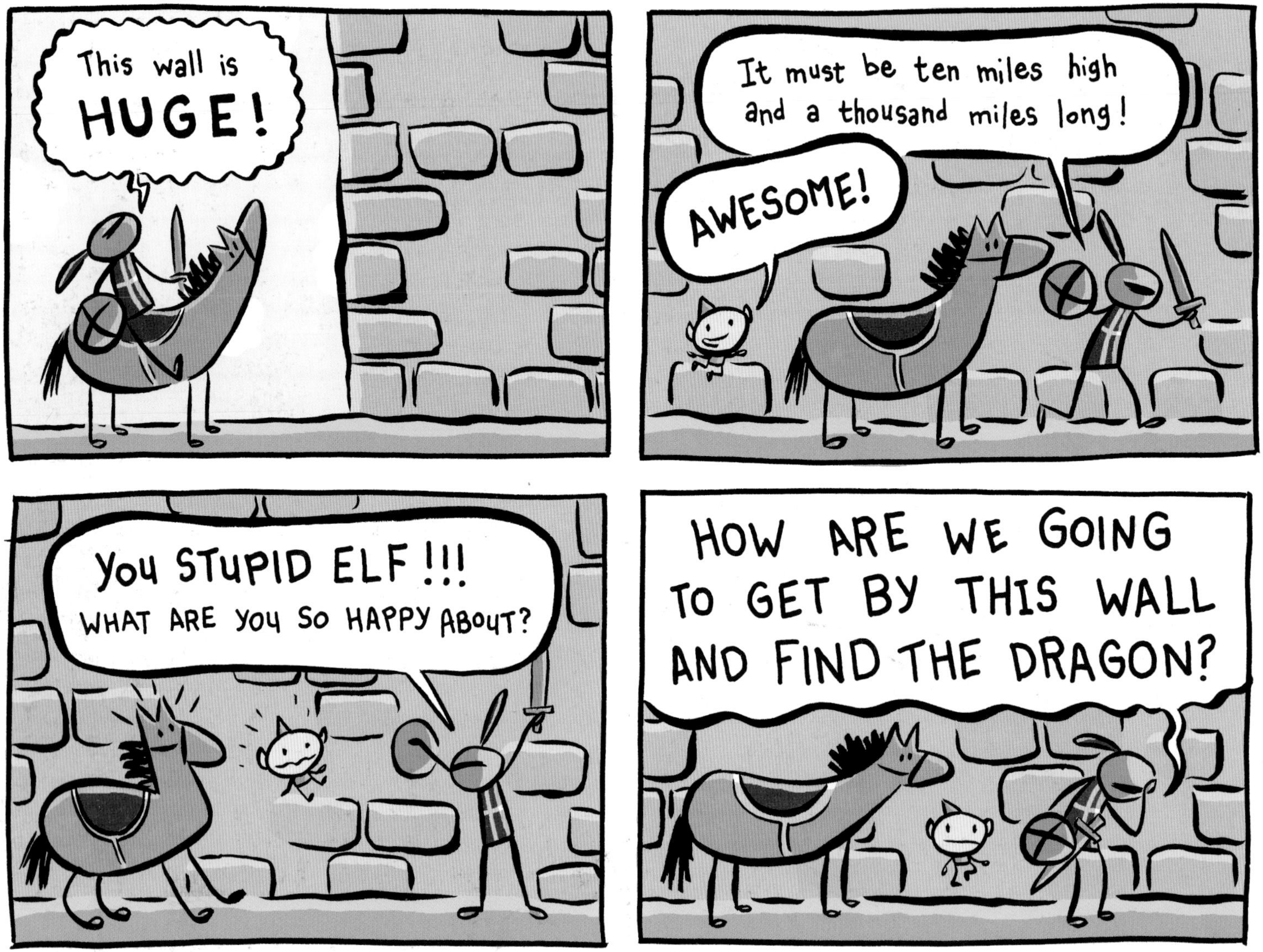
This wall is HUGE!
It must be ten miles high and a thousand miles long!
AWESOME!
You STUPID ELF!!! WHAT ARE YOU SO HAPPY ABOUT?
HOW ARE WE GOING TO GET BY THIS WALL AND FIND THE DRAGON?

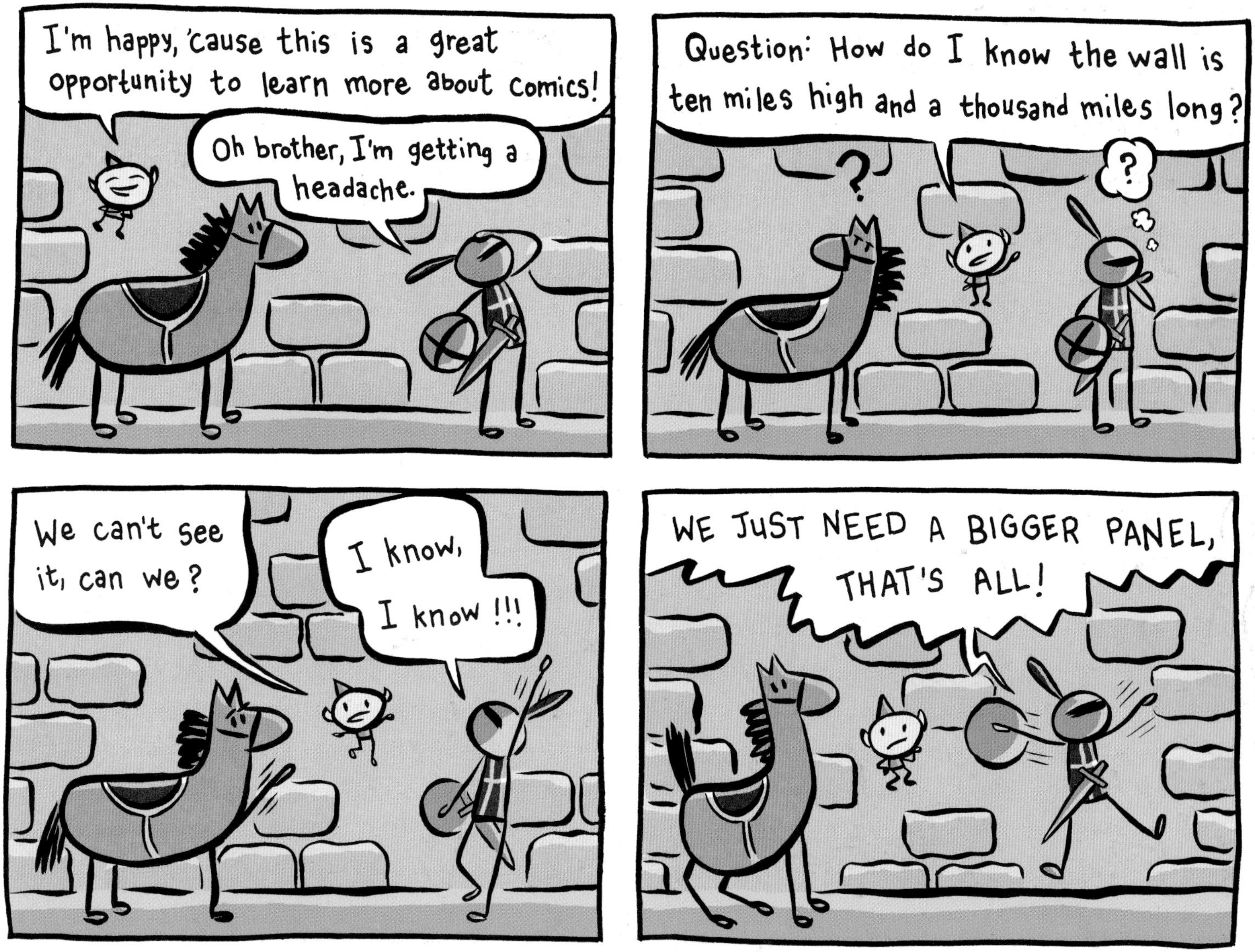
I'm happy, 'cause this is a great opportunity to learn more about comics!
Oh brother, I'm getting a headache.
Question: How do I know the wall is ten miles high and a thousand miles long?
?
?
We can't see it, can we?
I know,
I know!!!
WE JUST NEED A BIGGER PANEL, THAT'S ALL!

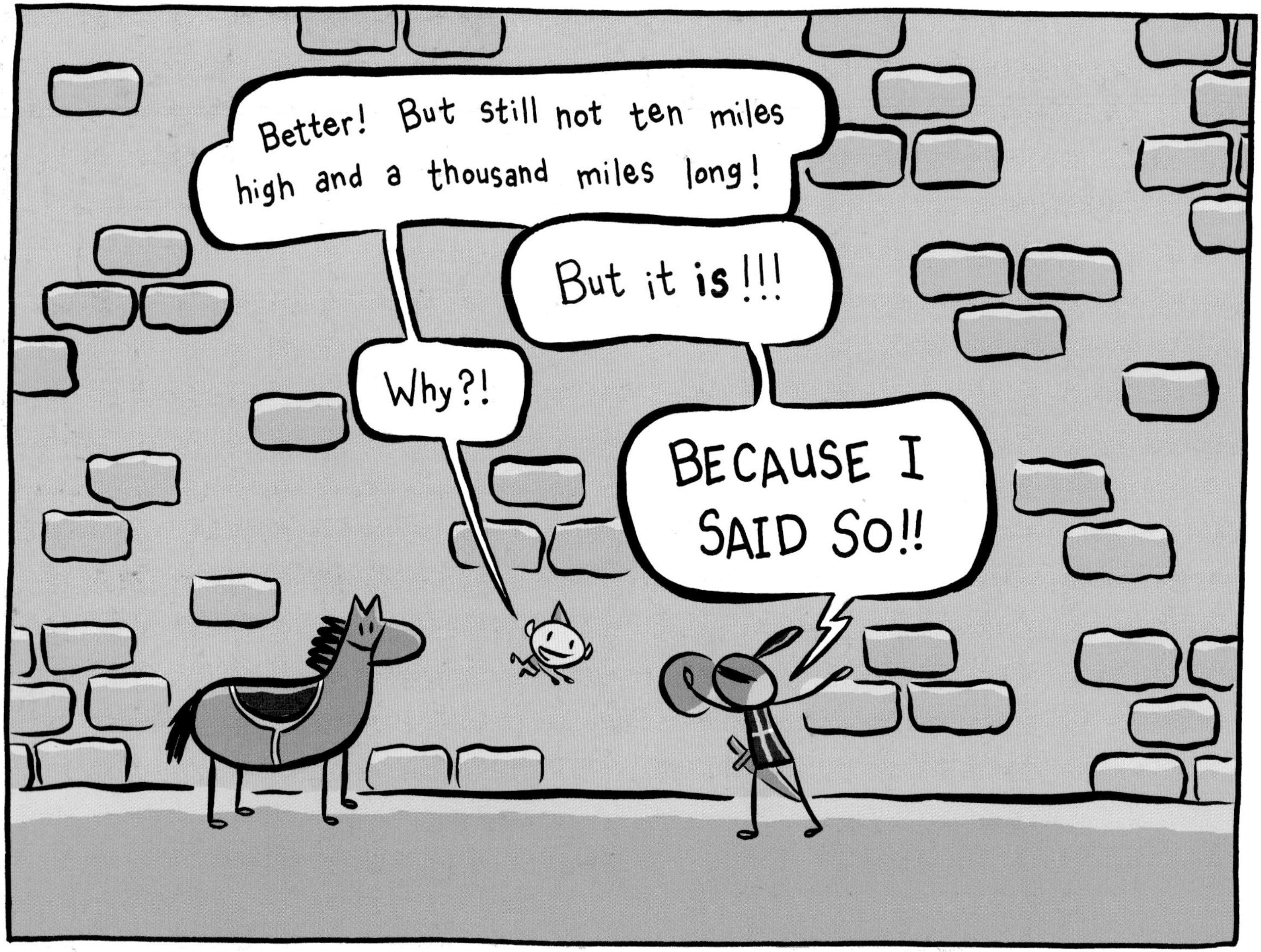
Better! But still not ten miles high and a thousand miles long!
Why?!
But it **is**!!!
BECAUSE I SAID SO!!

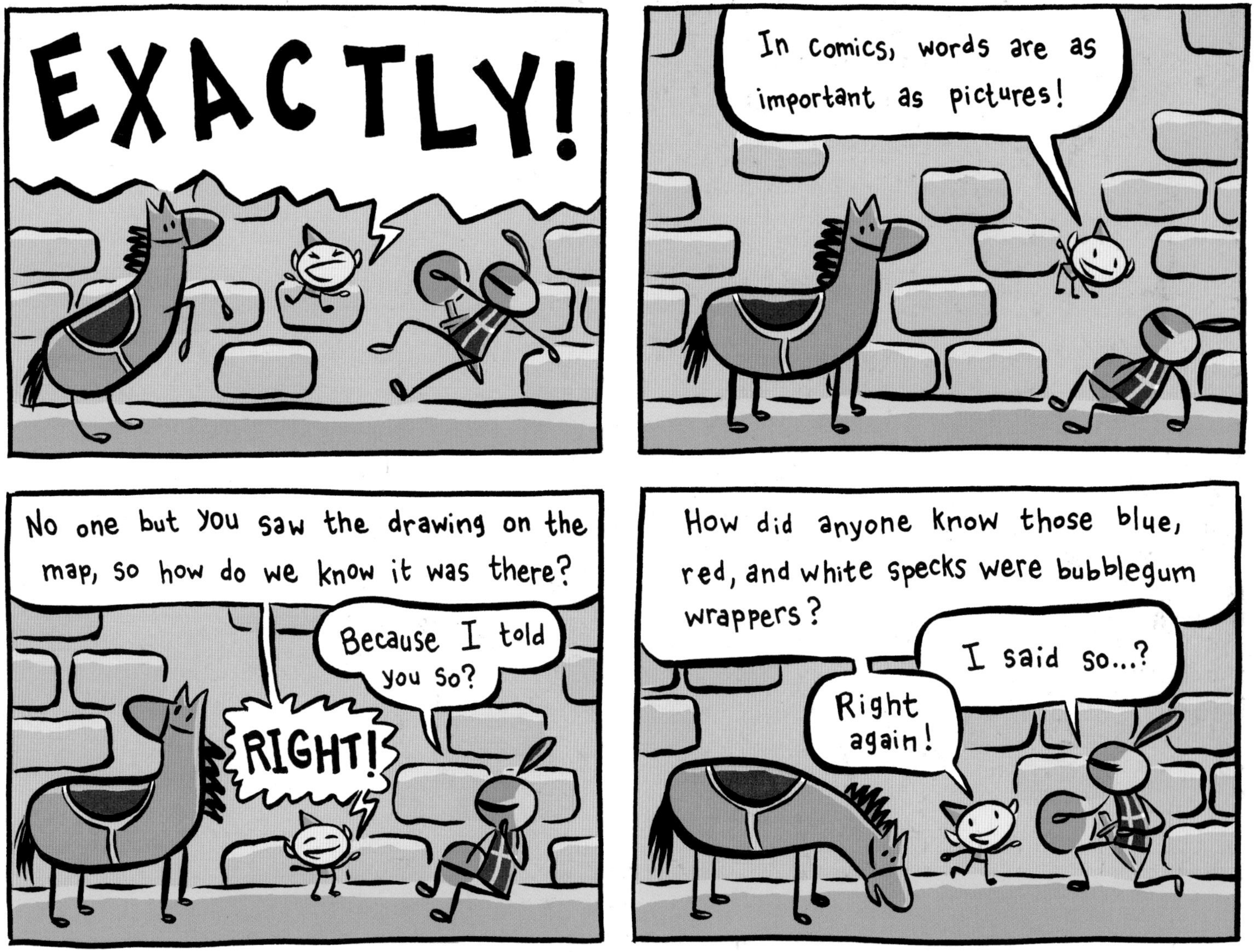
EXACTLY!
In comics, words are as important as pictures!
No one but you saw the drawing on the map, so how do we know it was there?
Because I told you so?
RIGHT!
How did anyone know those blue, red, and white specks were bubblegum wrappers?
I said so...?
Right again!

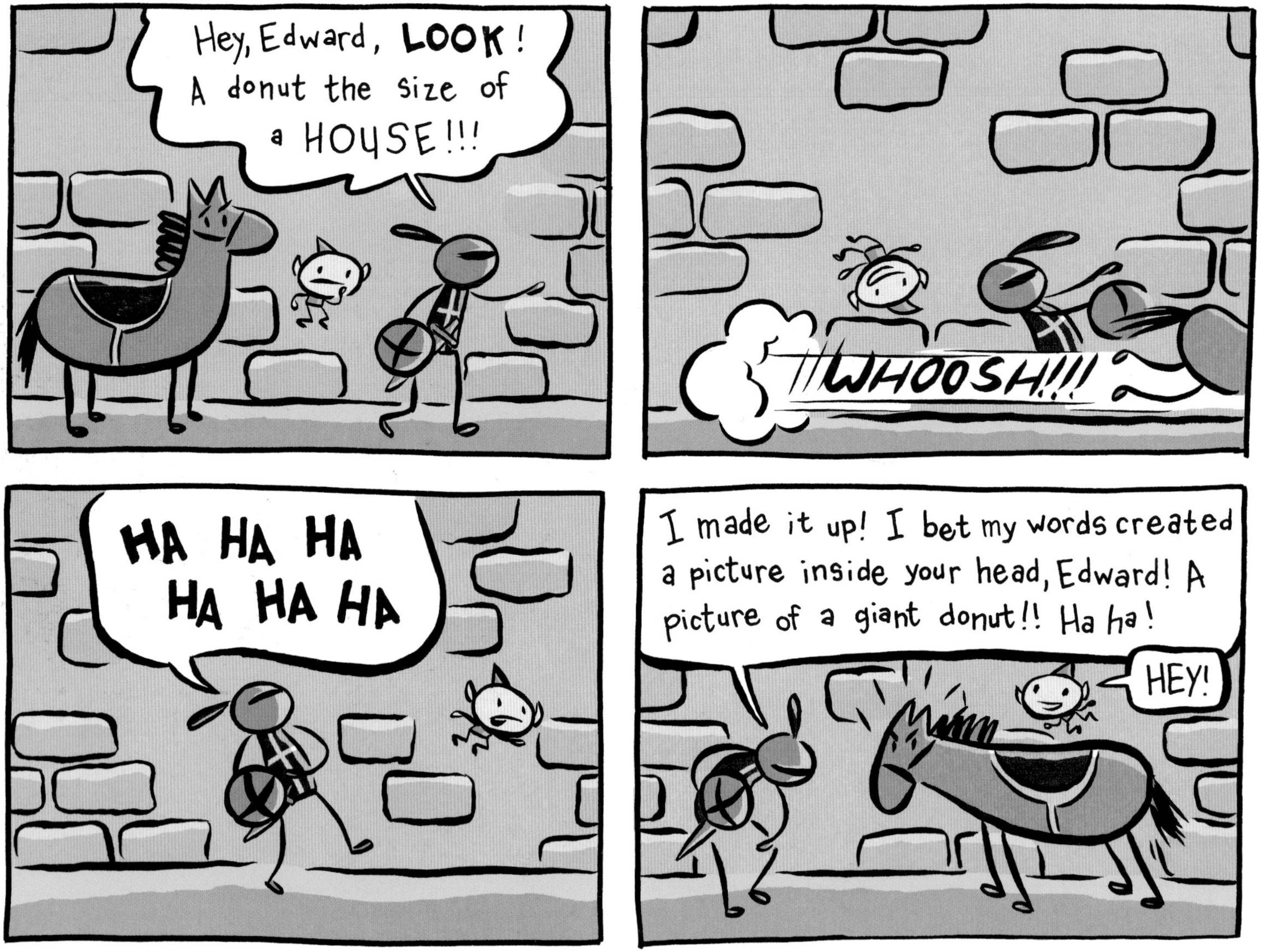
Hey, Edward, LOOK! A donut the size of a HOUSE!!!
WHOOSH!!!
HA HA HA HA HA HA
I made it up! I bet my words created a picture inside your head, Edward! A picture of a giant donut!! Ha ha!
HEY!

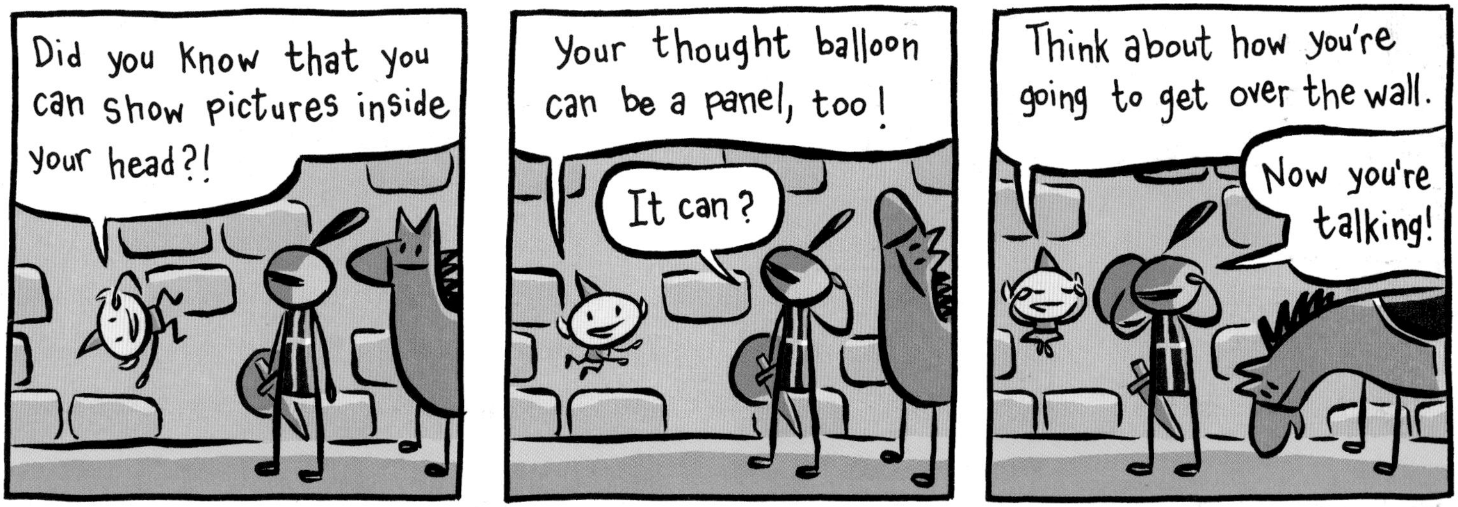
Did you know that you can show pictures inside your head?!
Your thought balloon can be a panel, too!
It can?
Think about how you're going to get over the wall.
Now you're talking!

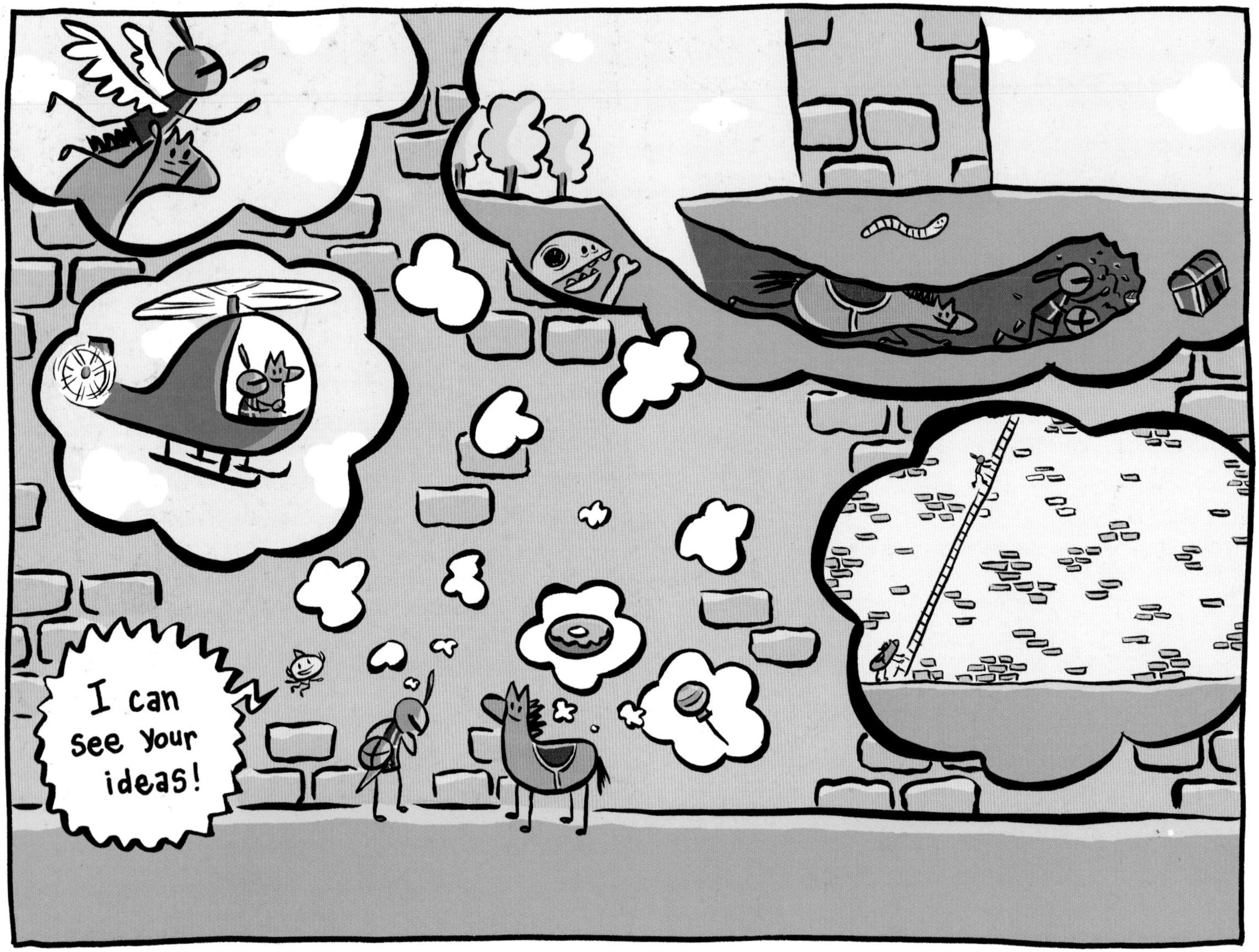
I can see your ideas!

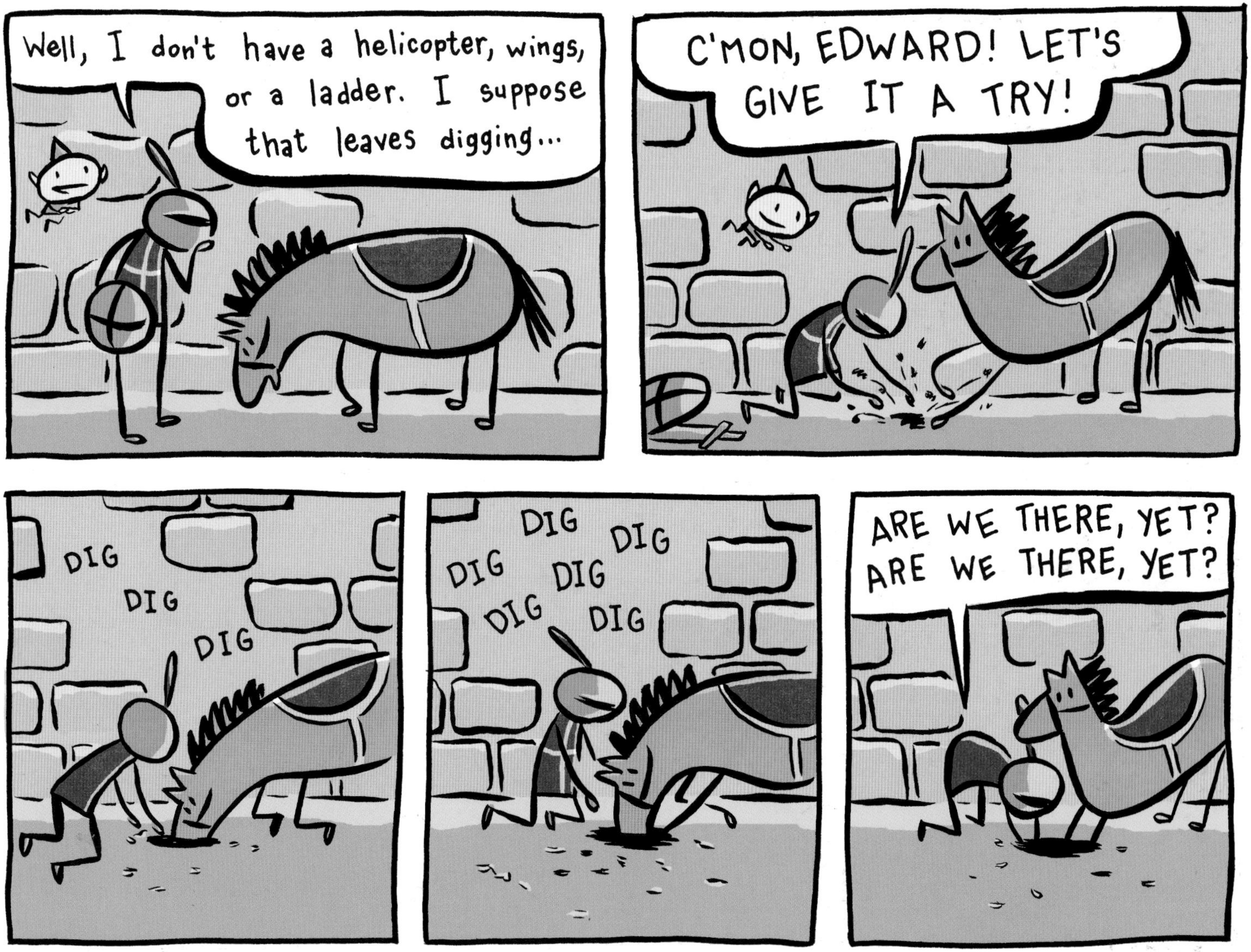
Well, I don't have a helicopter, wings, or a ladder. I suppose that leaves digging...
C'MON, EDWARD! LET'S GIVE IT A TRY!
DIG
DIG
DIG
DIG
DIG
DIG
DIG
DIG
DIG
ARE WE THERE, YET? ARE WE THERE, YET?

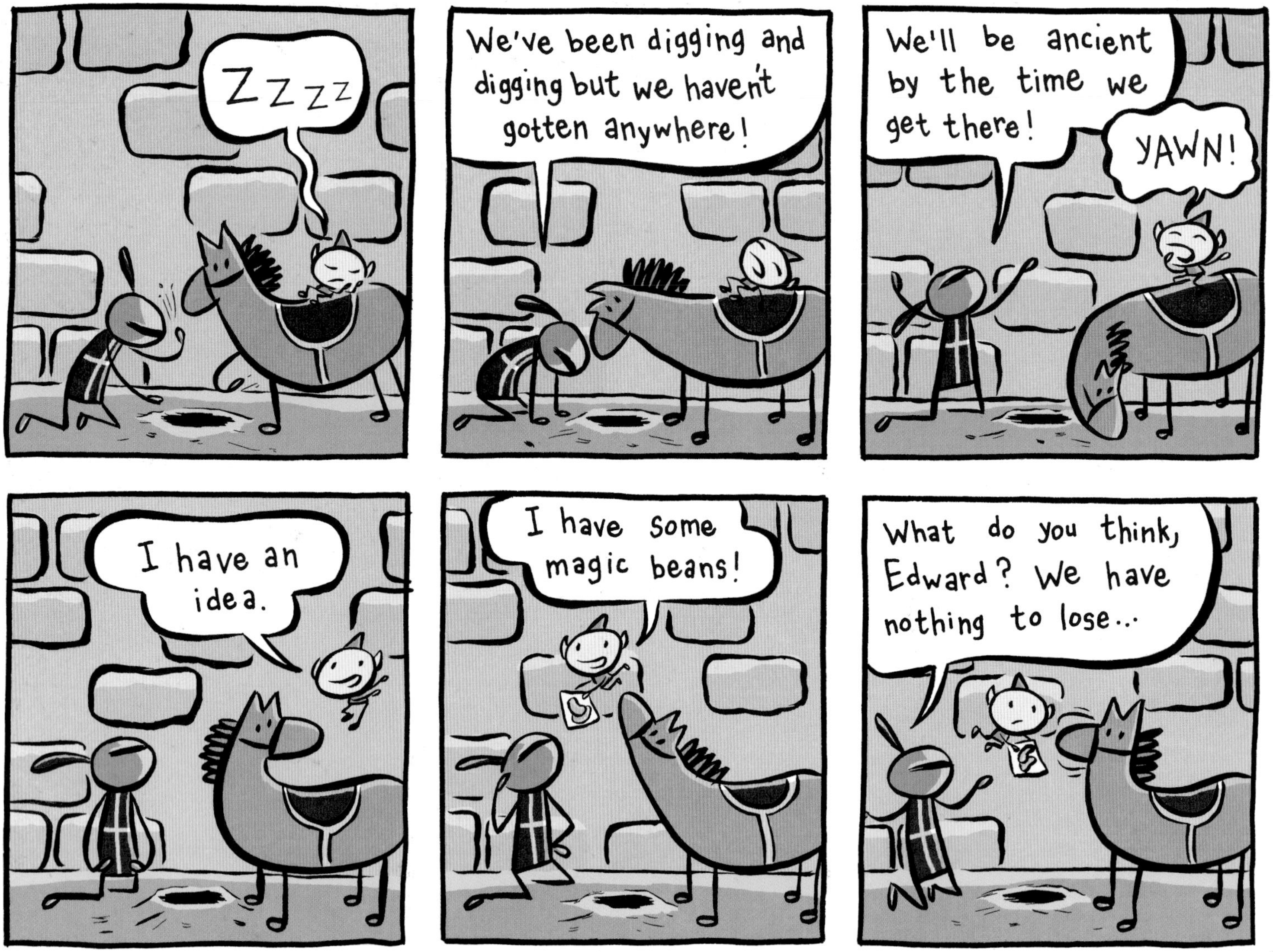
ZZZZZ
We've been digging and digging but we haven't gotten anywhere!
We'll be ancient by the time we get there!
YAWN!
I have an idea.
I have some magic beans!
What do you think, Edward? We have nothing to lose...

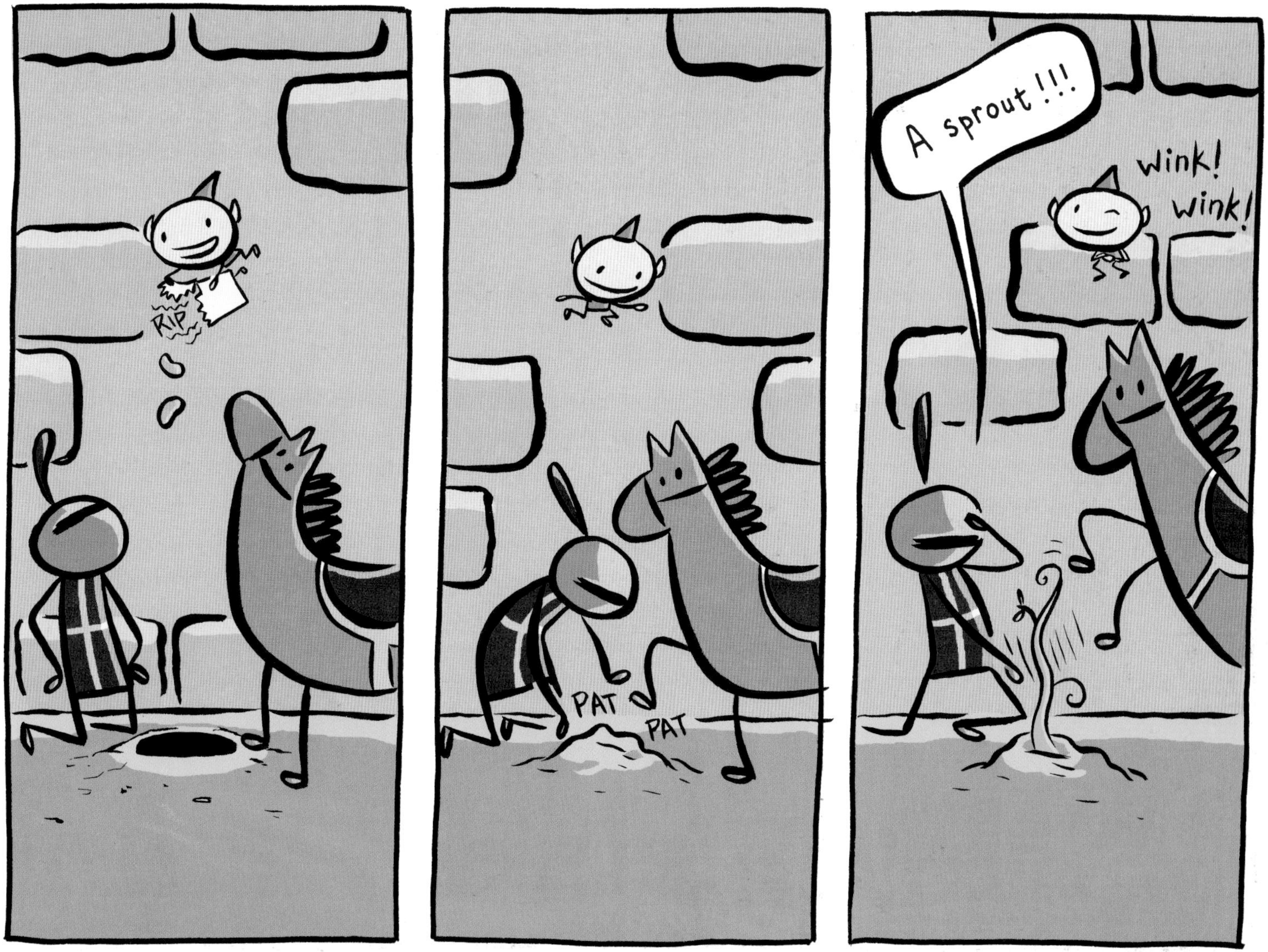
RIP
PAT
PAT
A sprout!!!
wink!
wink!

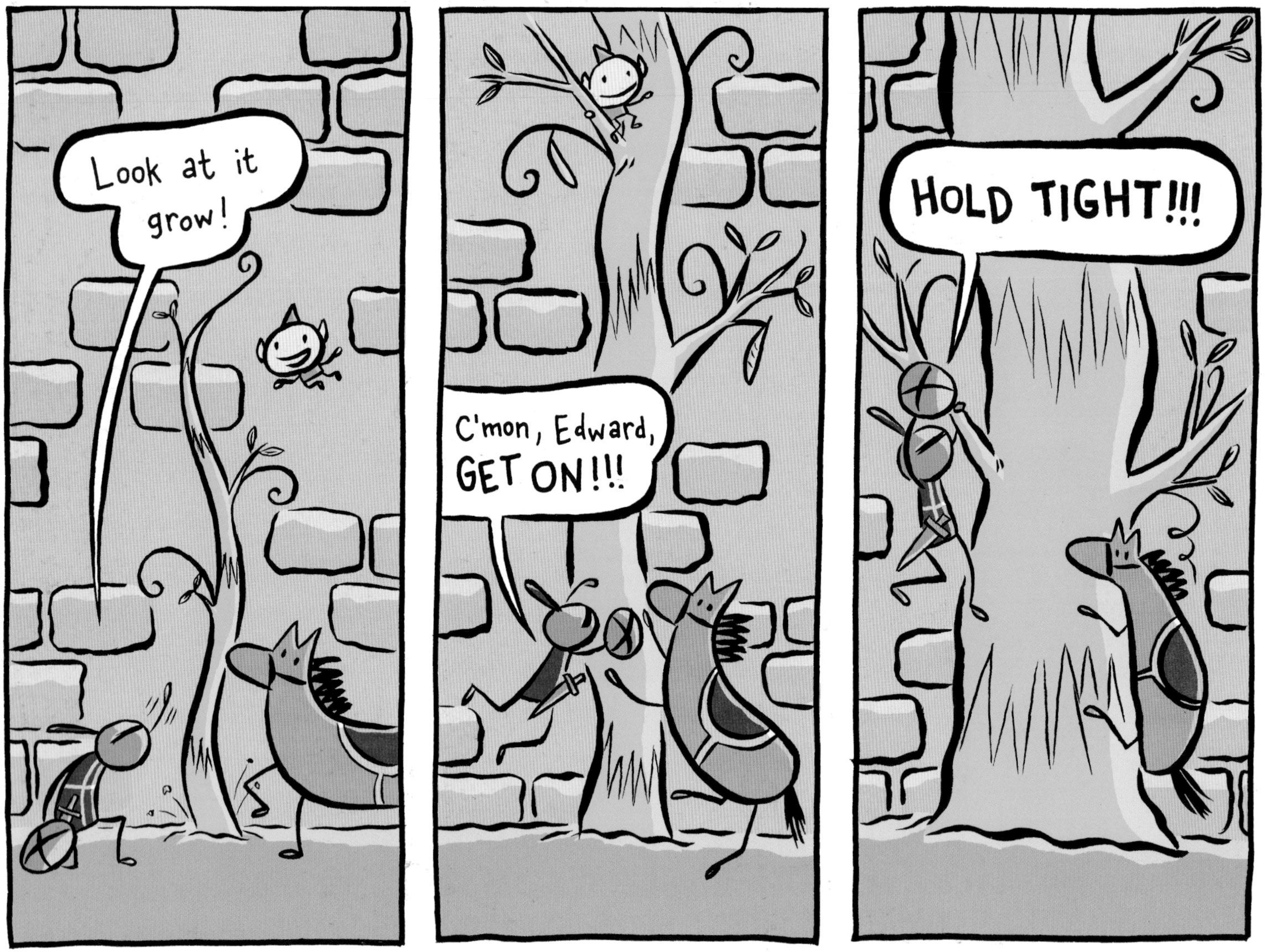
Look at it grow!
C'mon, Edward, GET ON!!!
HOLD TIGHT!!!

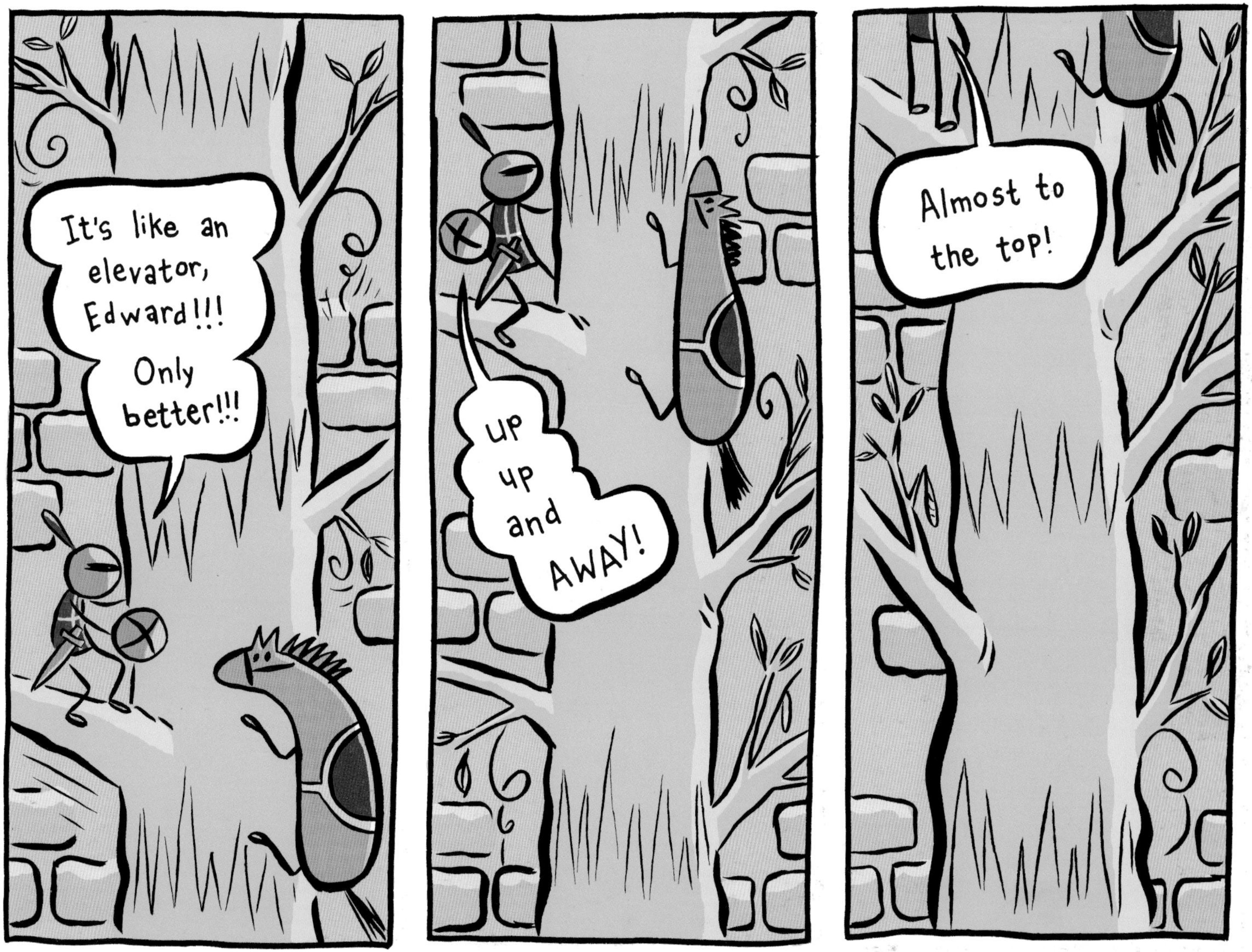
It's like an elevator, Edward!!!
Only better!!!
up up and AWAY!
Almost to the top!

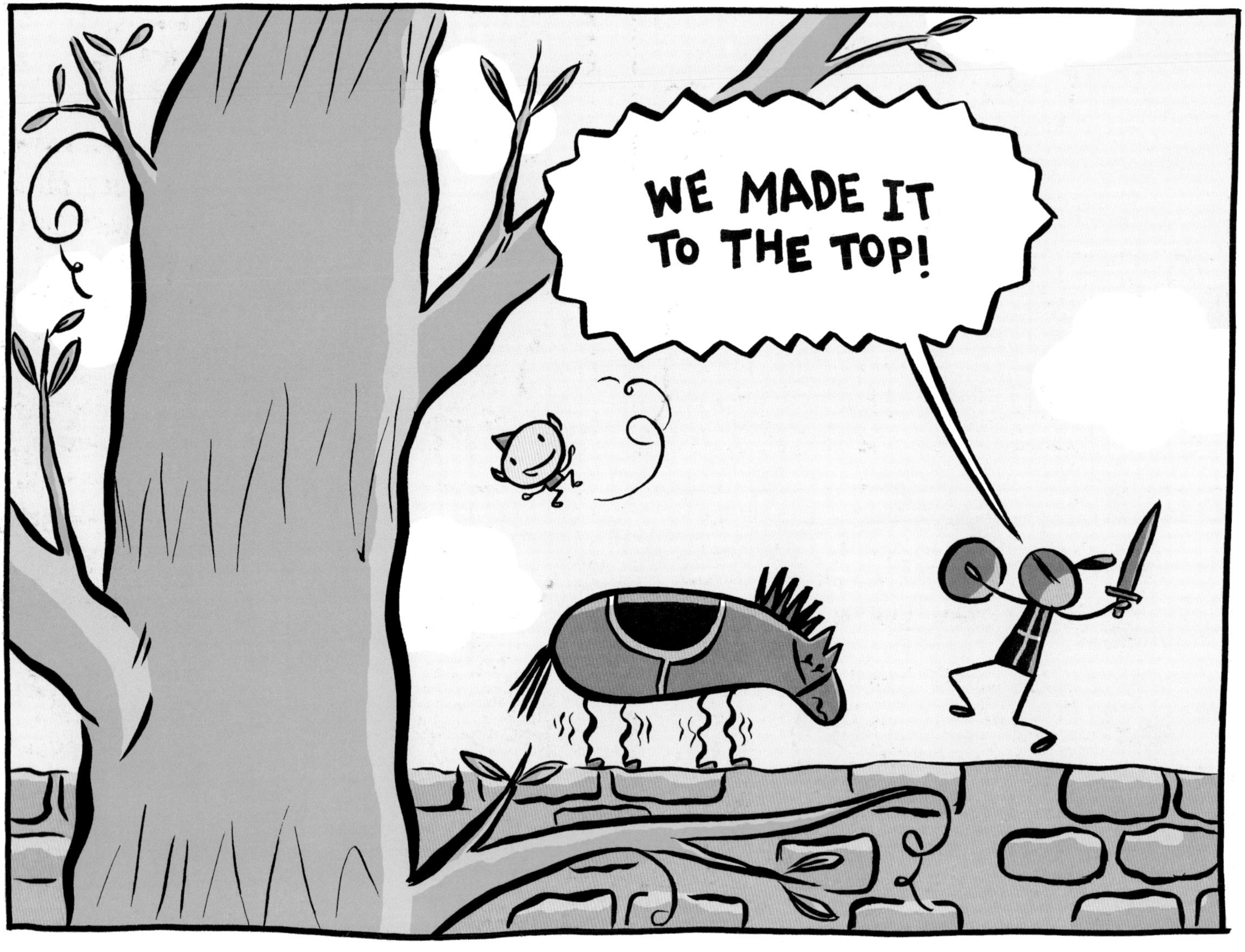
WE MADE IT TO THE TOP!

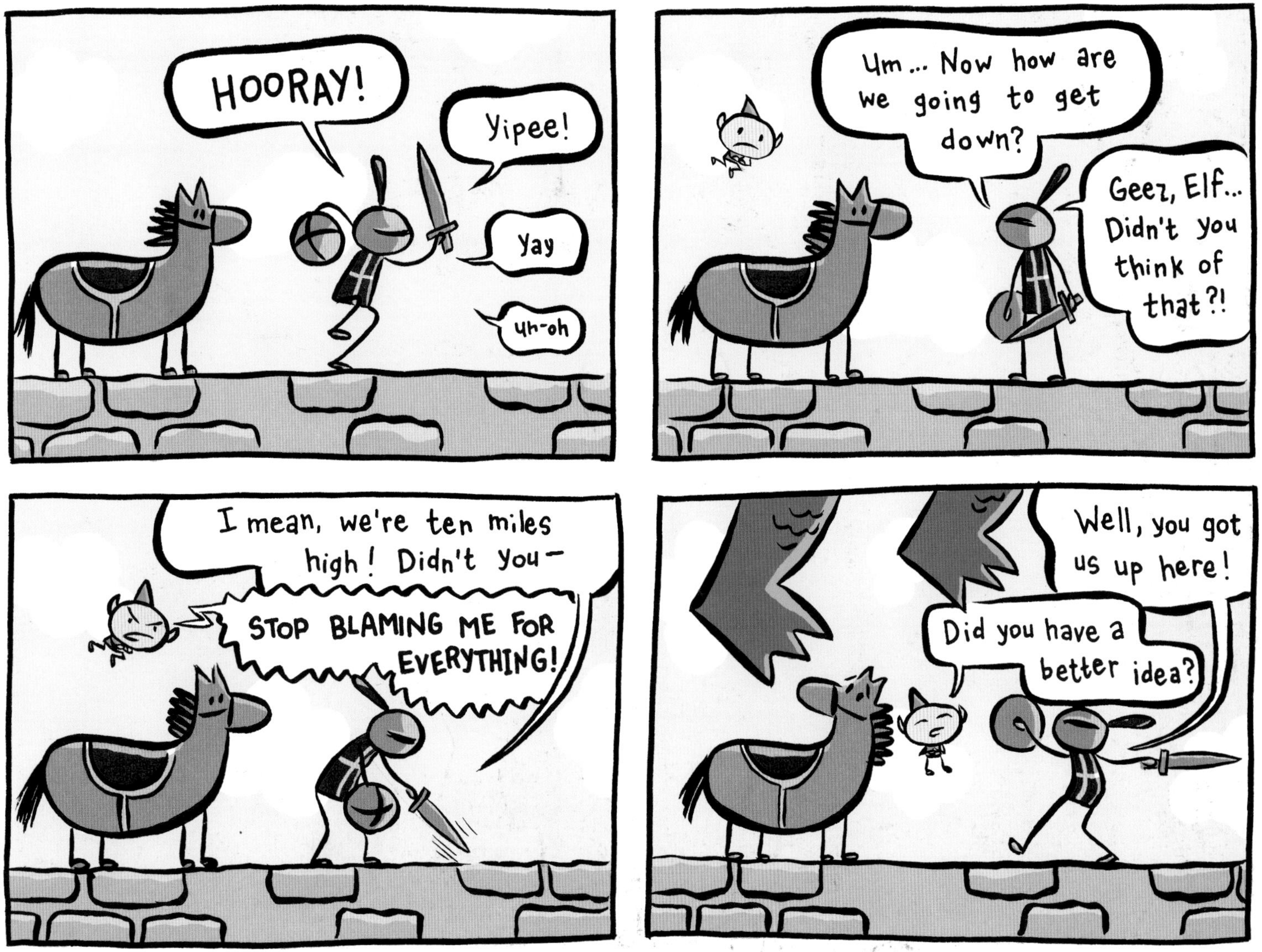
HOORAY!
Yipee!
Yay
Uh-oh
Um... Now how are we going to get down?
Geez, Elf... Didn't you think of that?!
I mean, we're ten miles high! Didn't you—
STOP BLAMING ME FOR EVERYTHING!
Well, you got us up here!
Did you have a better idea?

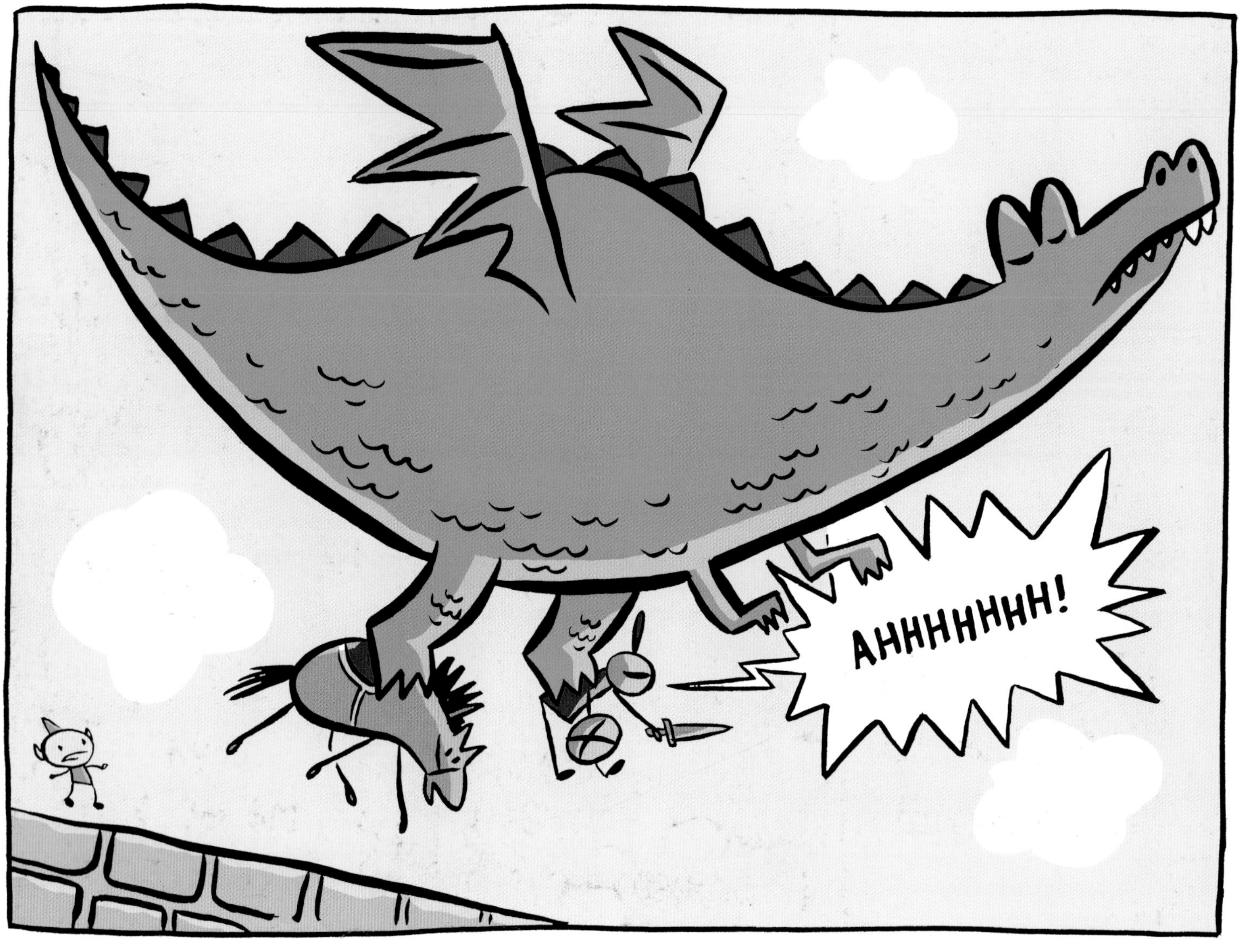
AHHHHHHH!

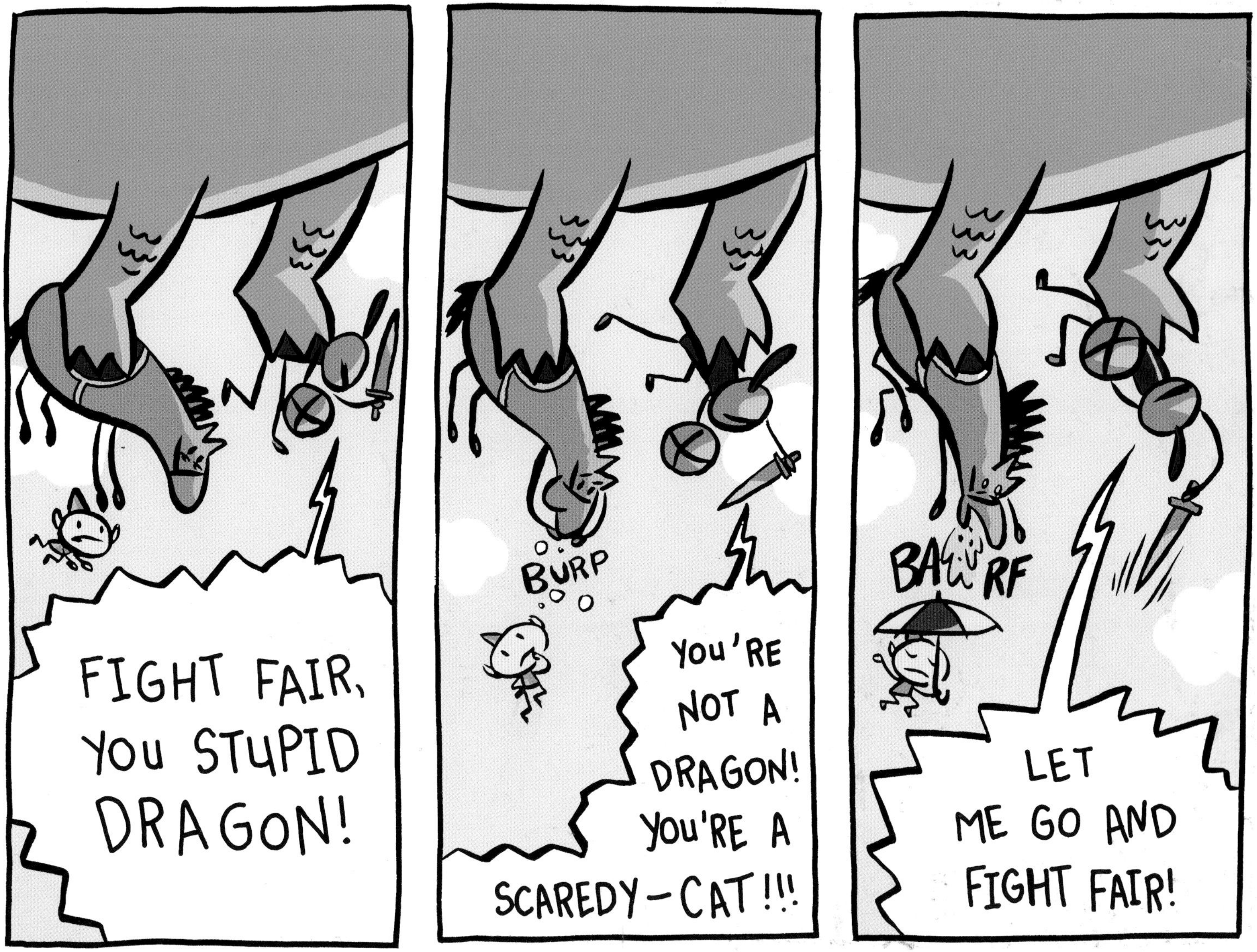
FIGHT FAIR, YOU STUPID DRAGON!
BURP
YOU'RE NOT A DRAGON! YOU'RE A SCAREDY-CAT!!!
BARF
LET ME GO AND FIGHT FAIR!

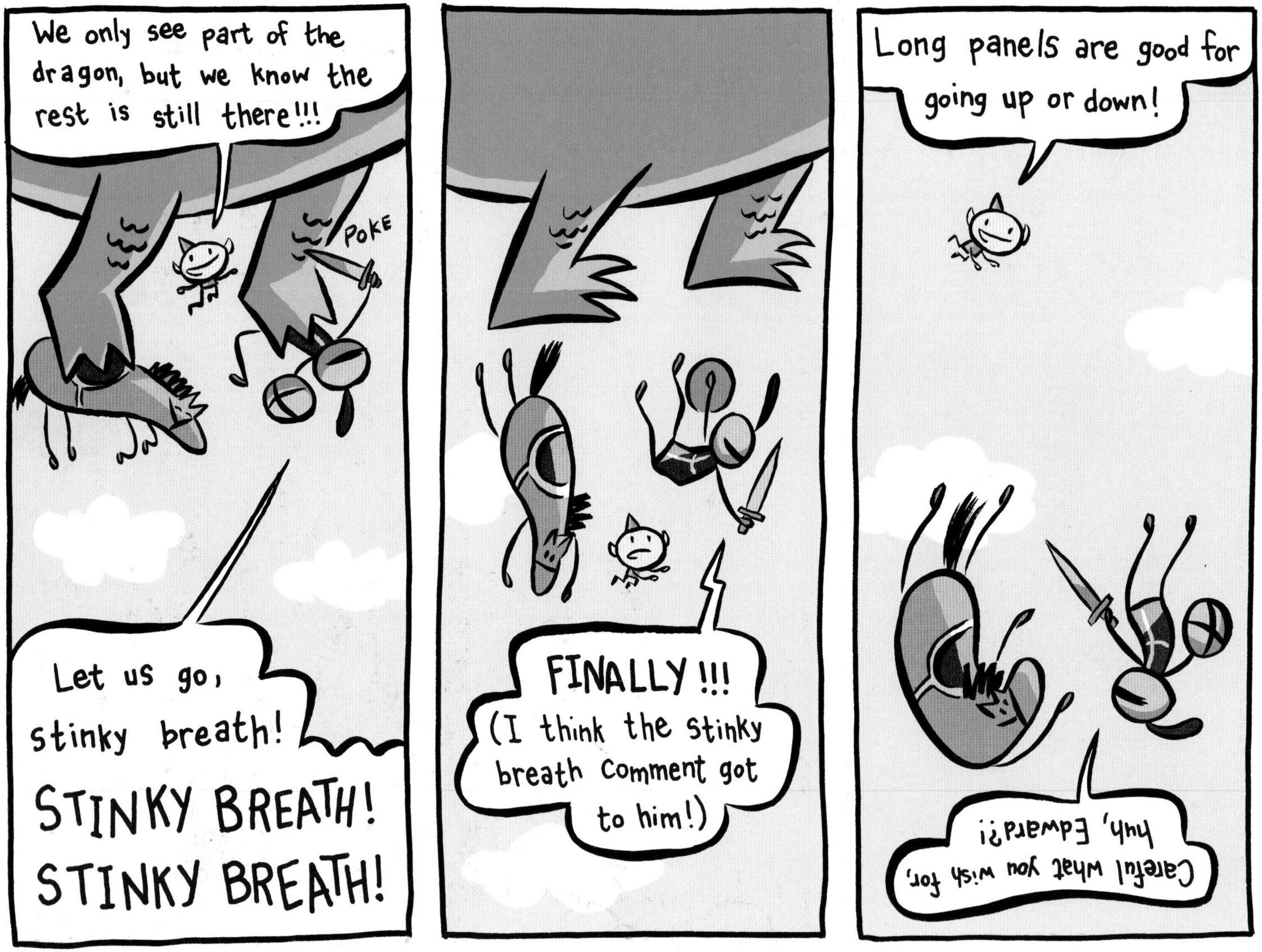
We only see part of the dragon, but we know the rest is still there!!!
POKE
Let us go, stinky breath!
STINKY BREATH! STINKY BREATH!
FINALLY!!!
(I think the stinky breath comment got to him!)
Long panels are good for going up or down!
Careful what you wish for, huh, Edward?!

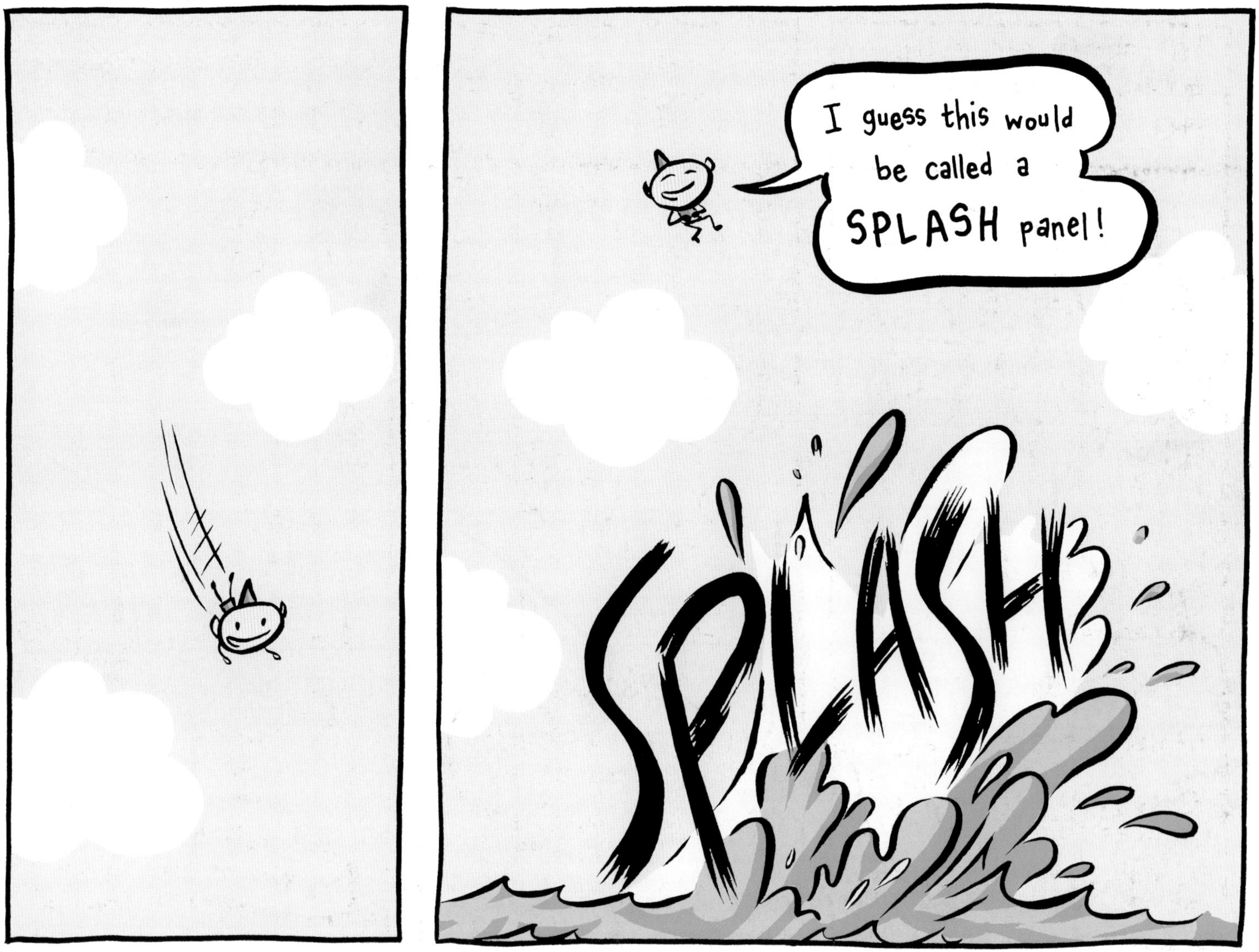
I guess this would be called a SPLASH panel!
SPLASH

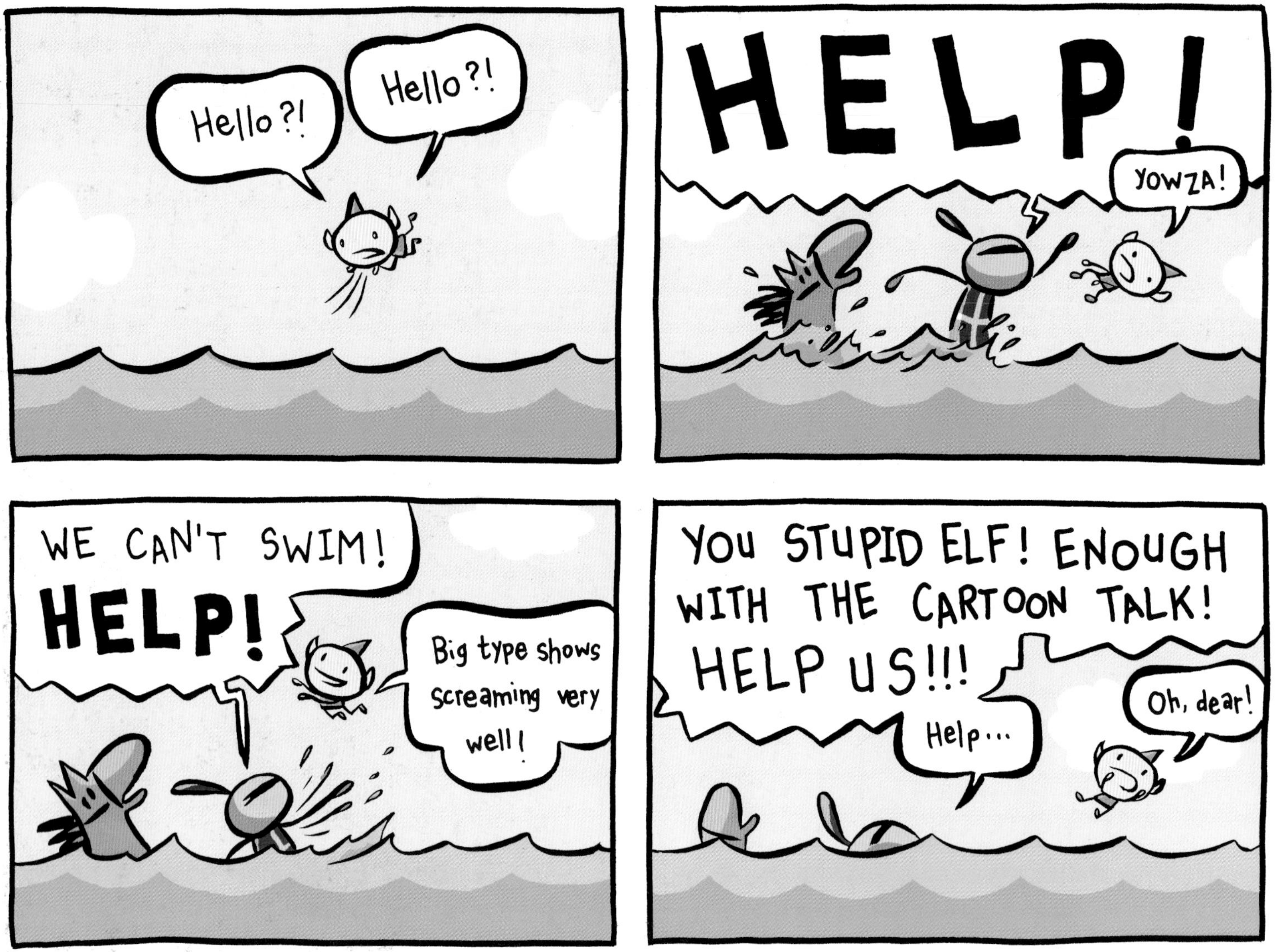
Hello?!
Hello?!
HELP!
YOWZA!
WE CAN'T SWIM! HELP!
Big type shows screaming very well!
YOU STUPID ELF! ENOUGH WITH THE CARTOON TALK! HELP US!!!
Help...
Oh, dear!

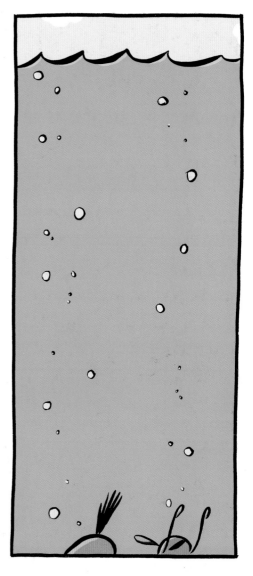

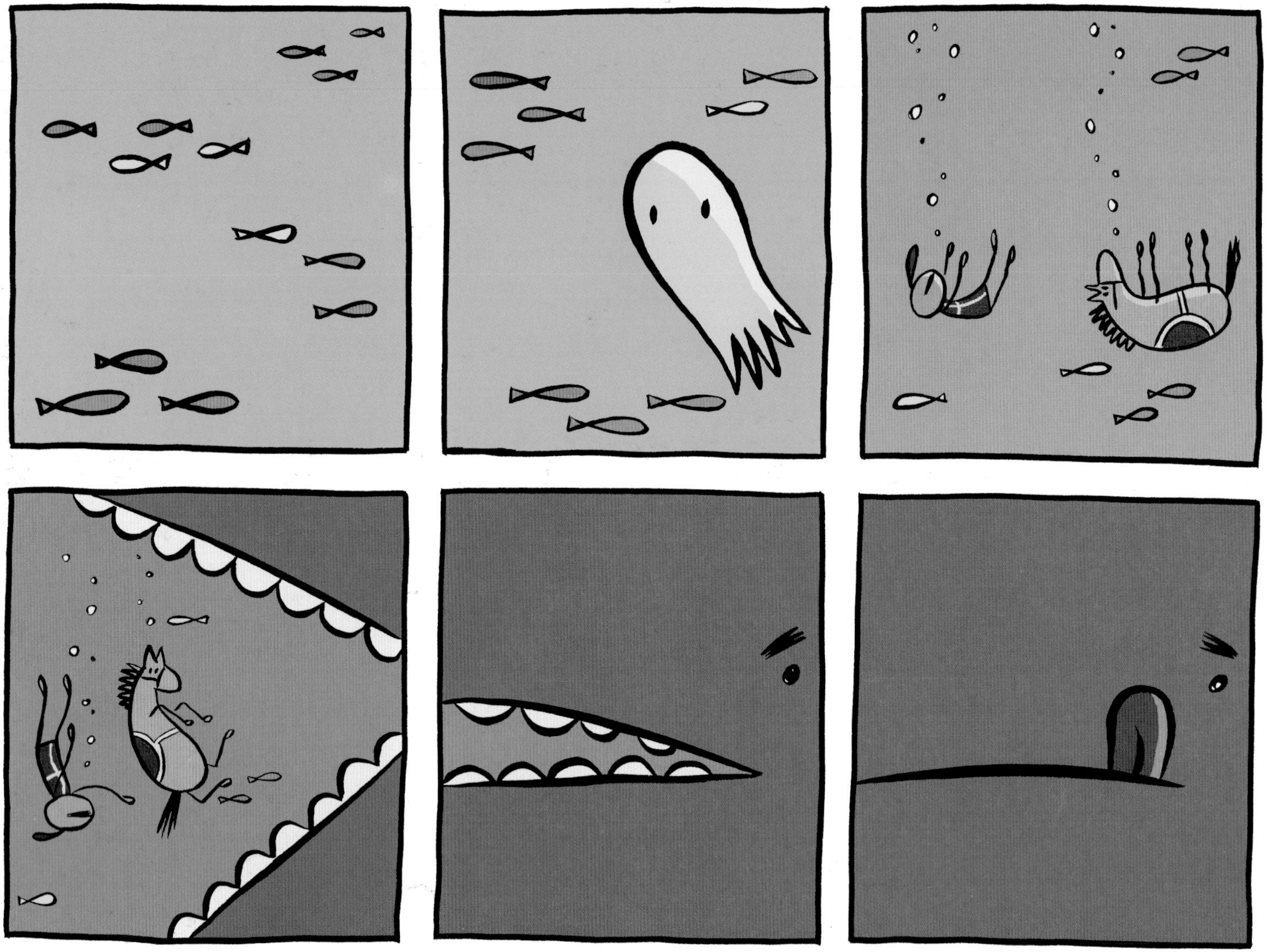

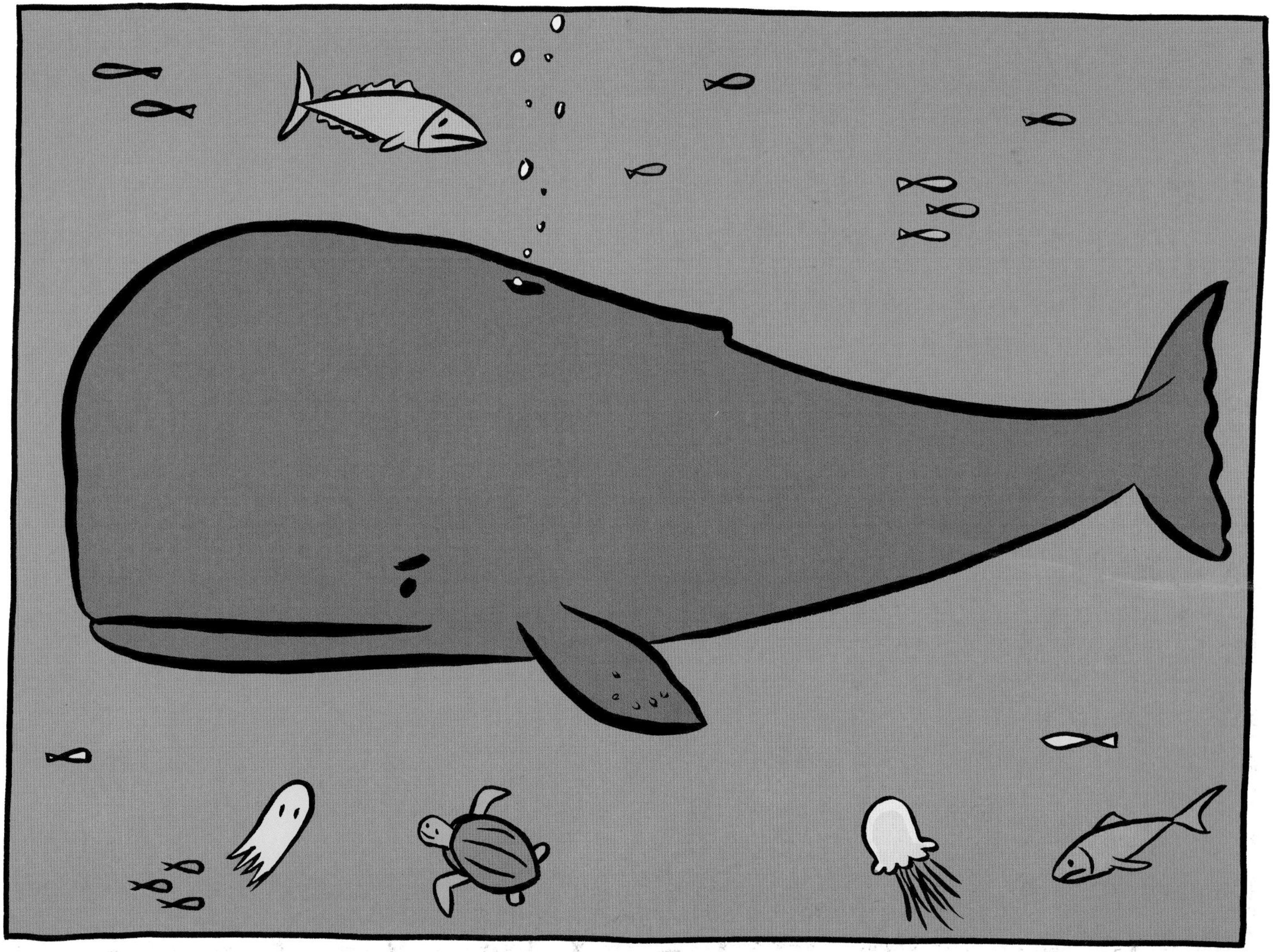

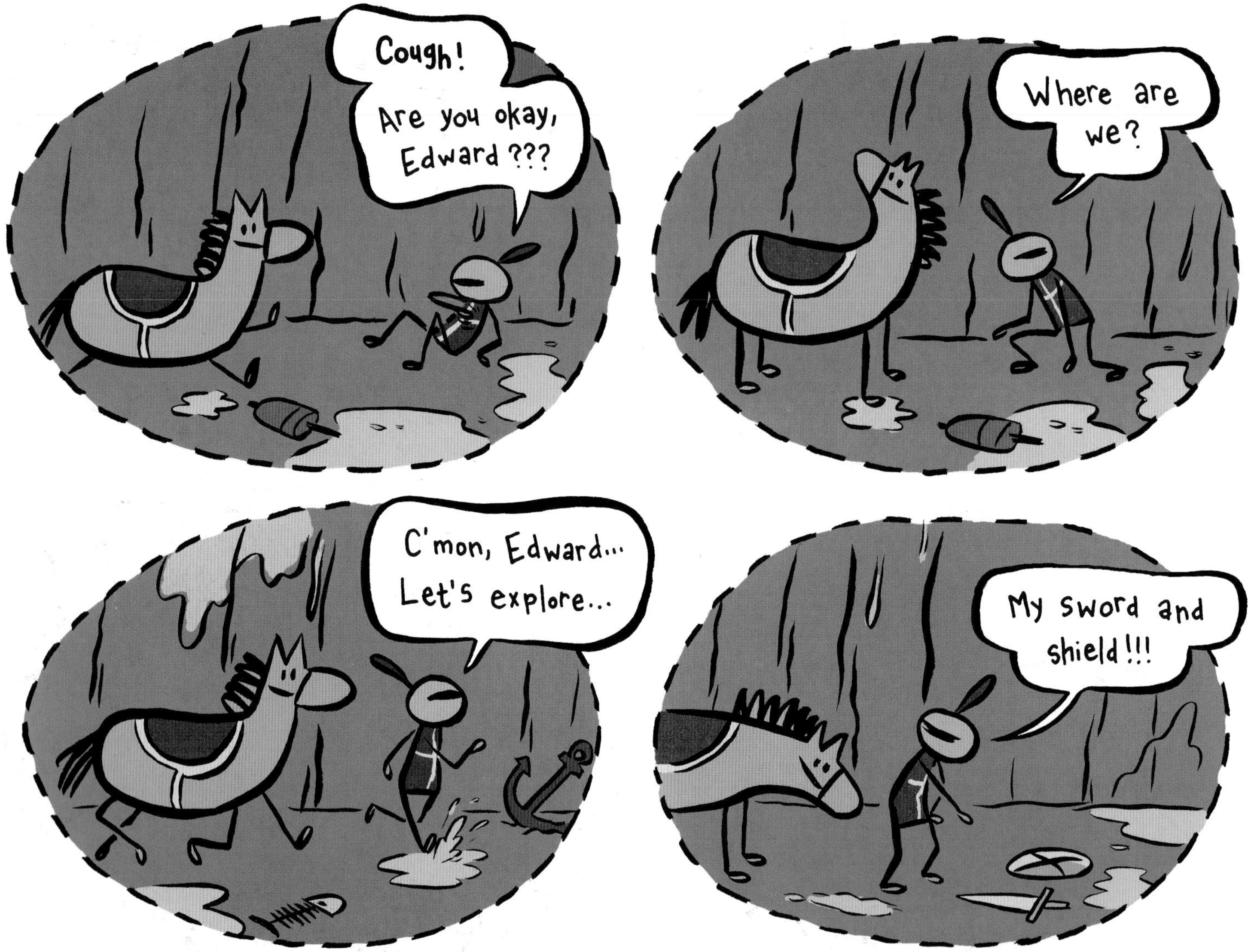
Cough!
Are you okay, Edward???
Where are we?
C'mon, Edward... Let's explore...
My sword and shield!!!

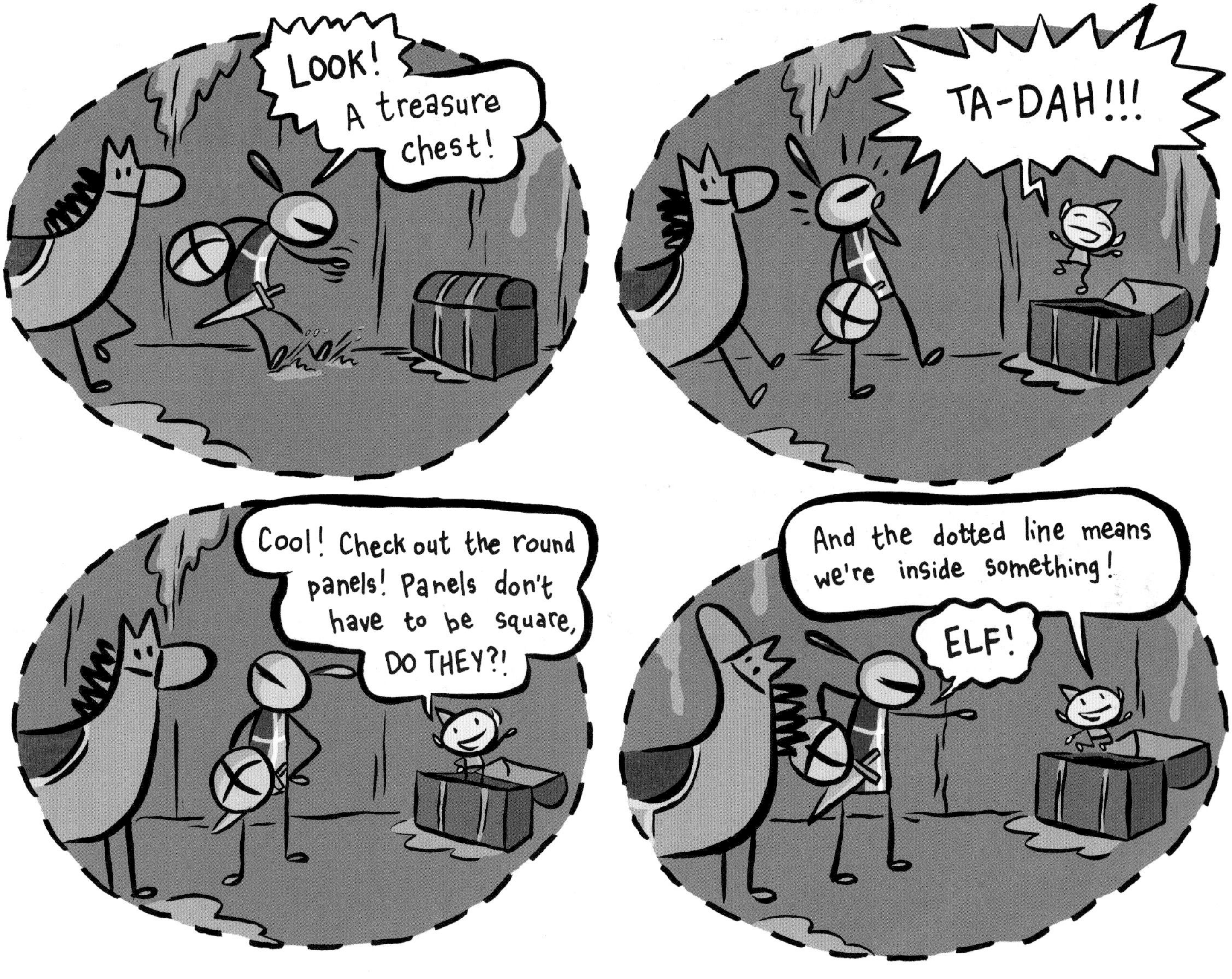
LOOK! A treasure chest!
TA-DAH!!!
Cool! Check out the round panels! Panels don't have to be square, DO THEY?!
And the dotted line means we're inside something!
ELF!

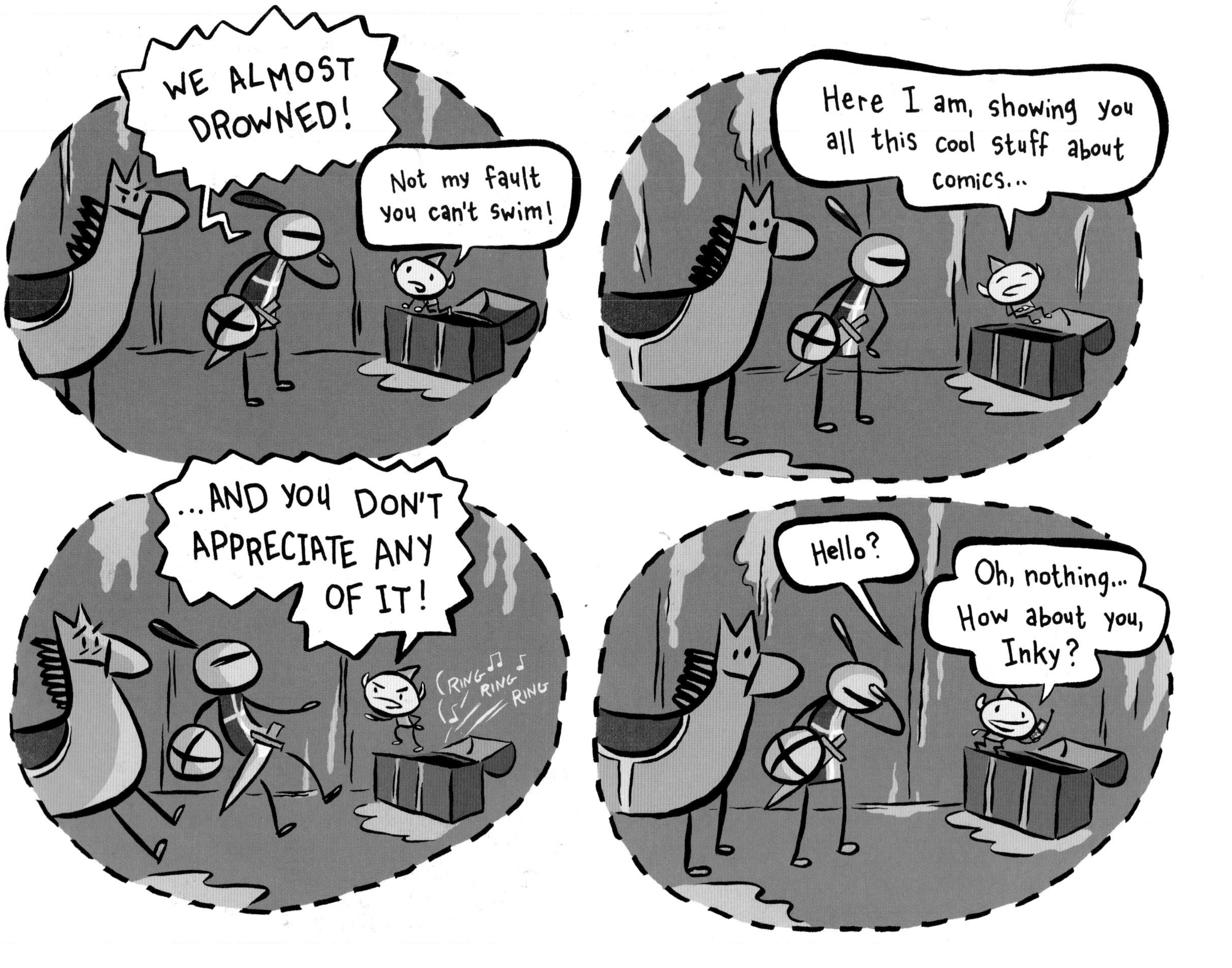
WE ALMOST DROWNED!
Not my fault you can't swim!
Here I am, showing you all this cool stuff about comics...
...AND YOU DON'T APPRECIATE ANY OF IT!
RING RING RING
Hello?
Oh, nothing... How about you, Inky?

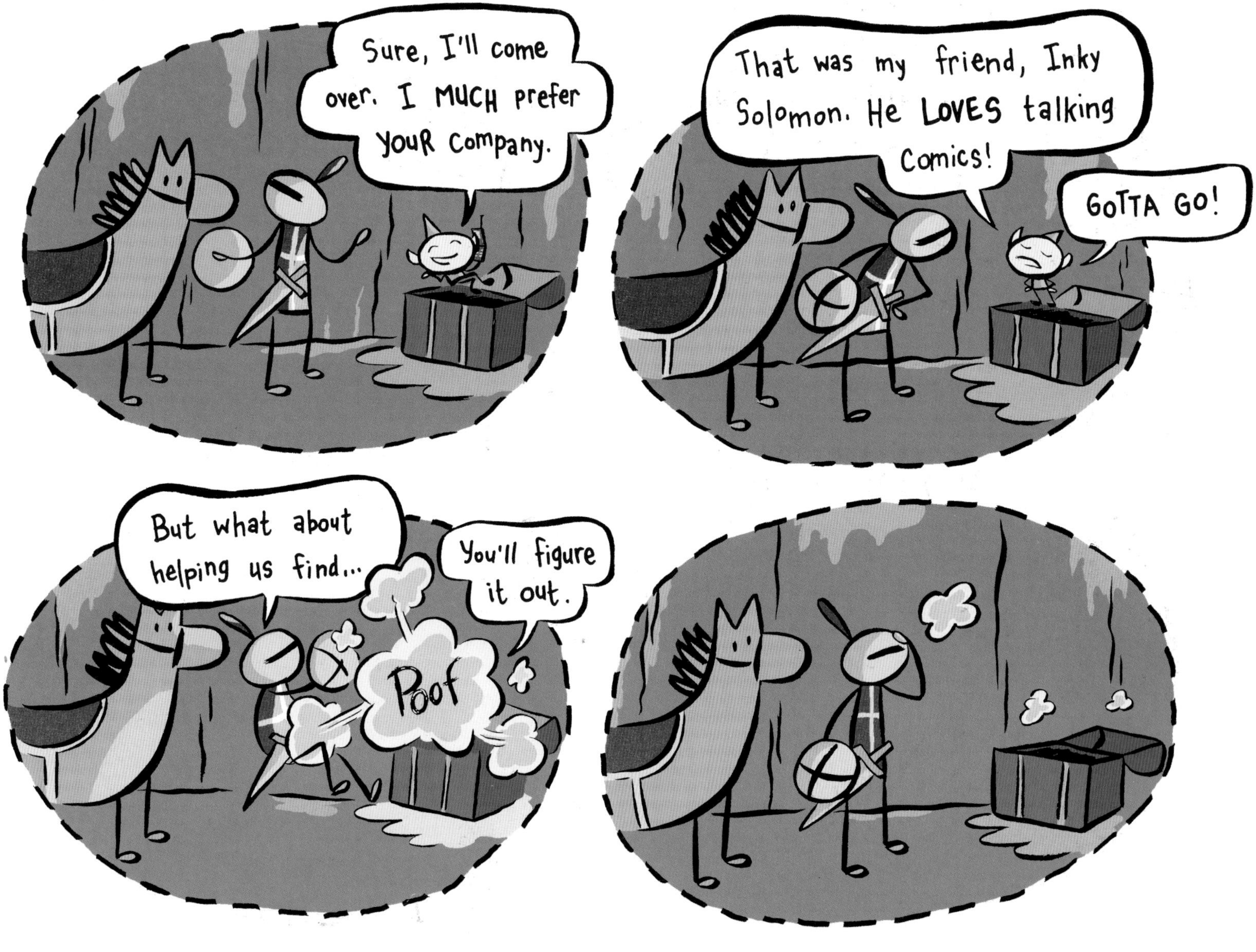
Sure, I'll come over. I MUCH prefer YOUR company.
That was my friend, Inky Solomon. He LOVES talking Comics!
GOTTA GO!
But what about helping us find...
You'll figure it out.
Poof

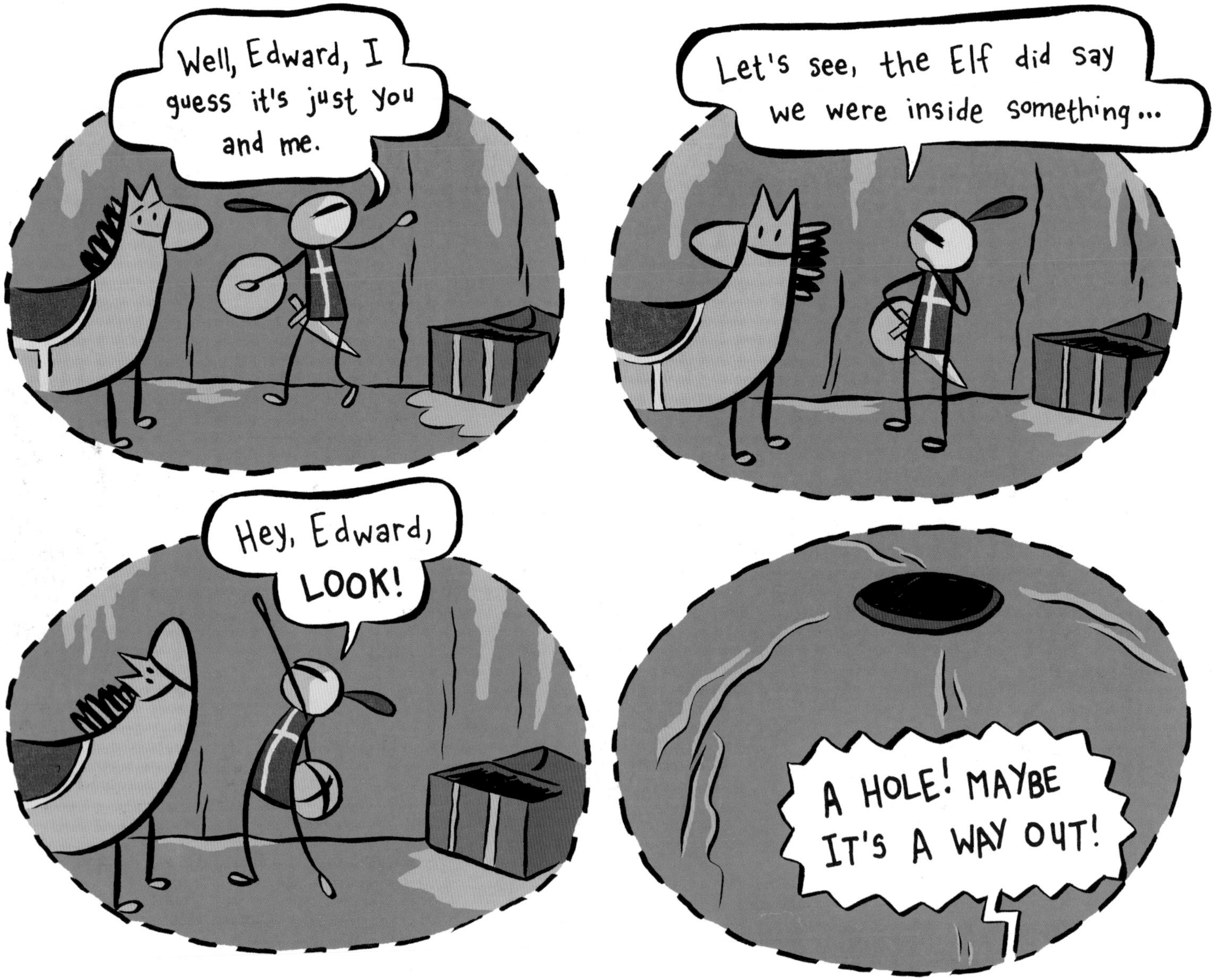
Well, Edward, I guess it's just you and me.
Let's see, the Elf did say we were inside something...
Hey, Edward, LOOK!
A HOLE! MAYBE IT'S A WAY OUT!

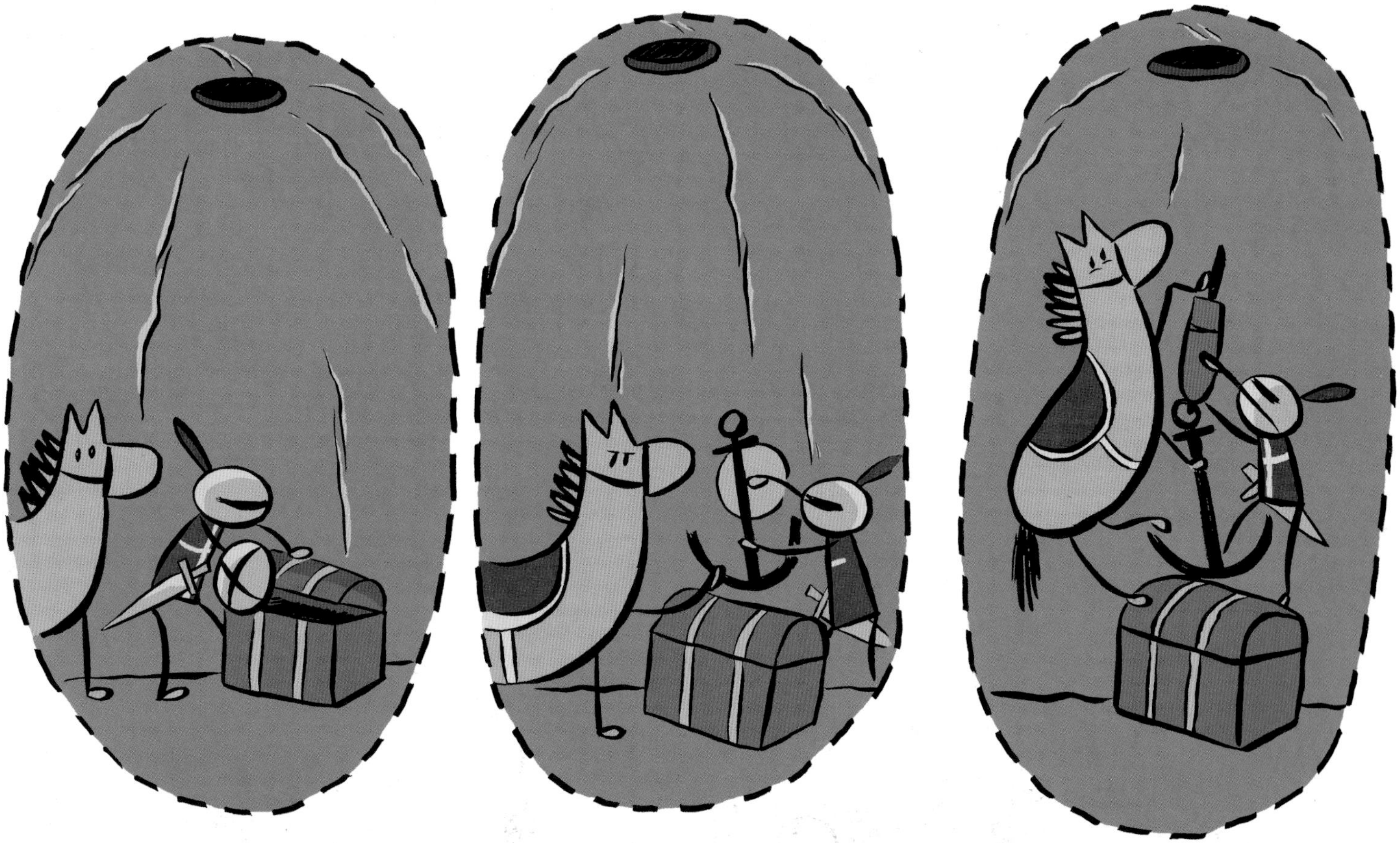

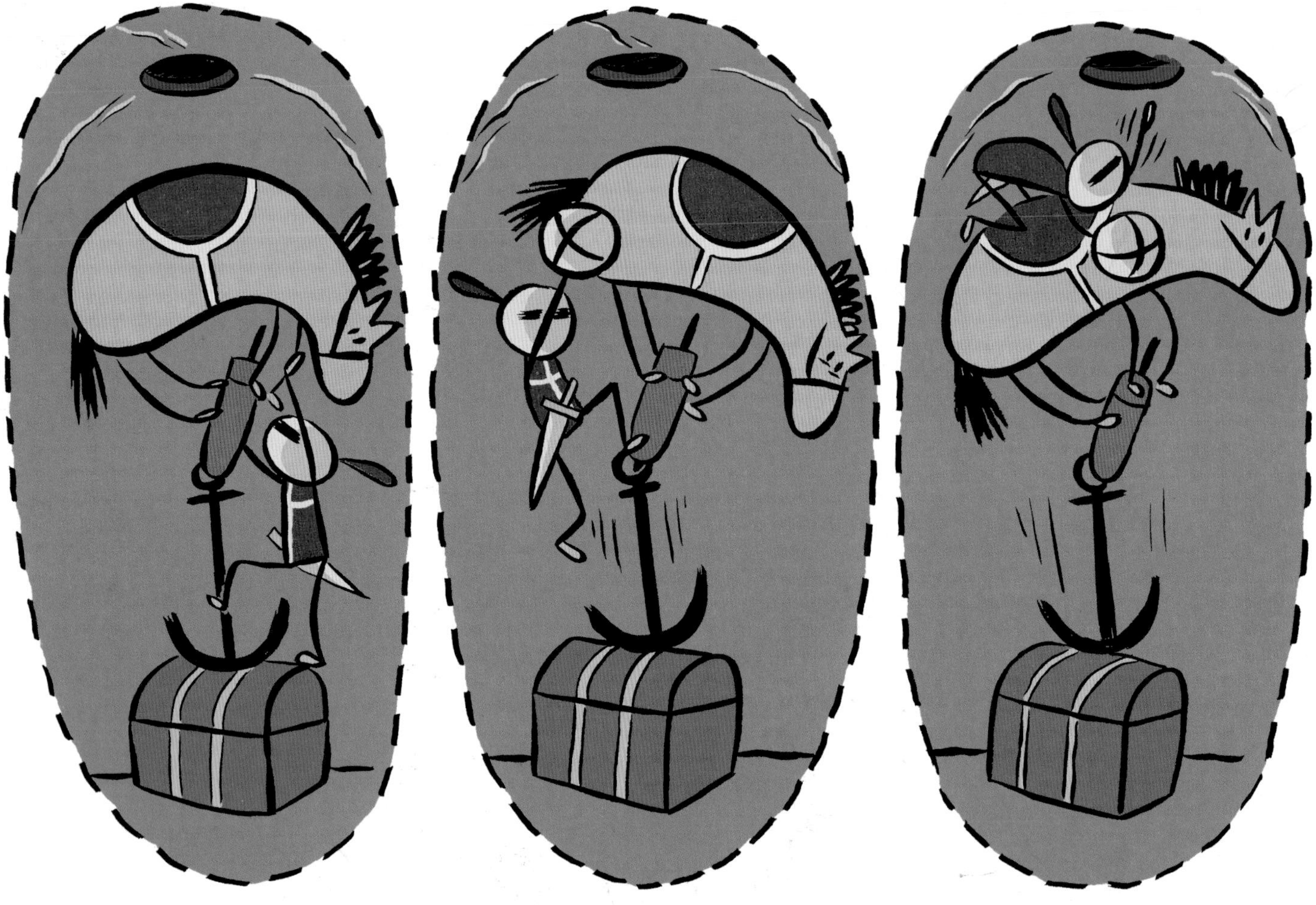

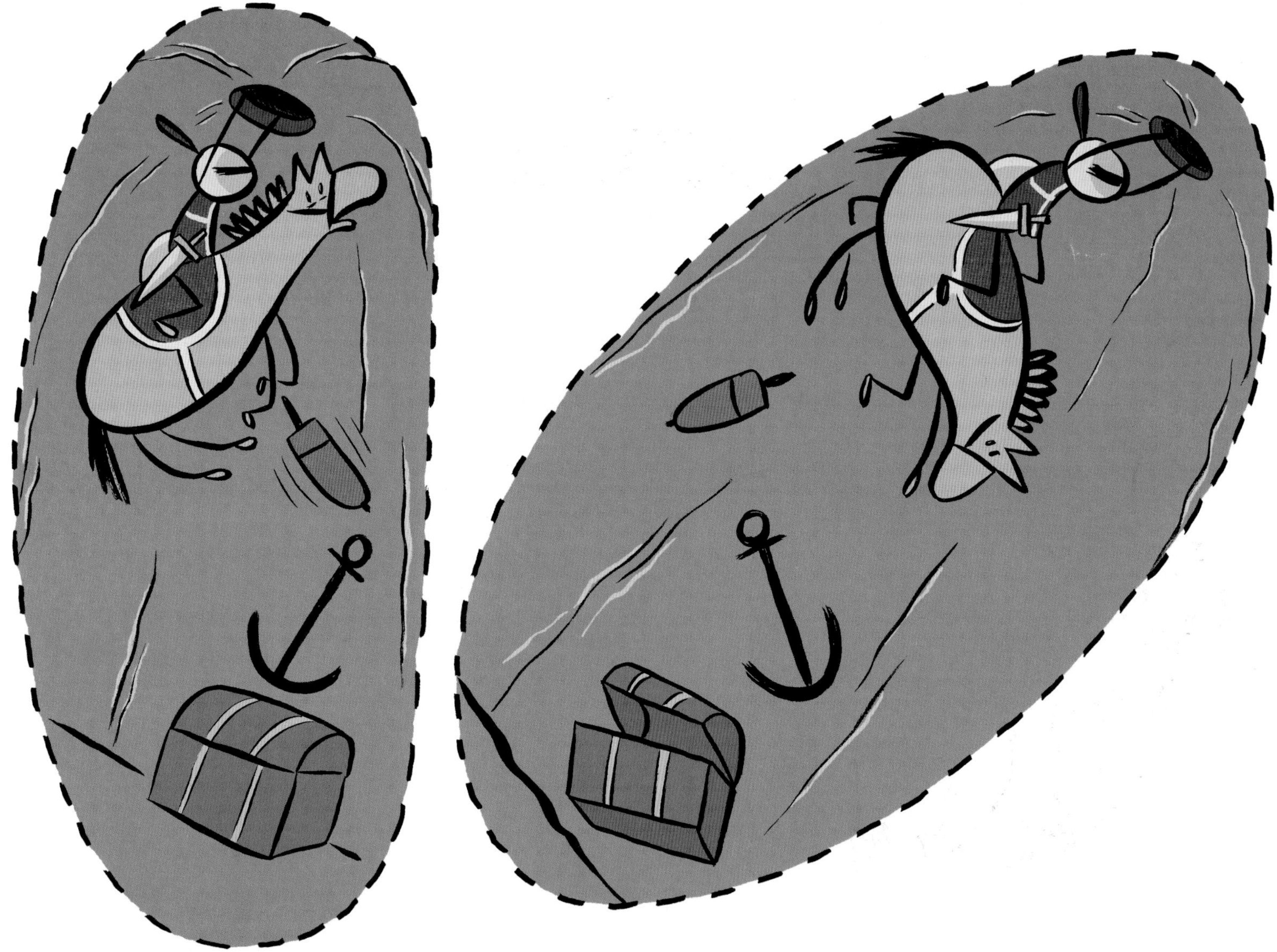

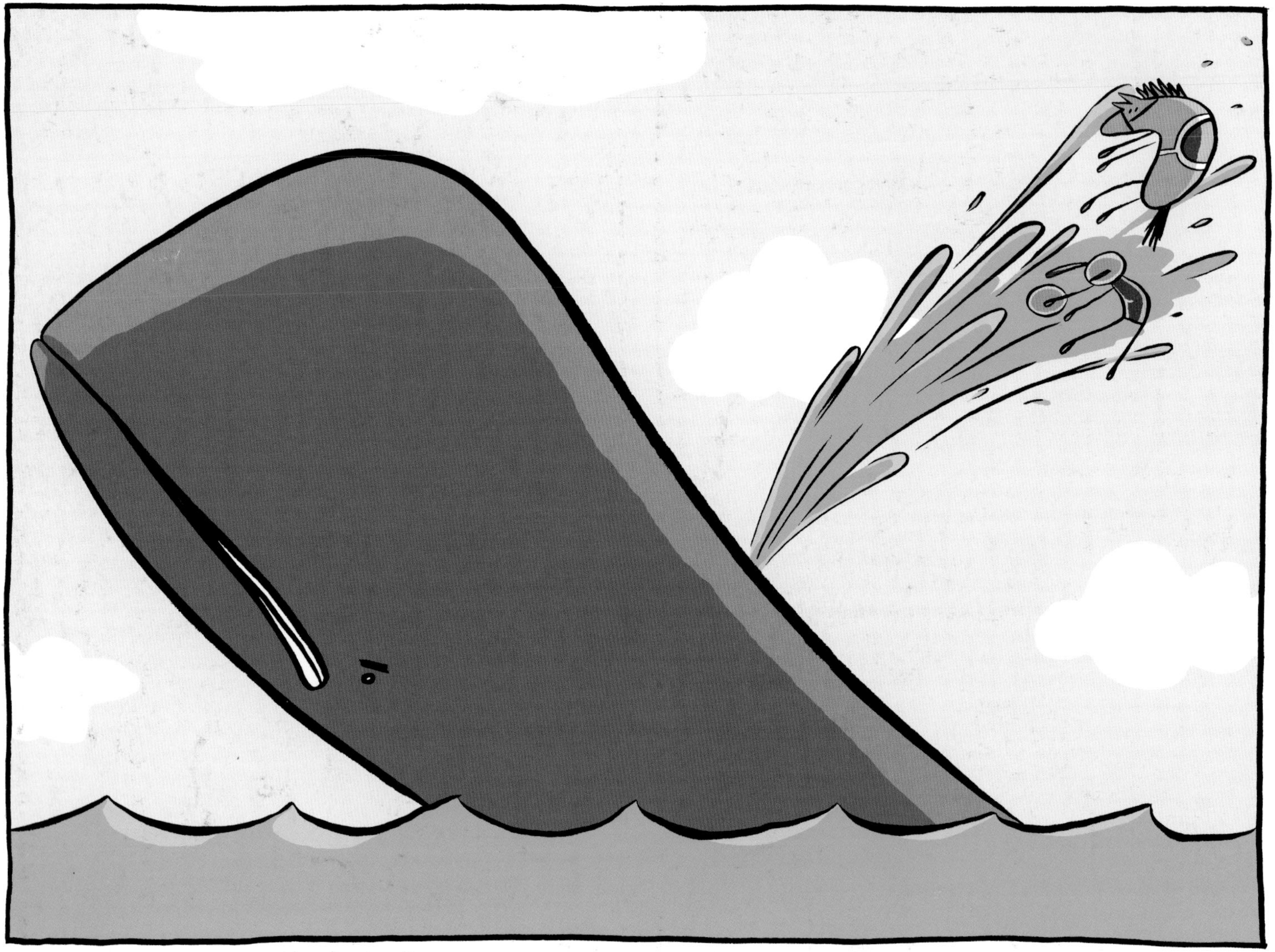

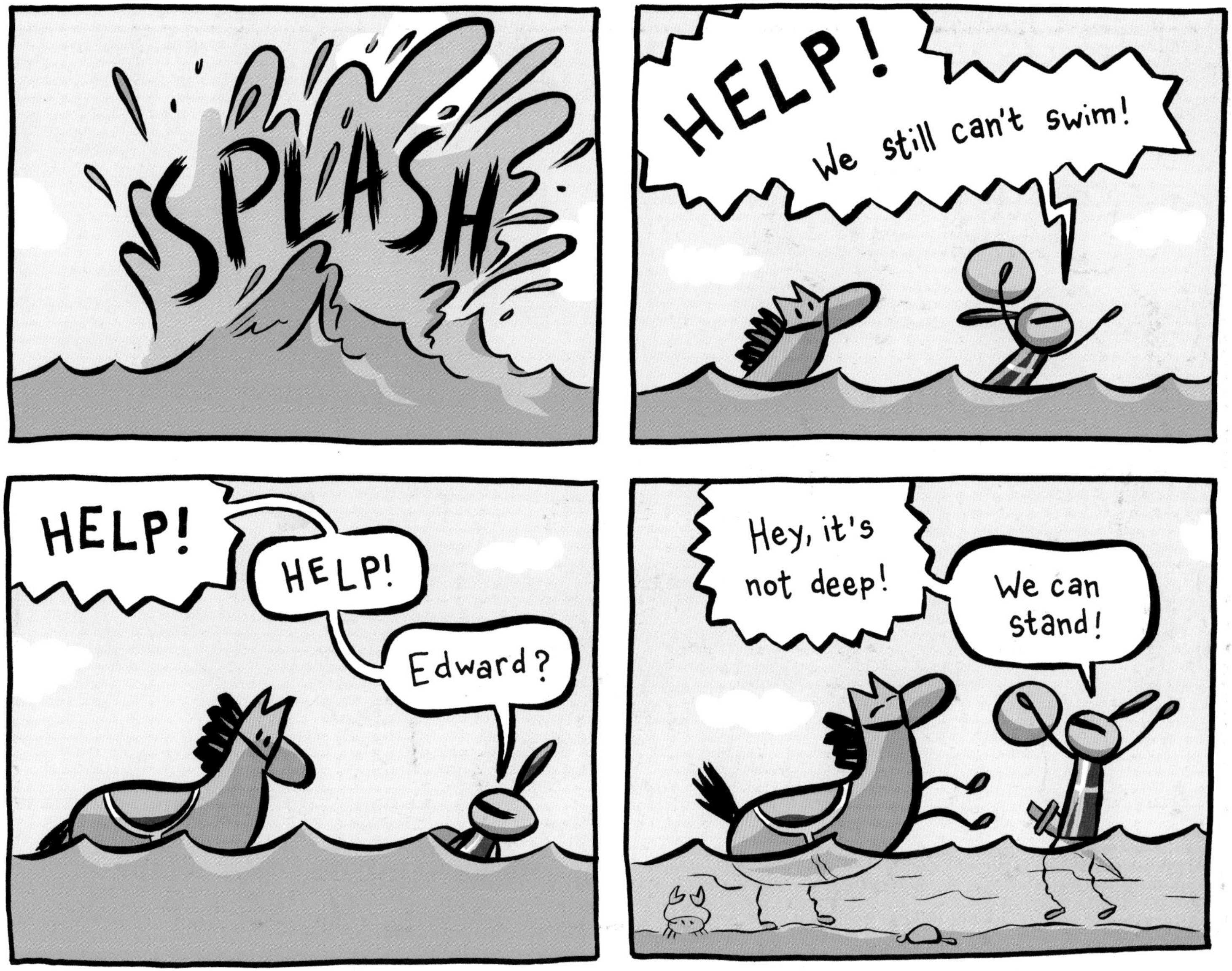
SPLASH
HELP! We still can't swim!
HELP!
HELP!
Edward?
Hey, it's not deep!
We can stand!

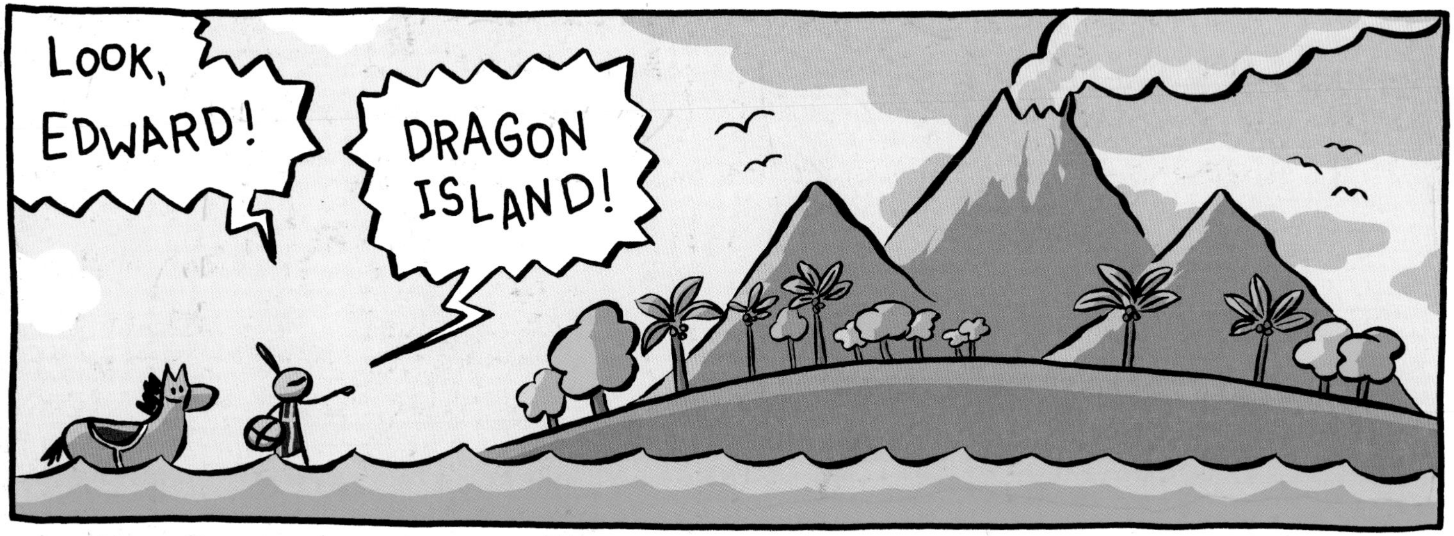
LOOK, EDWARD!
DRAGON ISLAND!

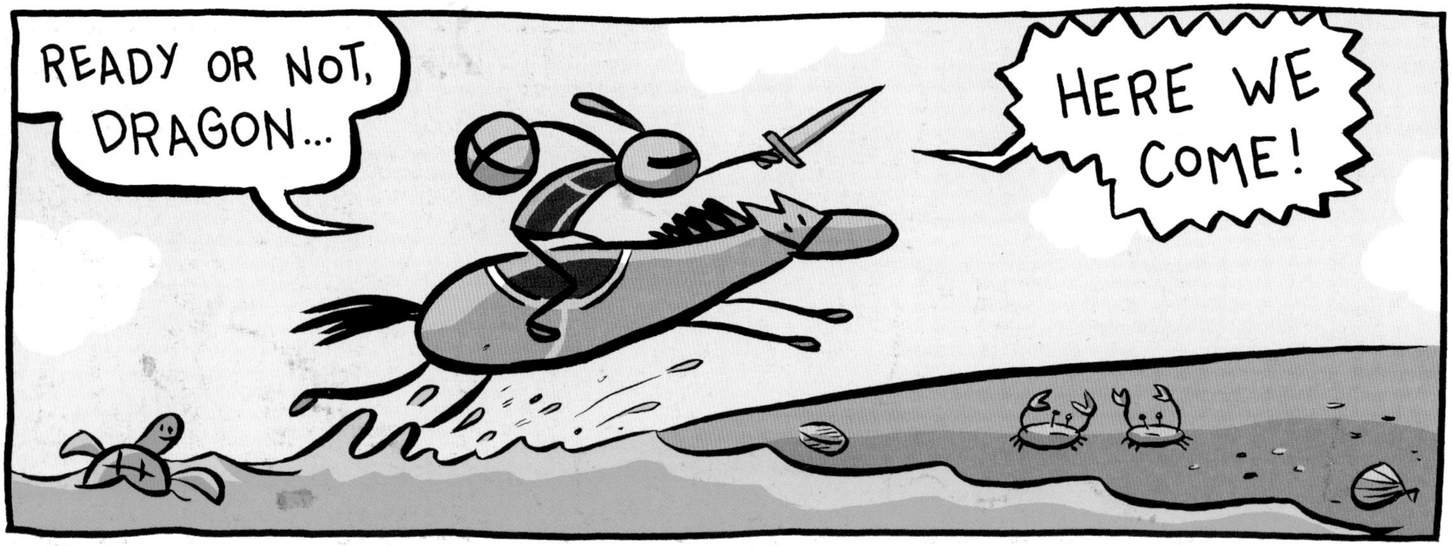
READY OR NOT, DRAGON...
HERE WE COME!

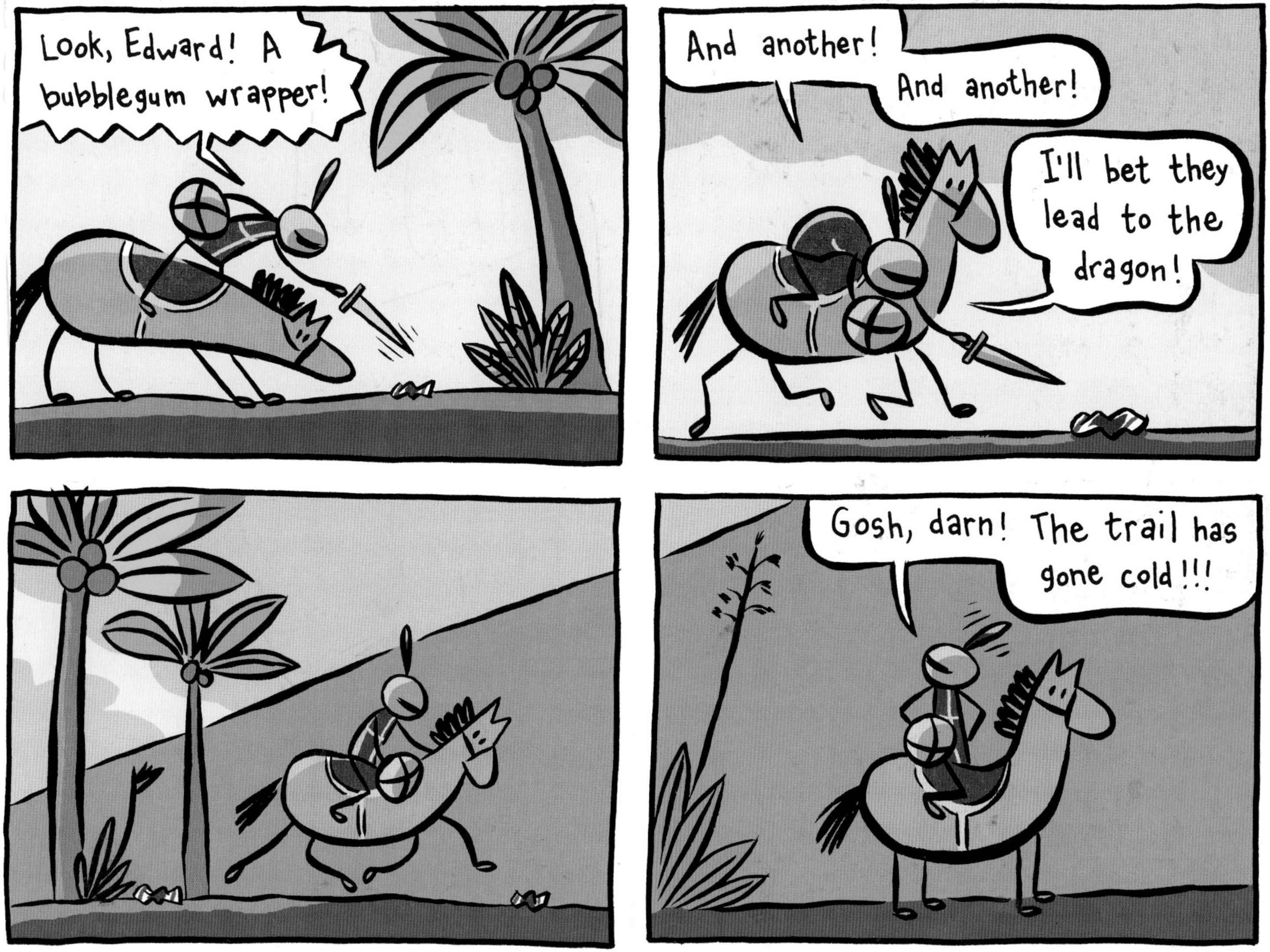

Look, Edward! A bubblegum wrapper!
And another!
And another!
I'll bet they lead to the dragon!
Gosh, darn! The trail has gone cold!!!

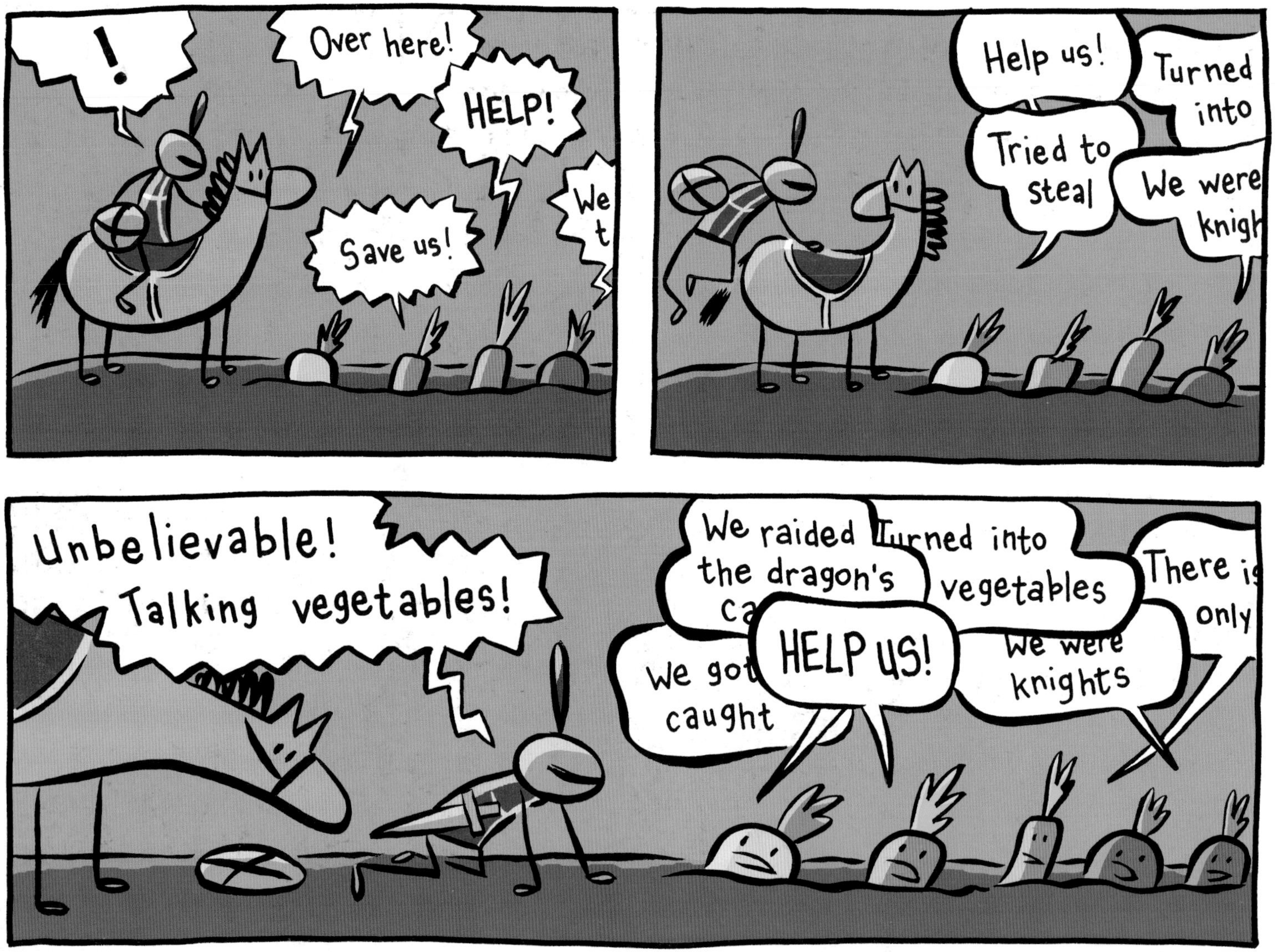

!
Over here!
HELP!
Save us!
We t
Help us!
Turned into
Tried to steal
We were knigh
Unbelievable! Talking vegetables!
We raided the dragon's ca
Turned into vegetables
There i only
We got caught
HELP US!
We were knights

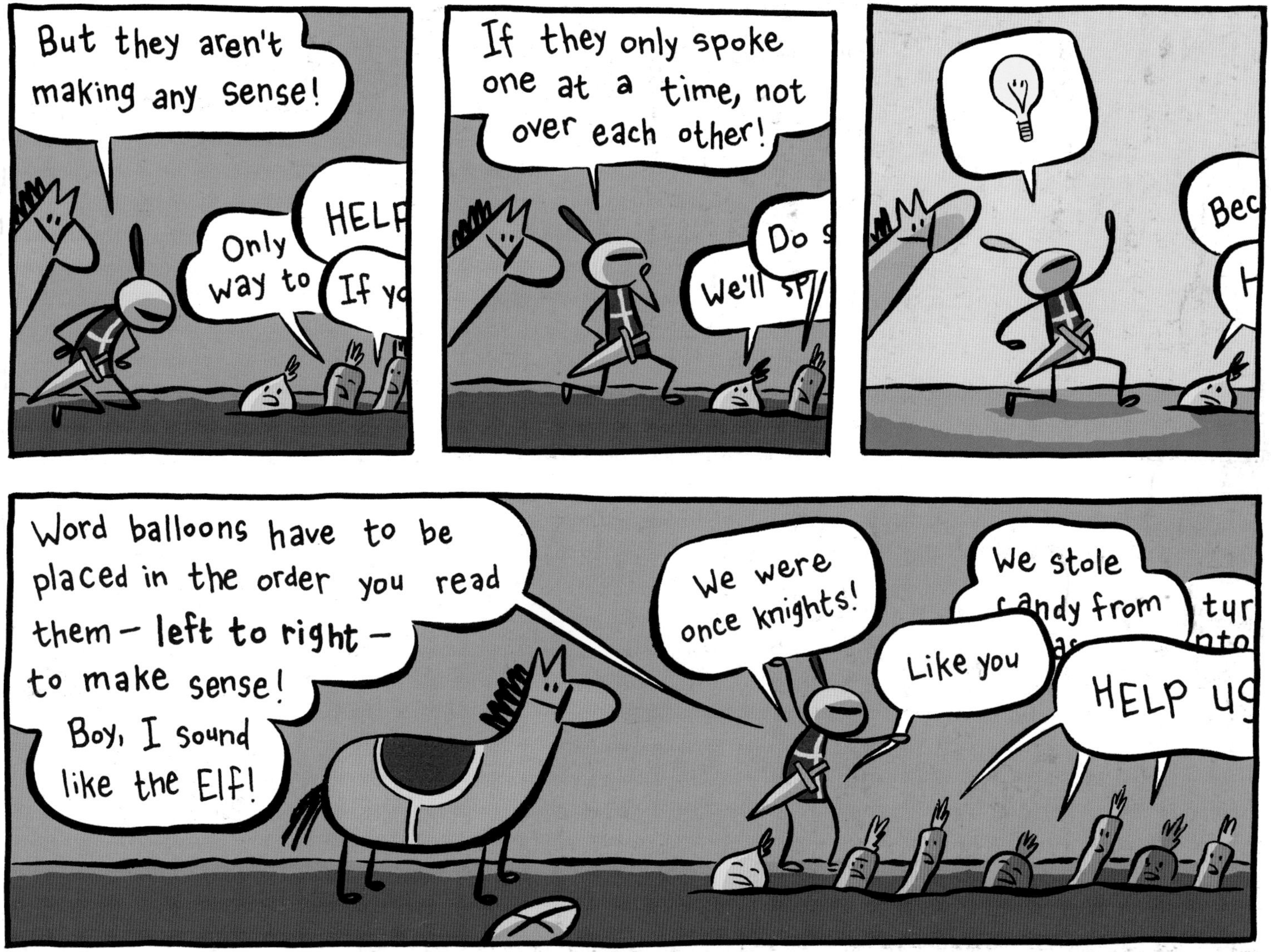
But they aren't making any sense!
Only way to
HELP
If
If they only spoke one at a time, not over each other!
We'll
Do
Word balloons have to be placed in the order you read them – **left to right** – to make sense!
Boy, I sound like the Elf!
We were once knights!
We stole candy from
Like you
HELP

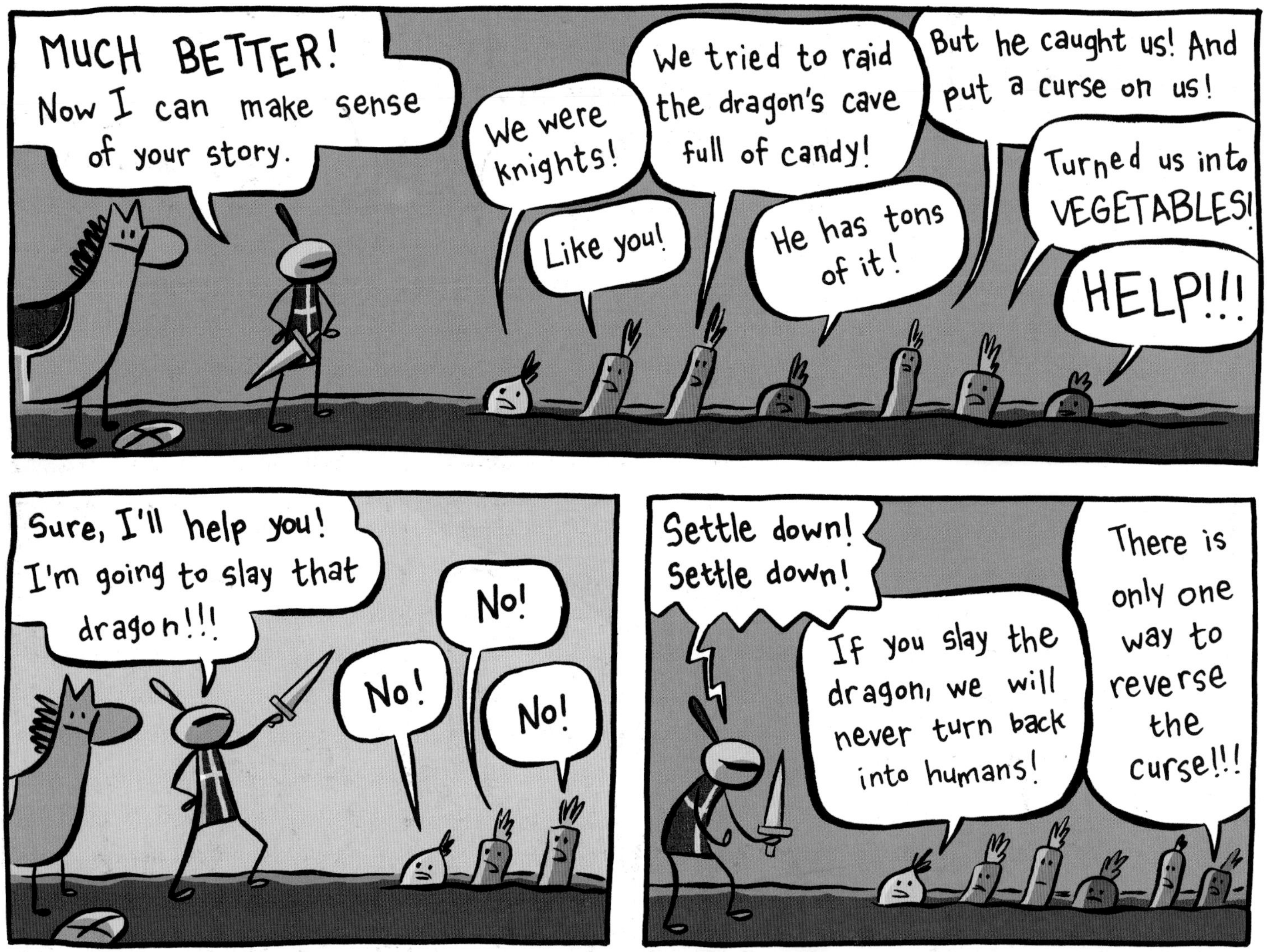
MUCH BETTER! Now I can make sense of your story.
We were knights!
Like you!
We tried to raid the dragon's cave full of candy!
He has tons of it!
But he caught us! And put a curse on us!
Turned us into VEGETABLES!
HELP!!!
Sure, I'll help you! I'm going to slay that dragon!!!
No!
No!
No!
Settle down! Settle down!
If you slay the dragon, we will never turn back into humans!
There is only one way to reverse the curse!!!

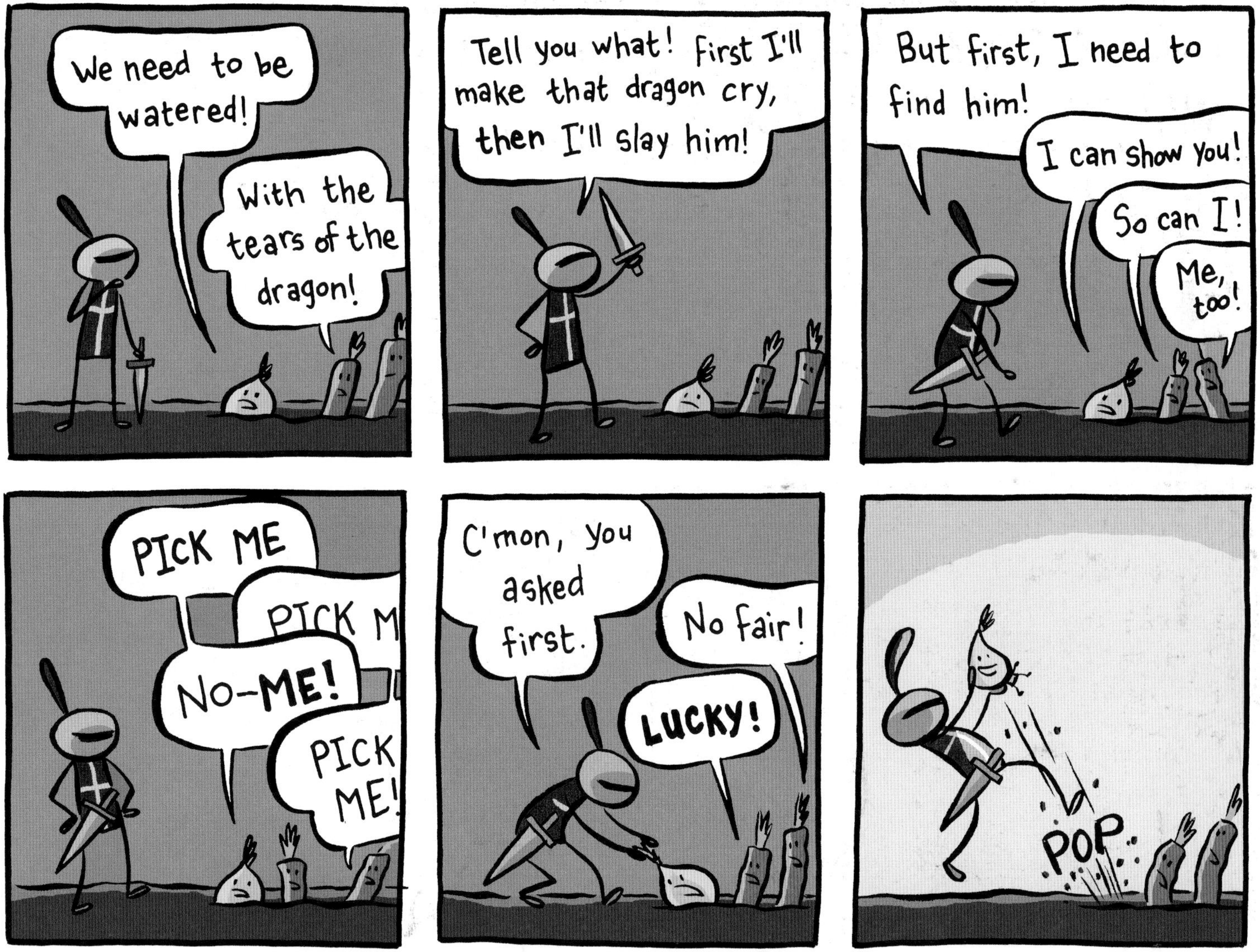
We need to be watered!
With the tears of the dragon!
Tell you what! First I'll make that dragon cry, then I'll slay him!
But first, I need to find him!
I can show you!
So can I!
Me, too!
PICK ME
PICK M
NO-ME!
PICK ME!
C'mon, you asked first.
No fair!
LUCKY!
POP

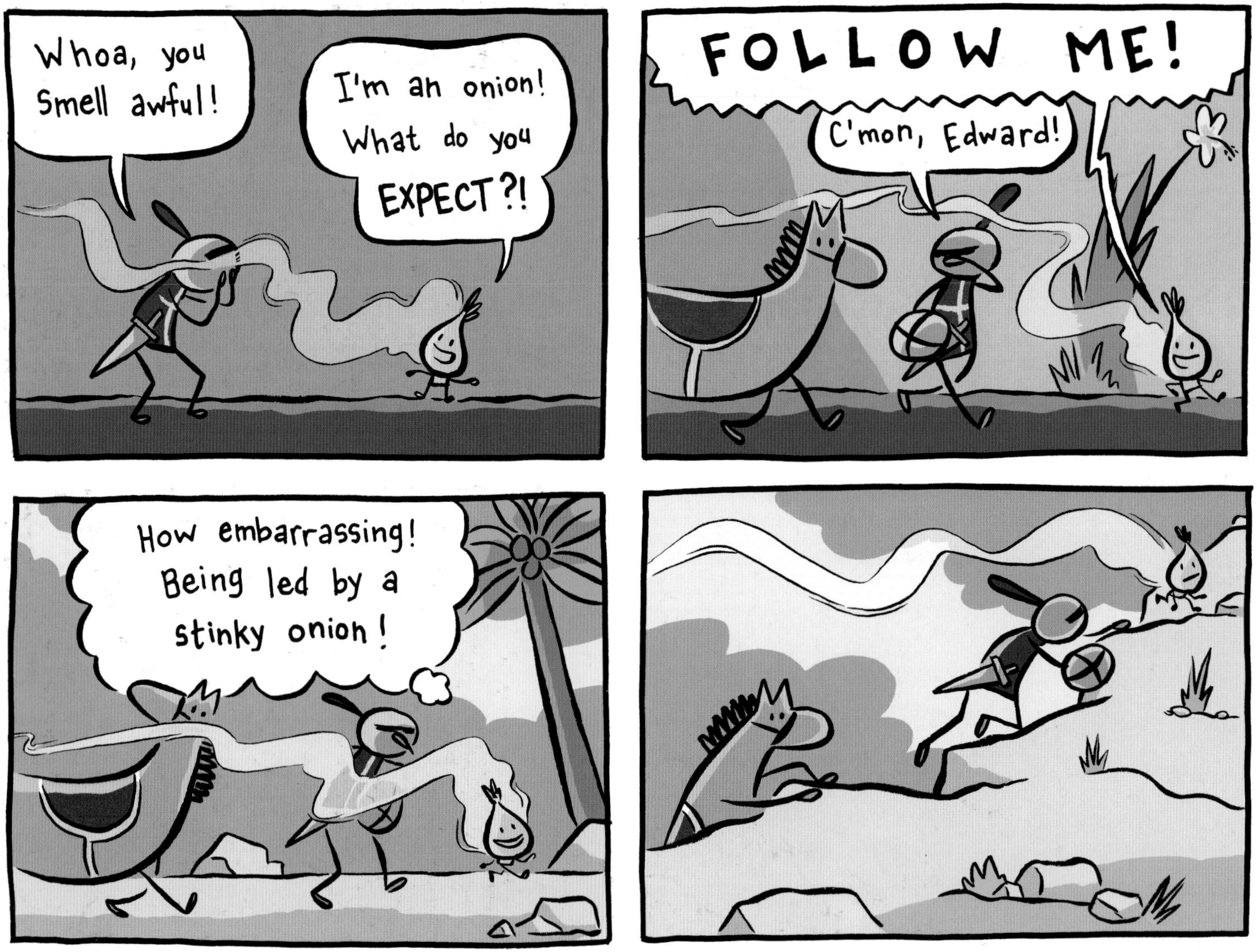
Whoa, you smell awful!
I'm an onion! What do you EXPECT?!
FOLLOW ME!
C'mon, Edward!
How embarrassing! Being led by a stinky onion!

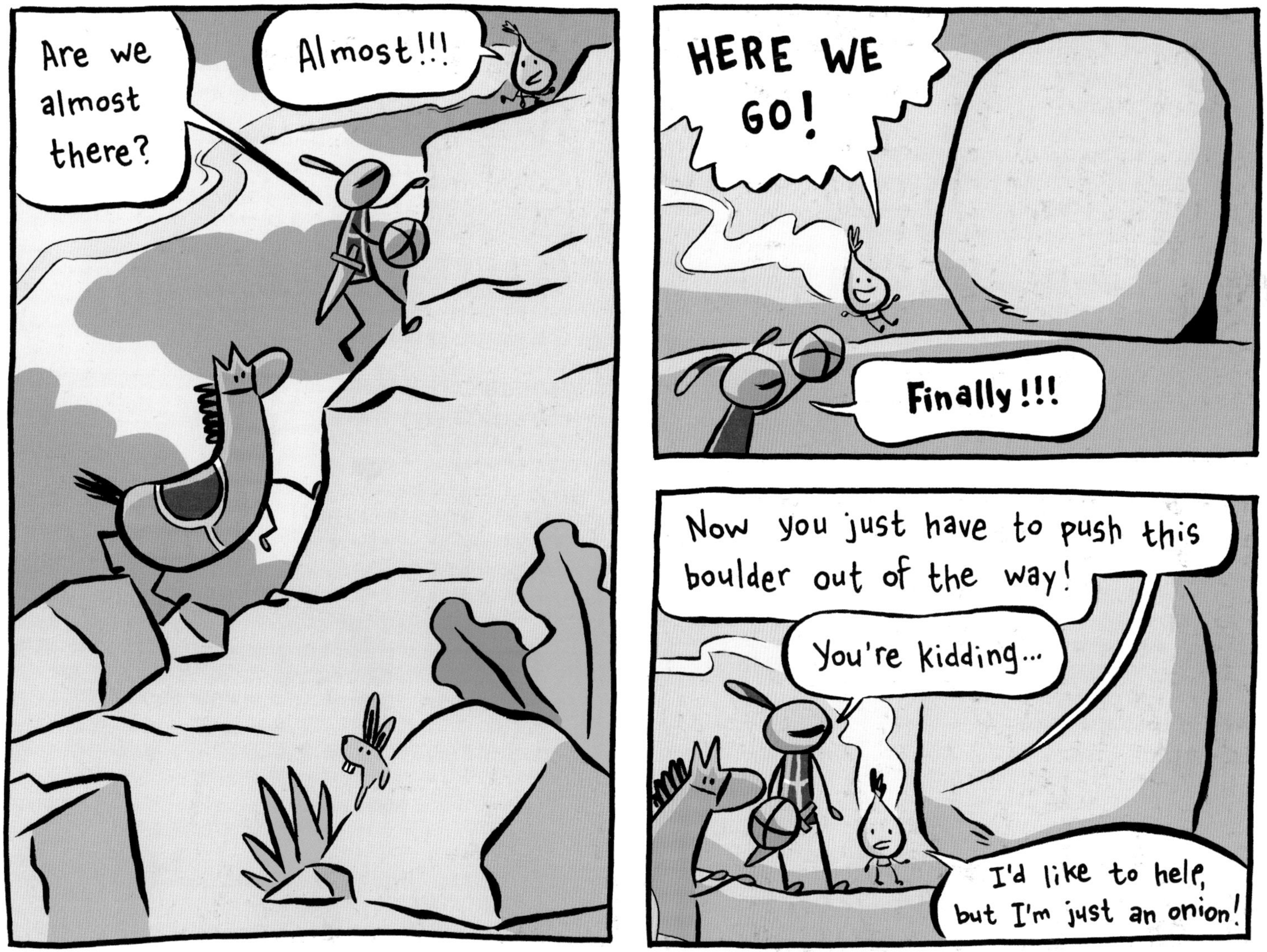
Are we almost there?
Almost!!!
HERE WE GO!
Finally!!!
Now you just have to push this boulder out of the way!
You're kidding...
I'd like to help, but I'm just an onion!

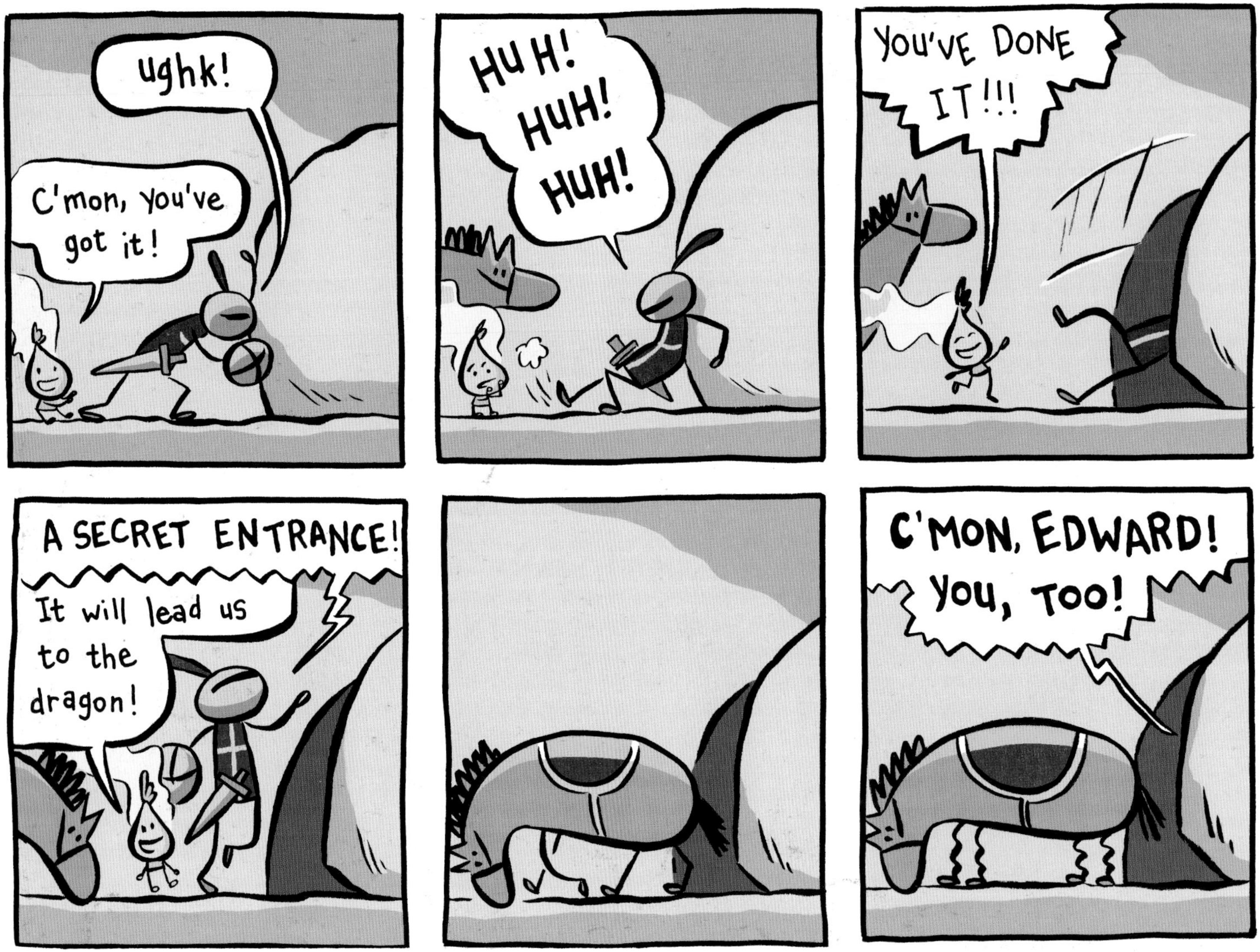
ughk!
C'mon, you've got it!
HUH! HUH! HUH!
YOU'VE DONE IT!!!
A SECRET ENTRANCE!
It will lead us to the dragon!
C'MON, EDWARD! YOU, TOO!

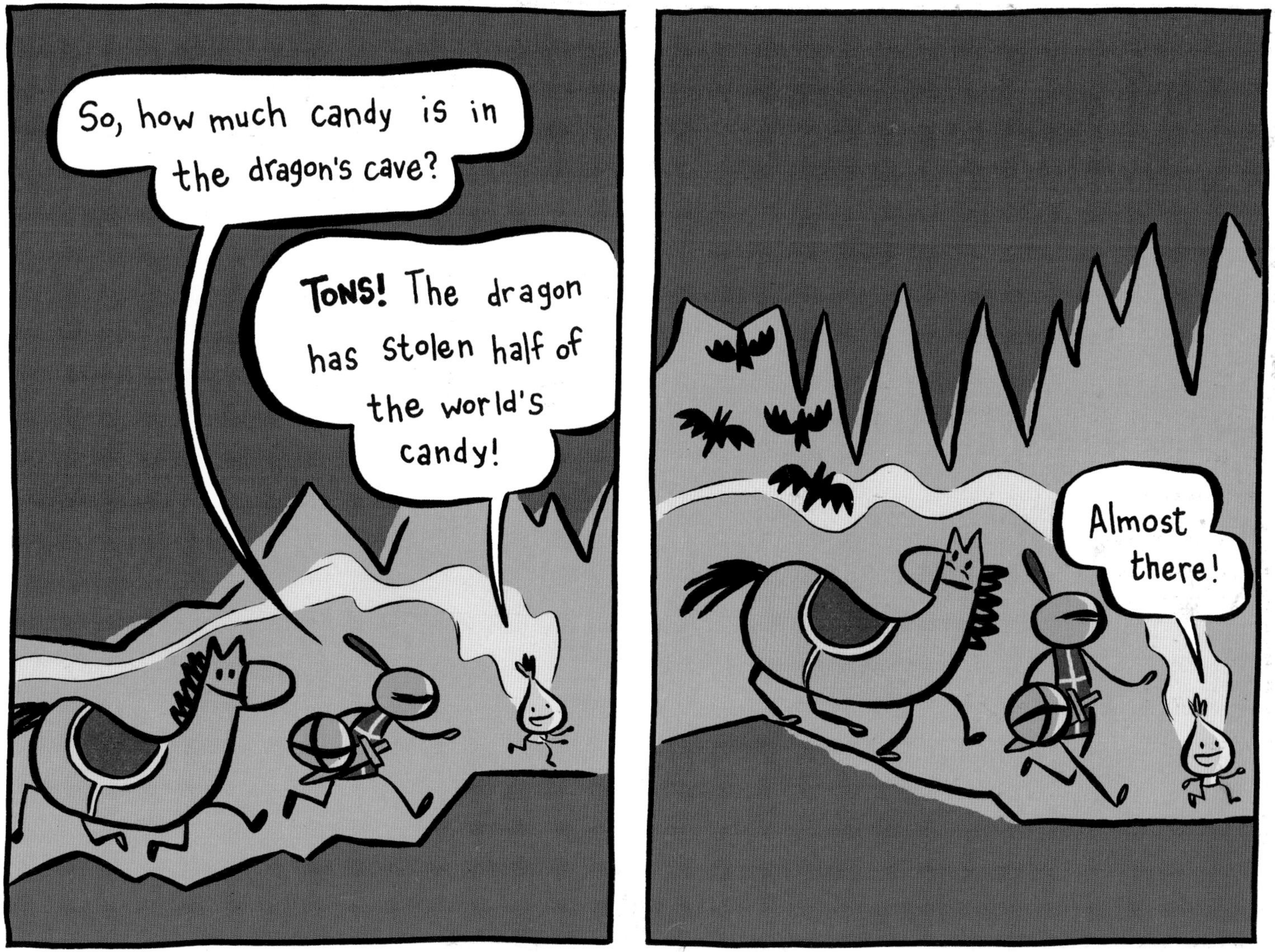
So, how much candy is in the dragon's cave?
TONS! The dragon has stolen half of the world's candy!
Almost there!

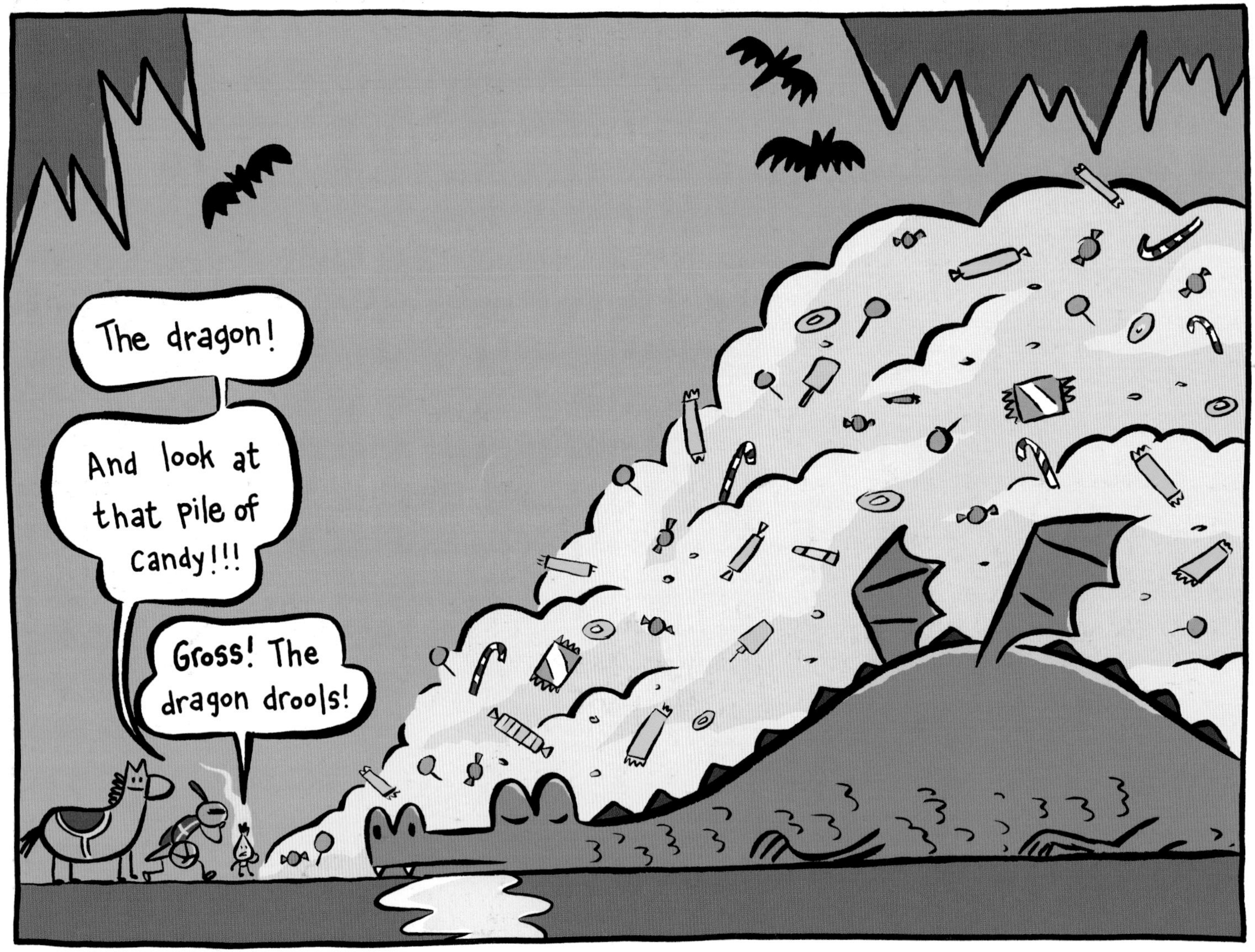
The dragon!
And look at that pile of candy!!!
Gross! The dragon drools!

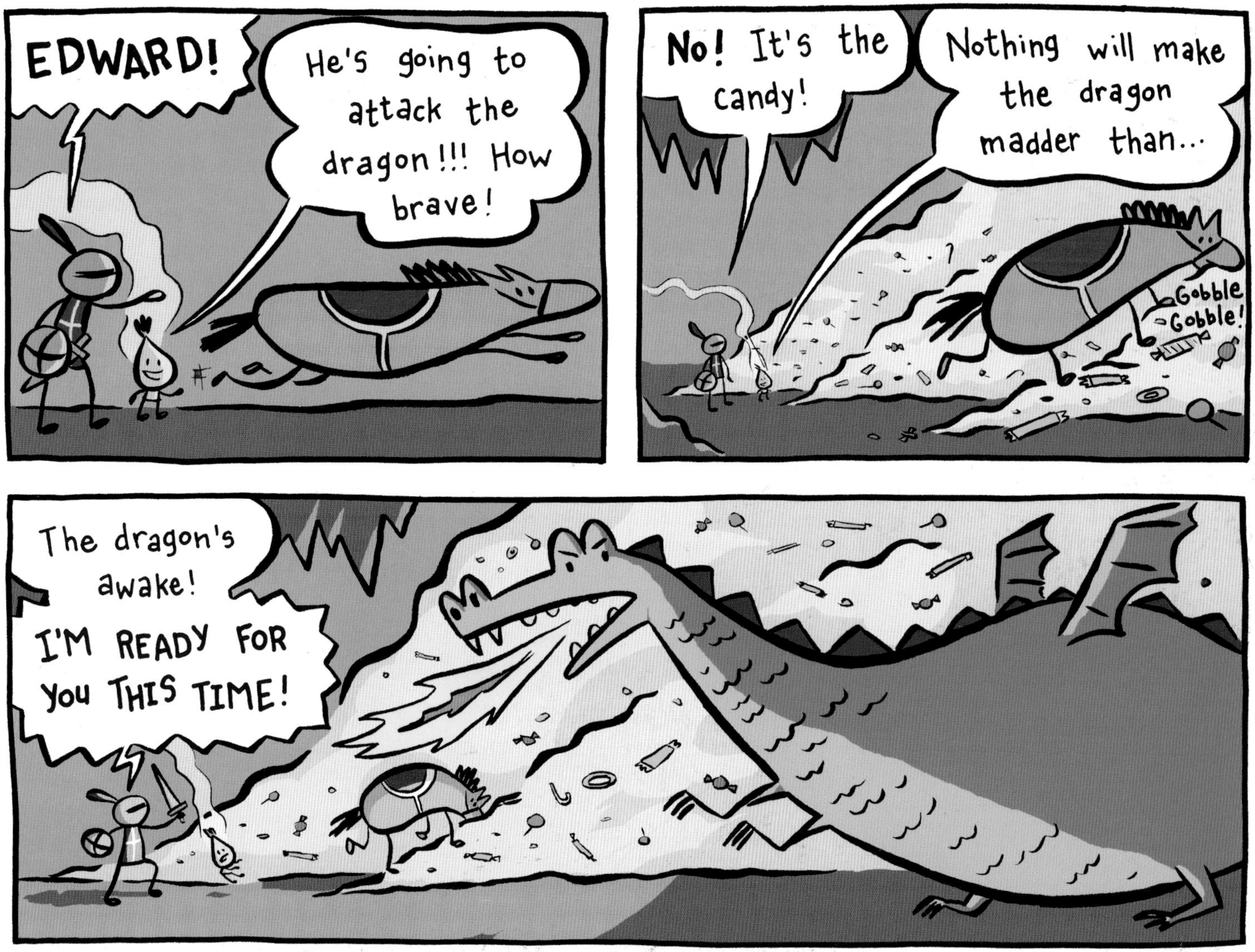

EDWARD!
He's going to attack the dragon!!! How brave!
No! It's the candy!
Nothing will make the dragon madder than...
Gobble Gobble!
The dragon's awake!
I'M READY FOR YOU THIS TIME!

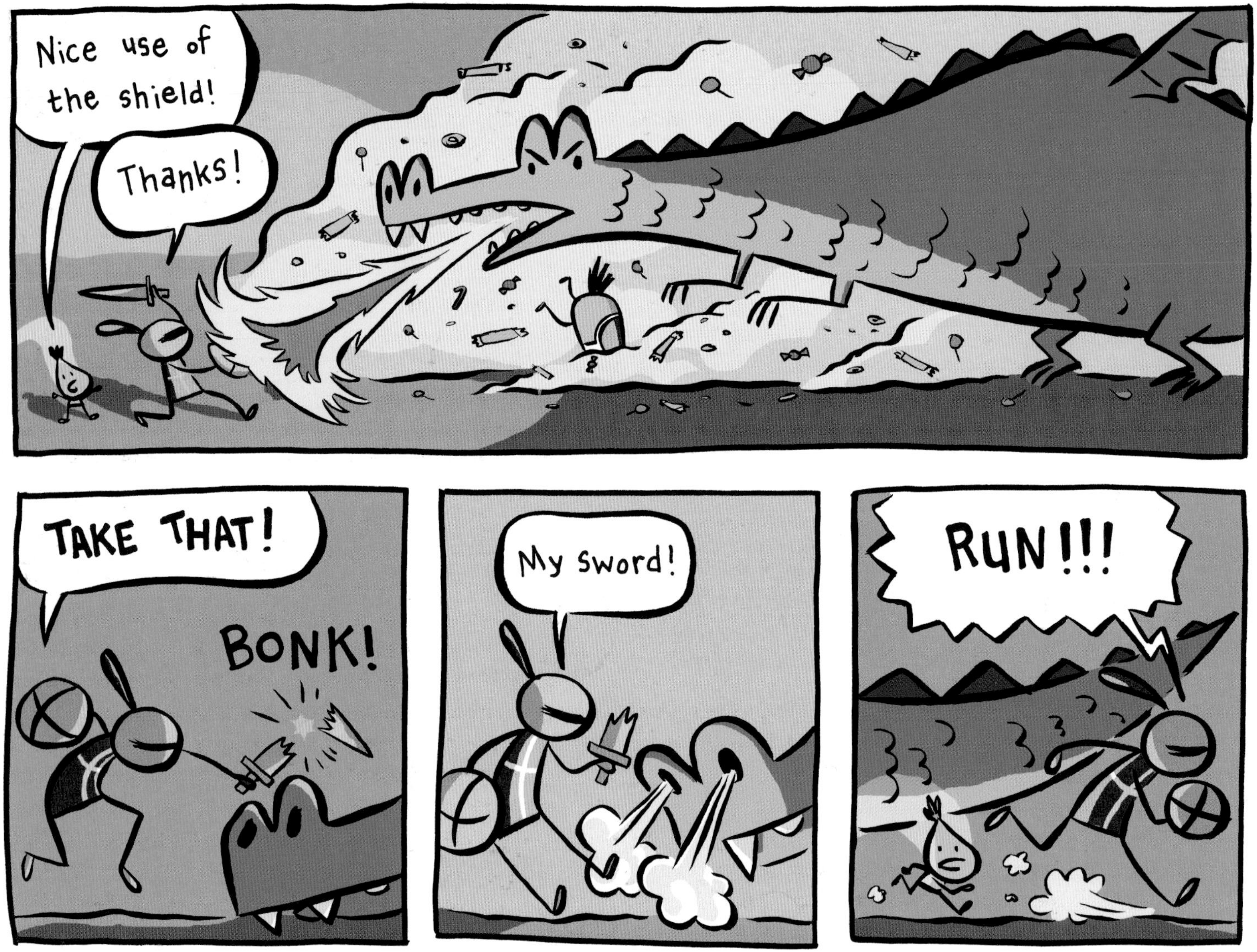
Nice use of the shield!
Thanks!
TAKE THAT!
BONK!
My sword!
RUN!!!

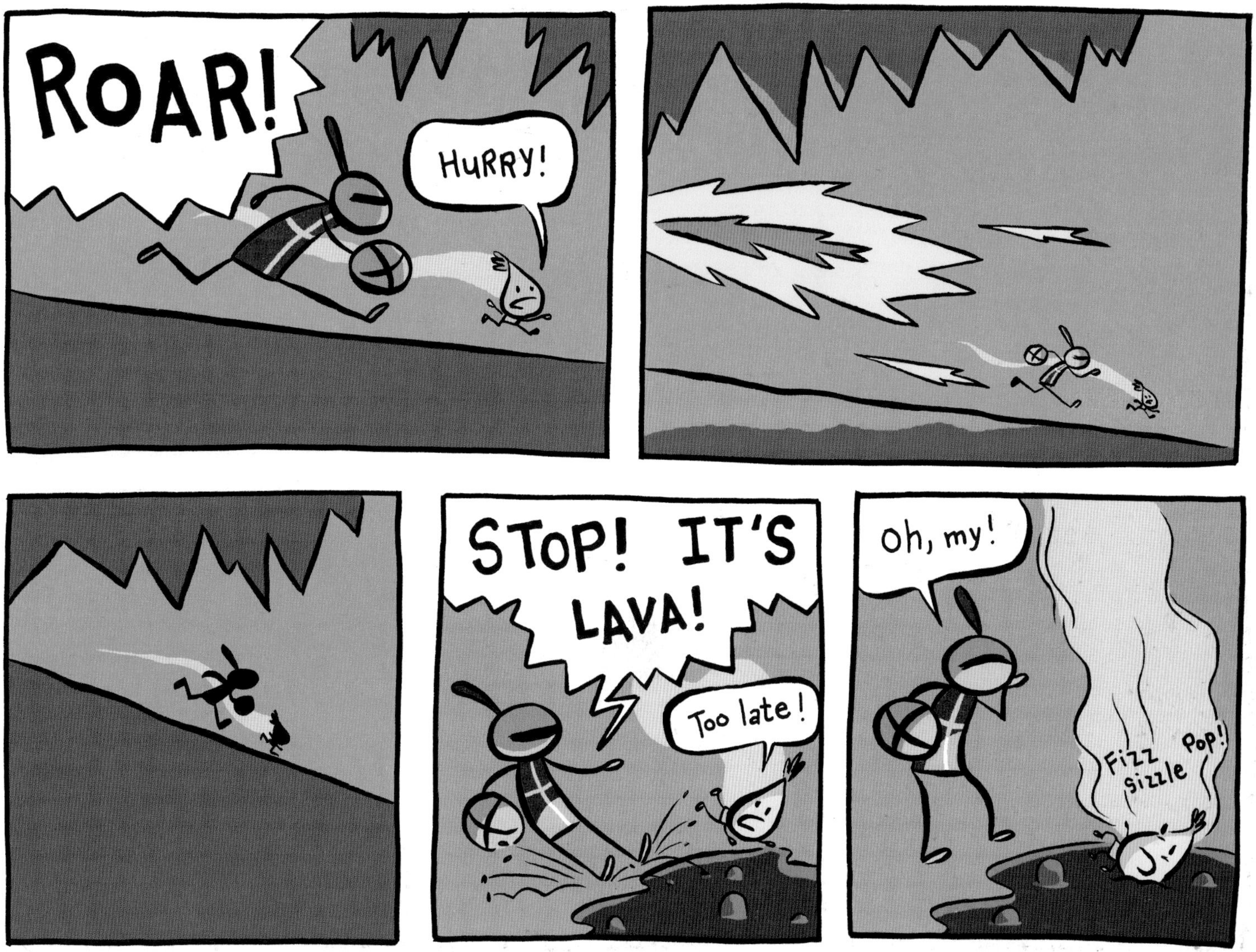
ROAR!
HURRY!
STOP! IT'S LAVA!
Too late!
Oh, my!
Fizz sizzle Pop!

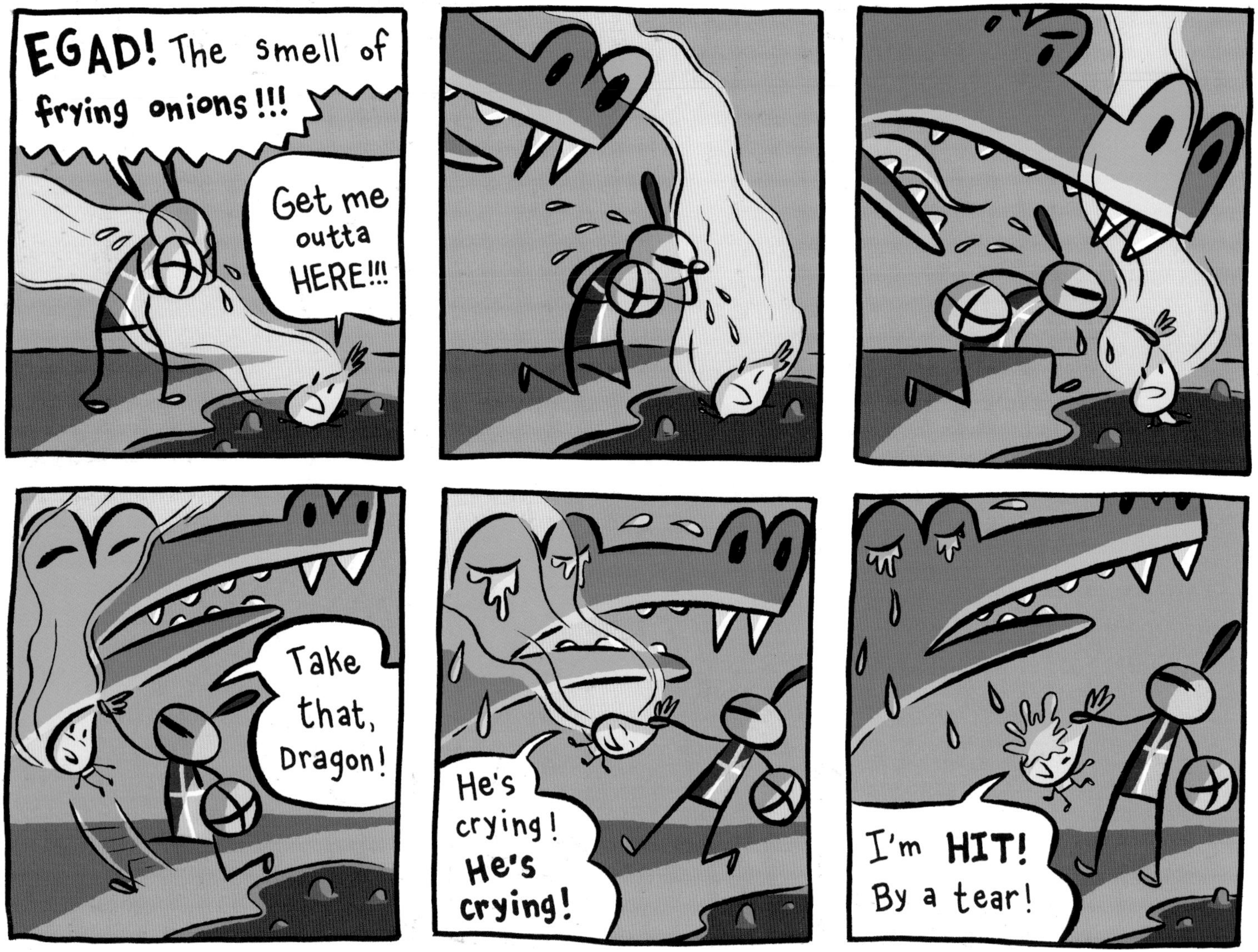
EGAD! The smell of frying onions!!!
Get me outta HERE!!!
Take that, Dragon!
He's crying! He's crying!
I'm HIT! By a tear!

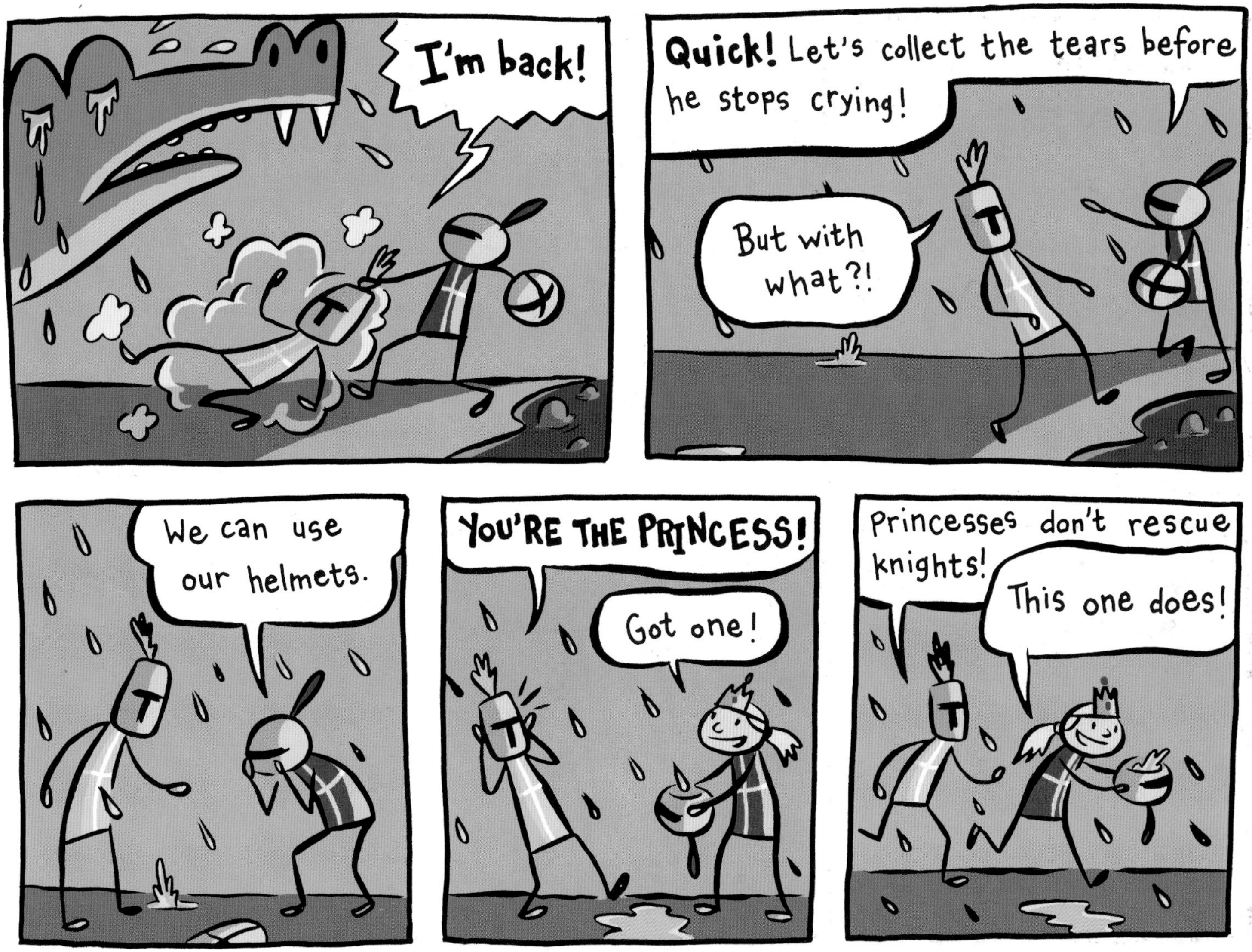
I'm back!
Quick! Let's collect the tears before he stops crying!
But with what?!
We can use our helmets.
YOU'RE THE PRINCESS!
Got one!
Princesses don't rescue knights!
This one does!

BACK TO THE VEGETABLES!
Once we change them back to knights, there will be enough of us to beat the dragon!
Unless he eats us first!

THIS WAY!
This tunnel is too small for the dragon to follow!
ROAR!

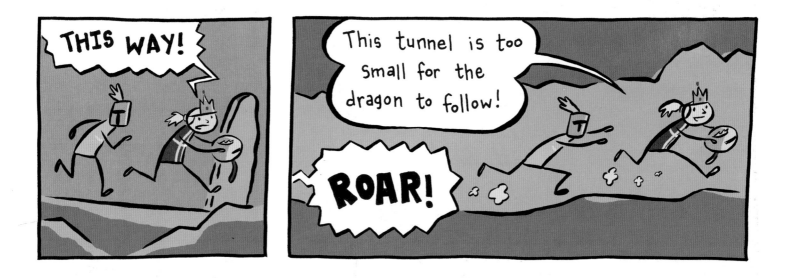

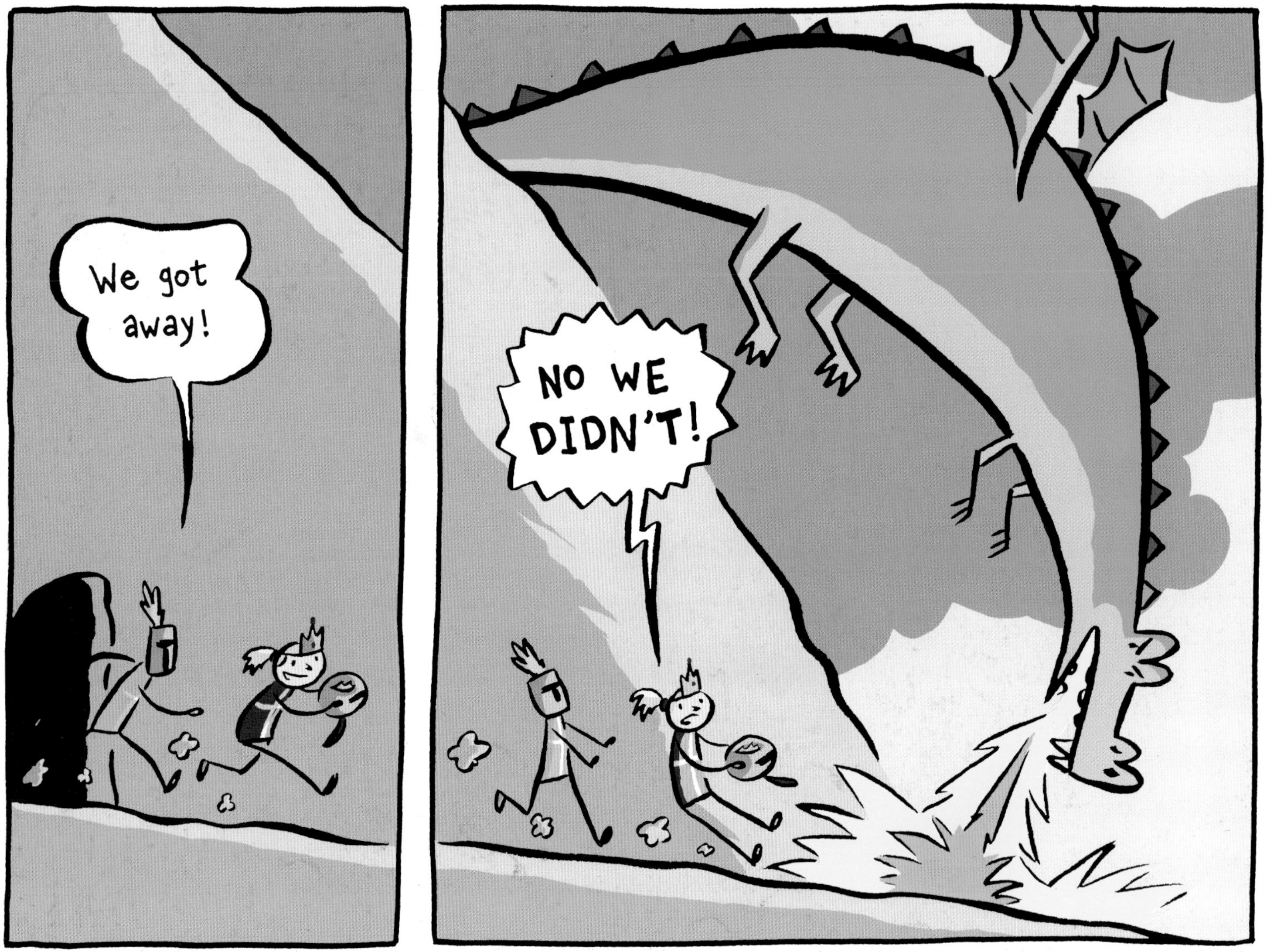
We got away!
NO WE DIDN'T!

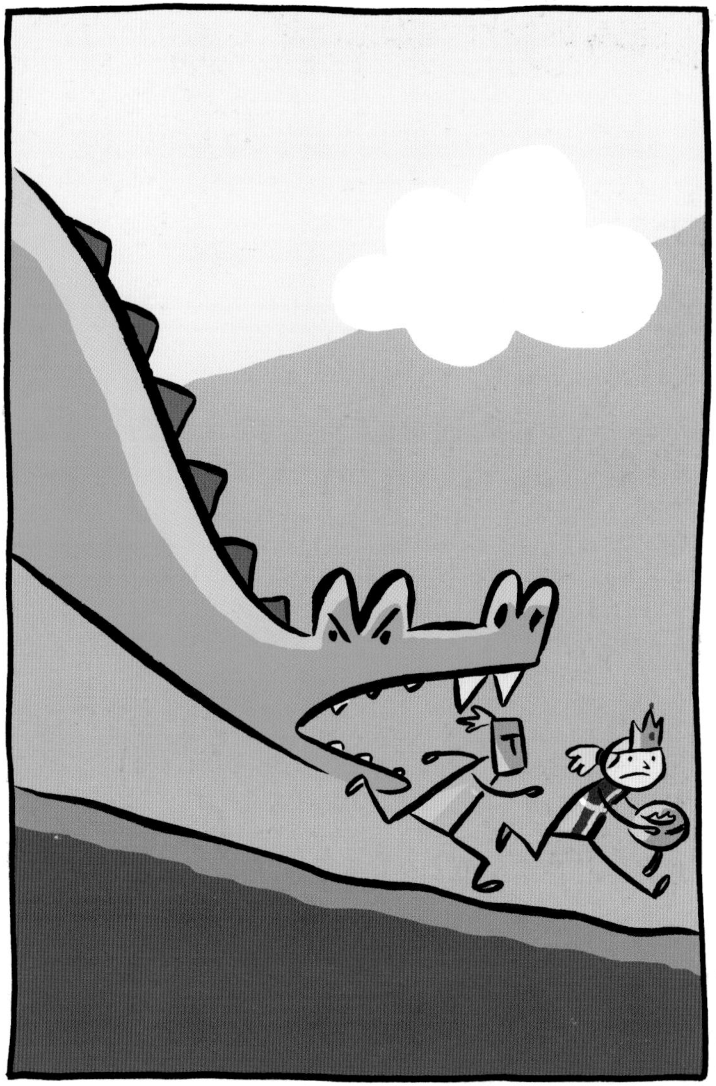

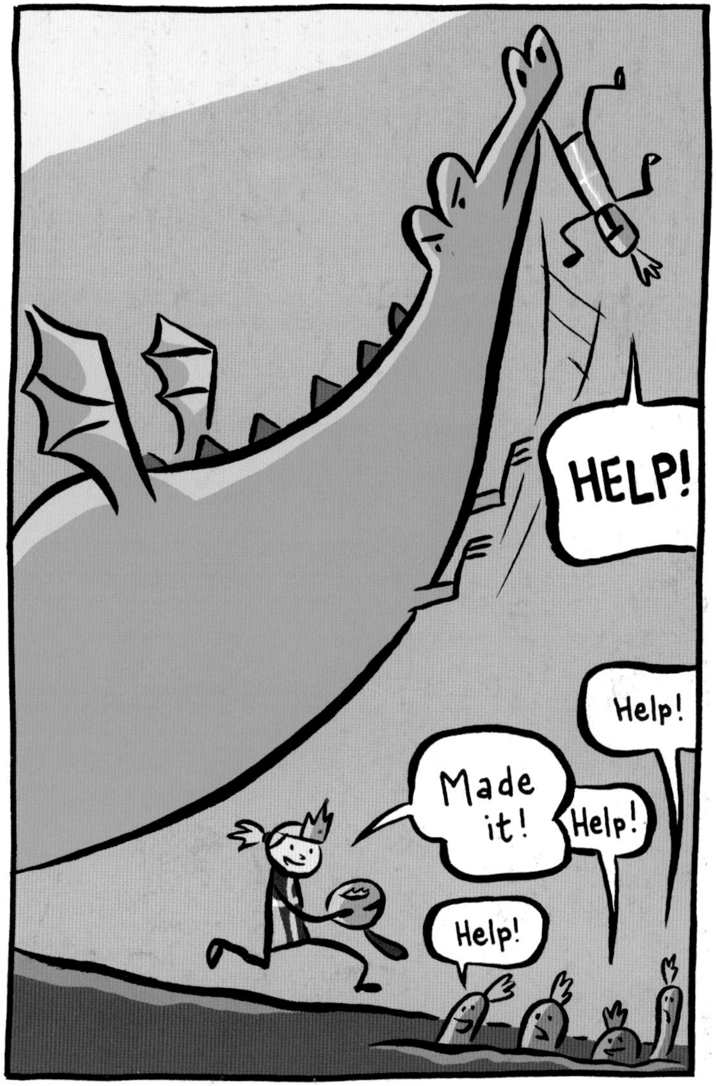
HELP!
Help!
Made it!
Help!
Help!

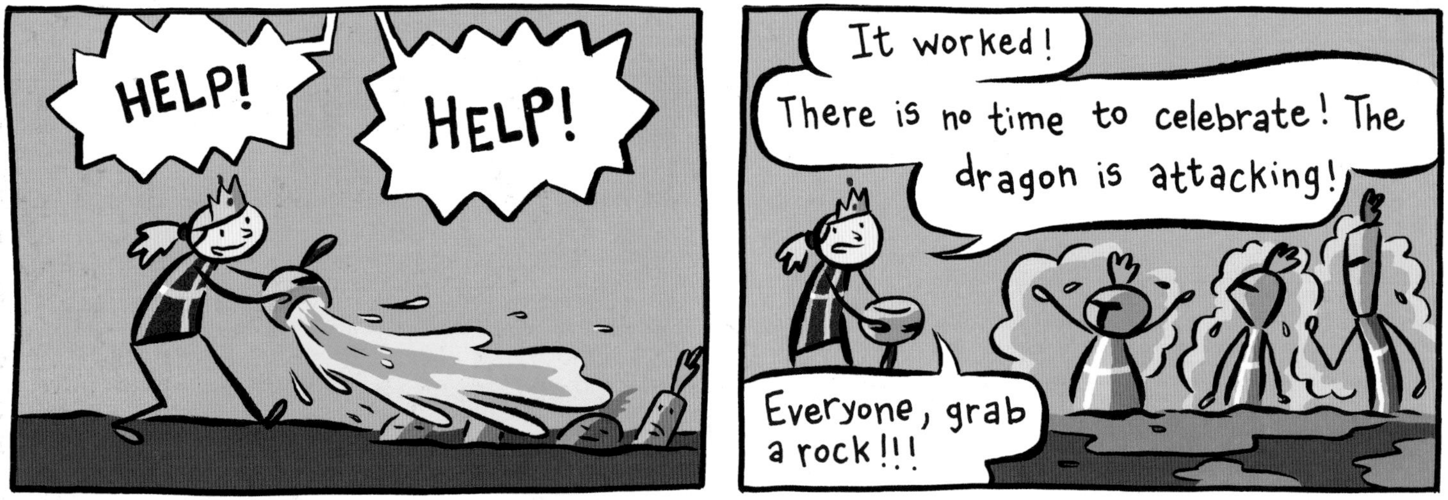
HELP!
HELP!
It worked!
There is no time to celebrate! The dragon is attacking!
Everyone, grab a rock!!!

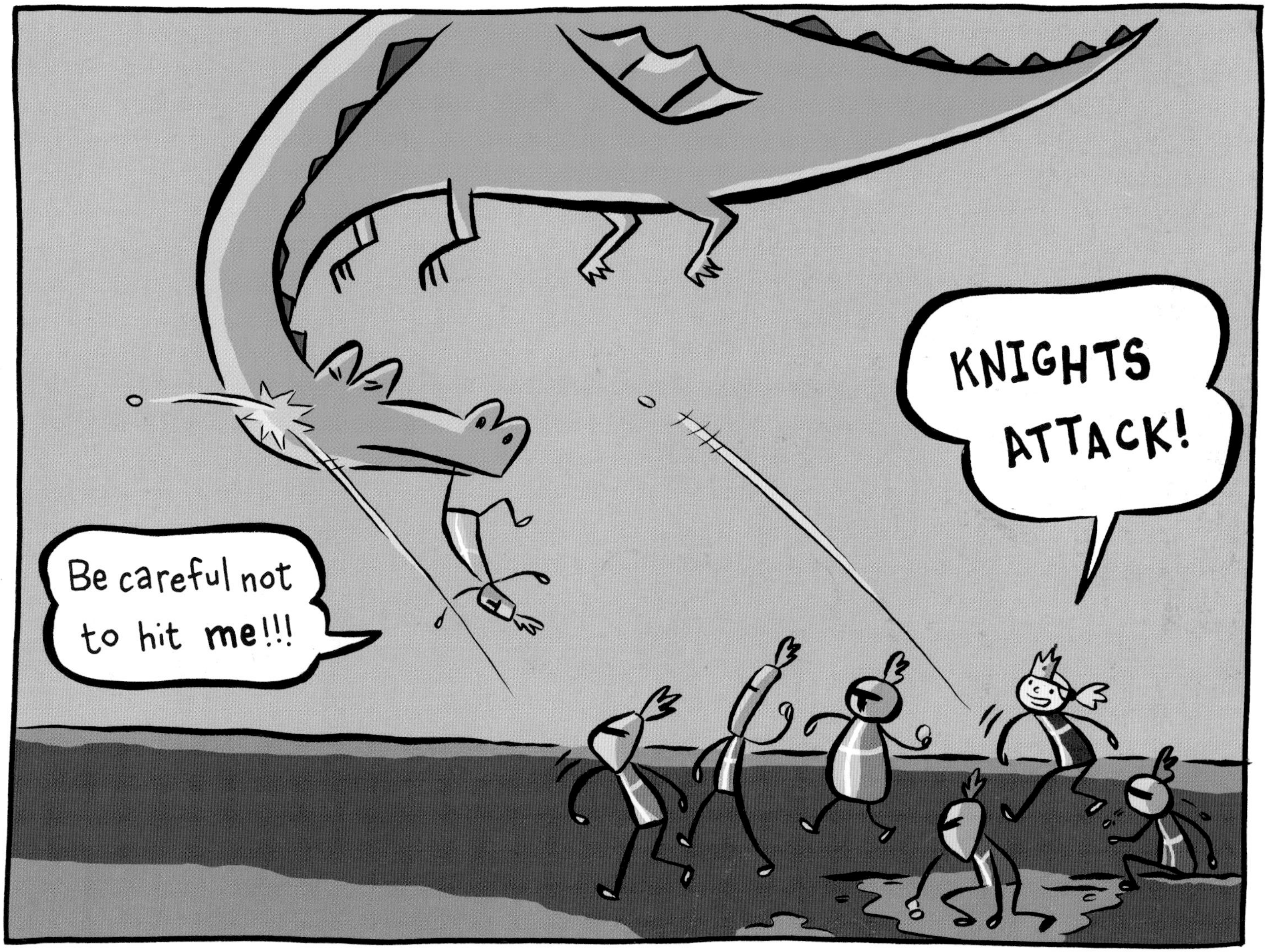
KNIGHTS ATTACK!
Be careful not to hit me!!!

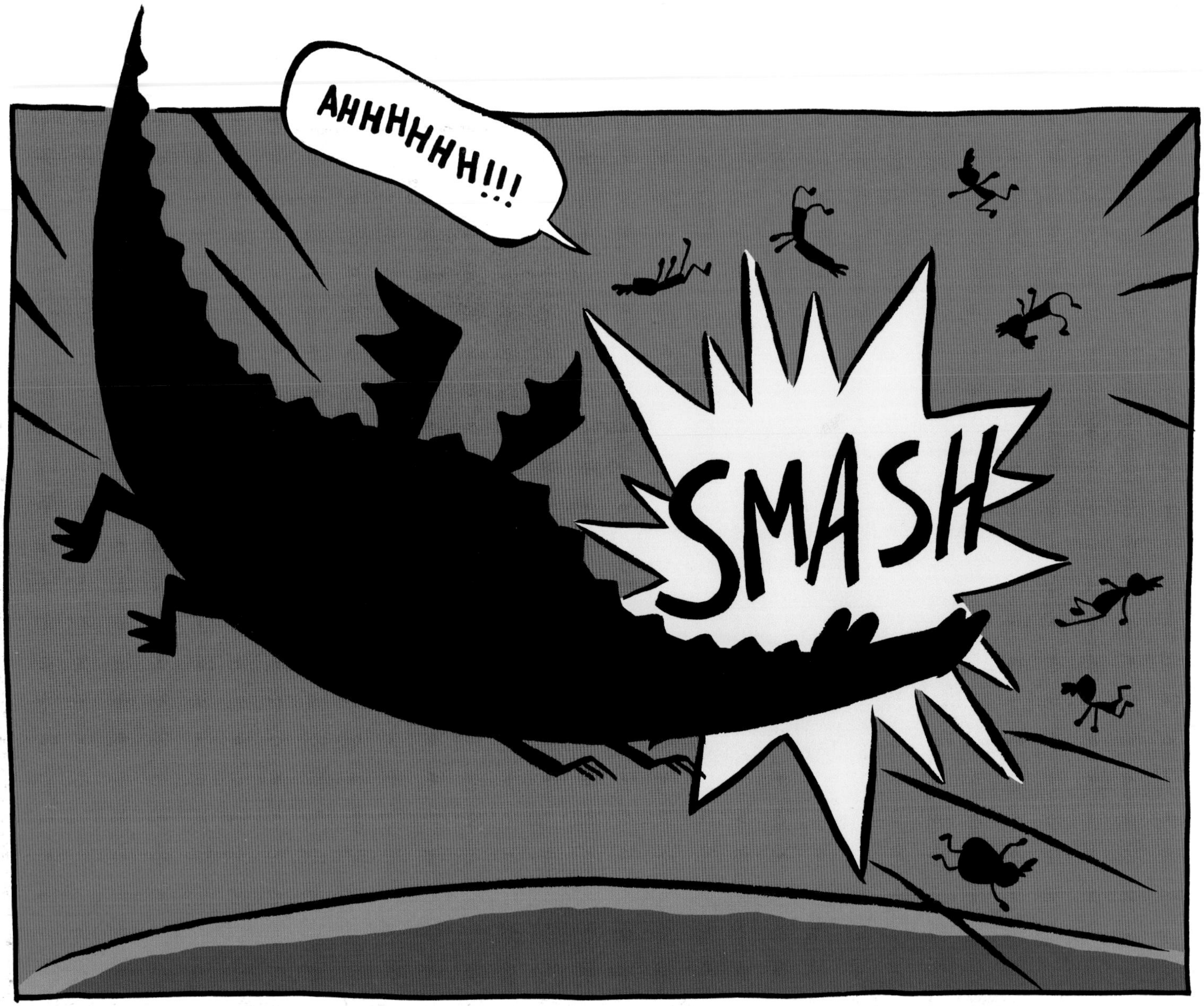
AHHHHHHH!!!
SMASH

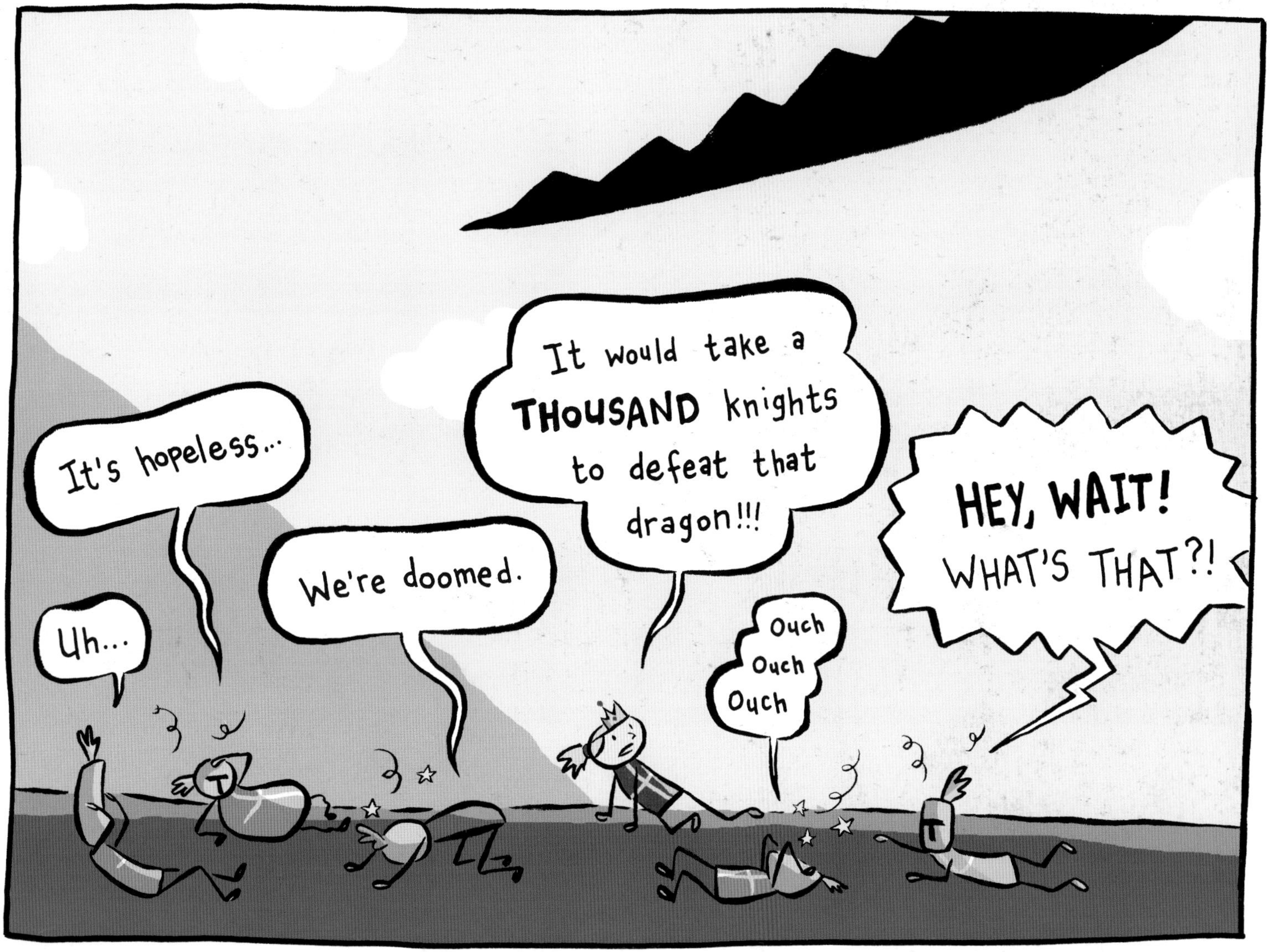
It's hopeless...
Uh...
We're doomed.
It would take a THOUSAND knights to defeat that dragon!!!
Ouch
Ouch
Ouch
HEY, WAIT! WHAT'S THAT?!

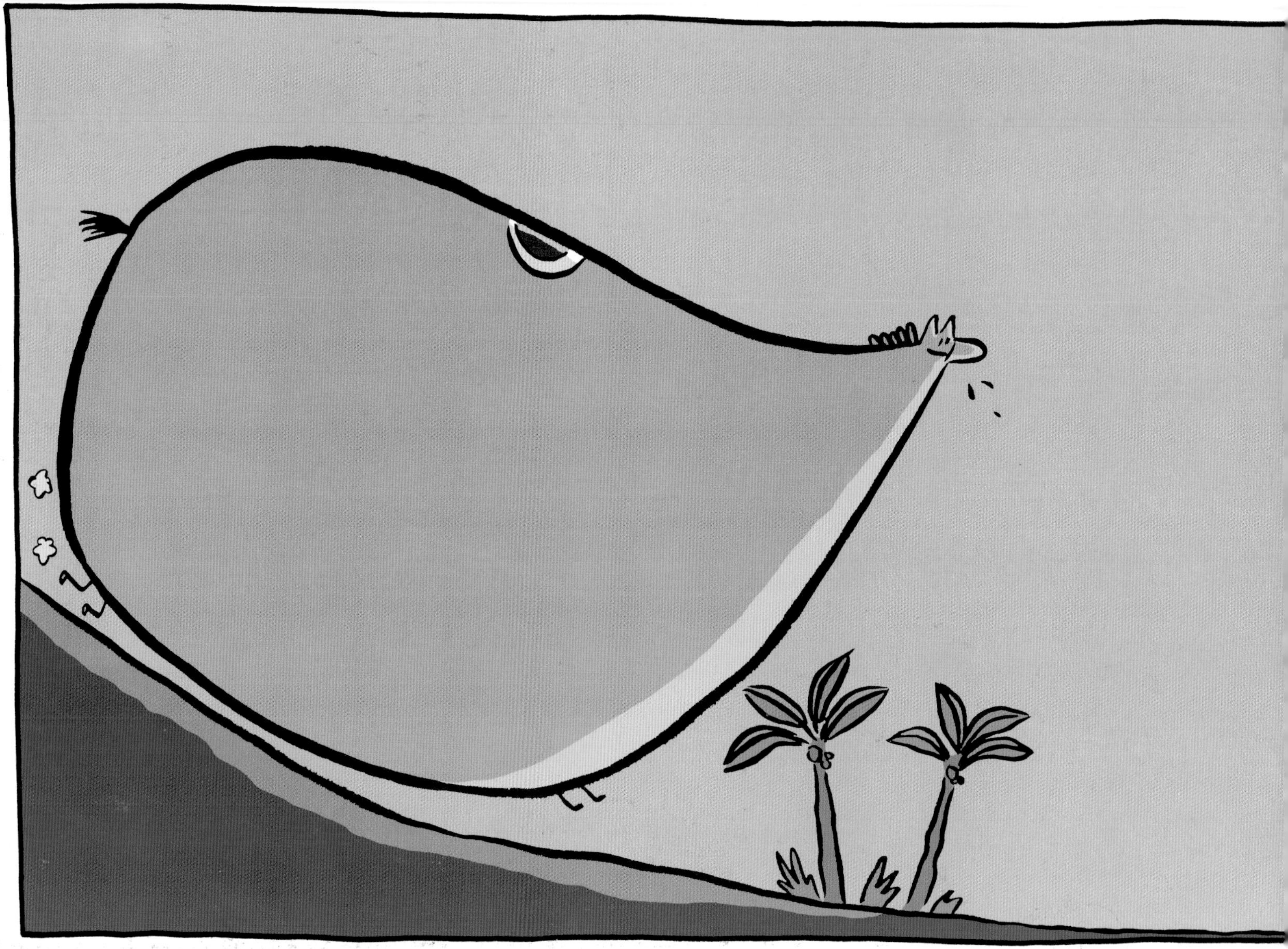

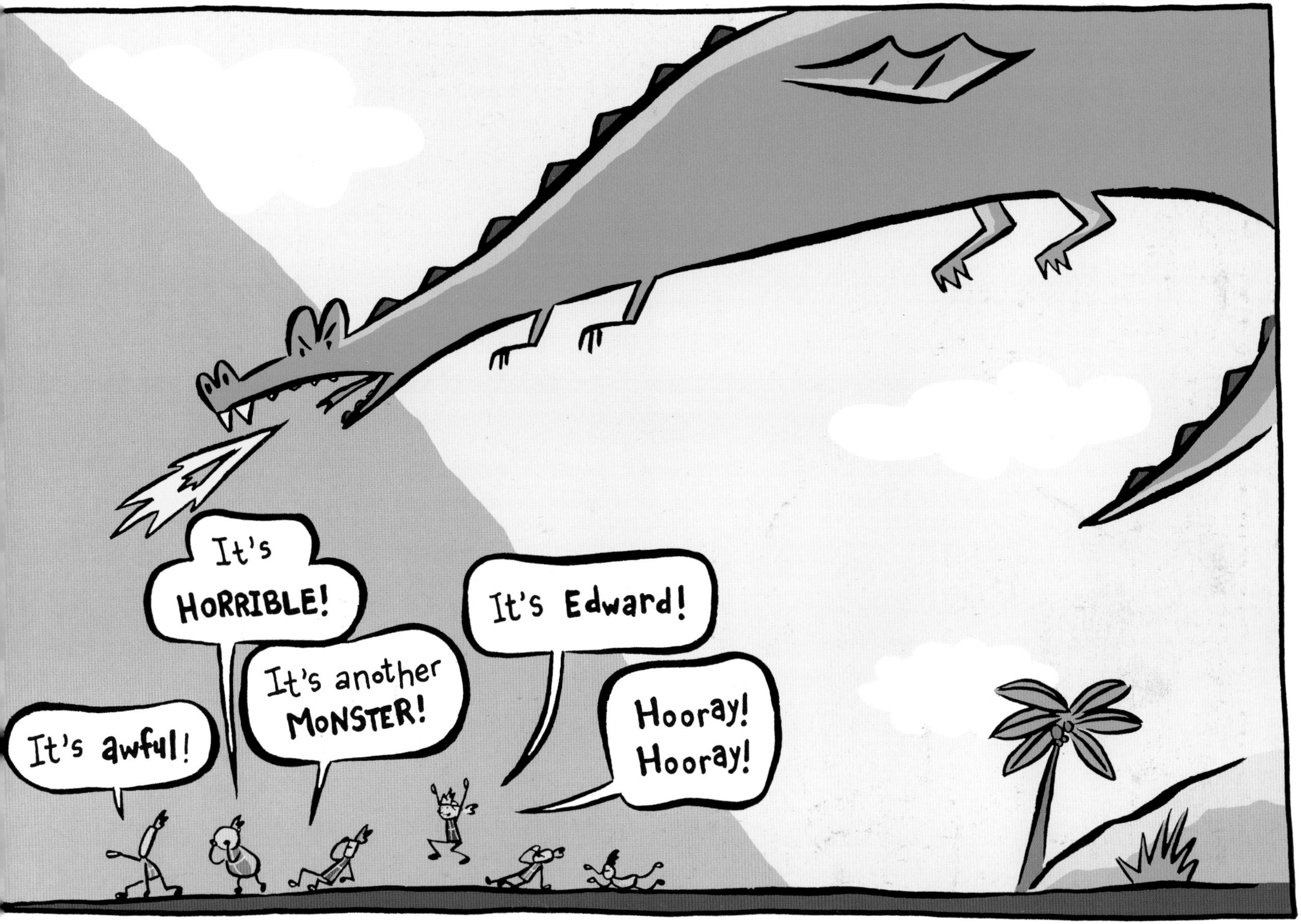
It's awful!
It's HORRIBLE!
It's another MONSTER!
It's Edward!
Hooray! Hooray!

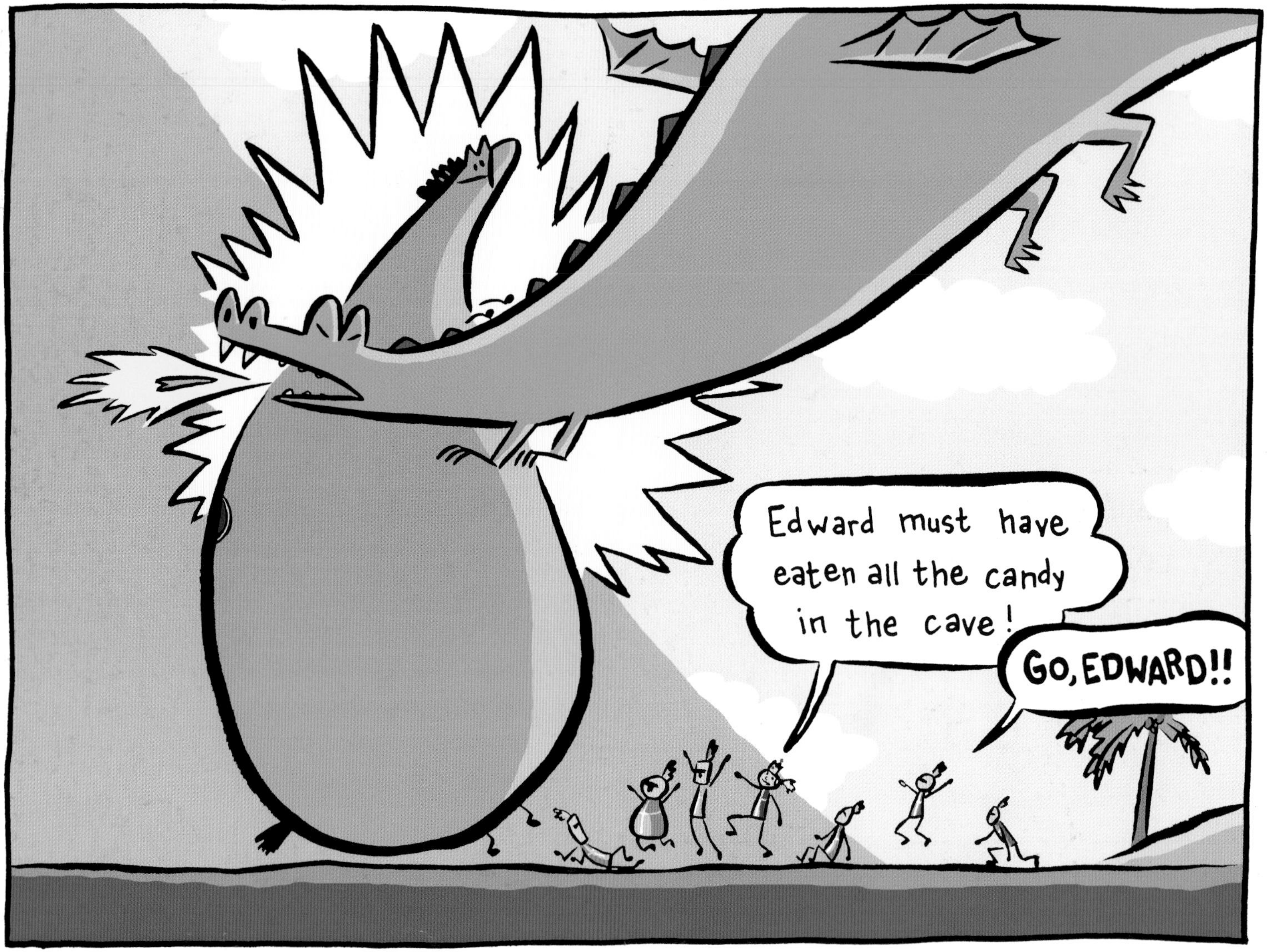
Edward must have eaten all the candy in the cave!
GO, EDWARD!!

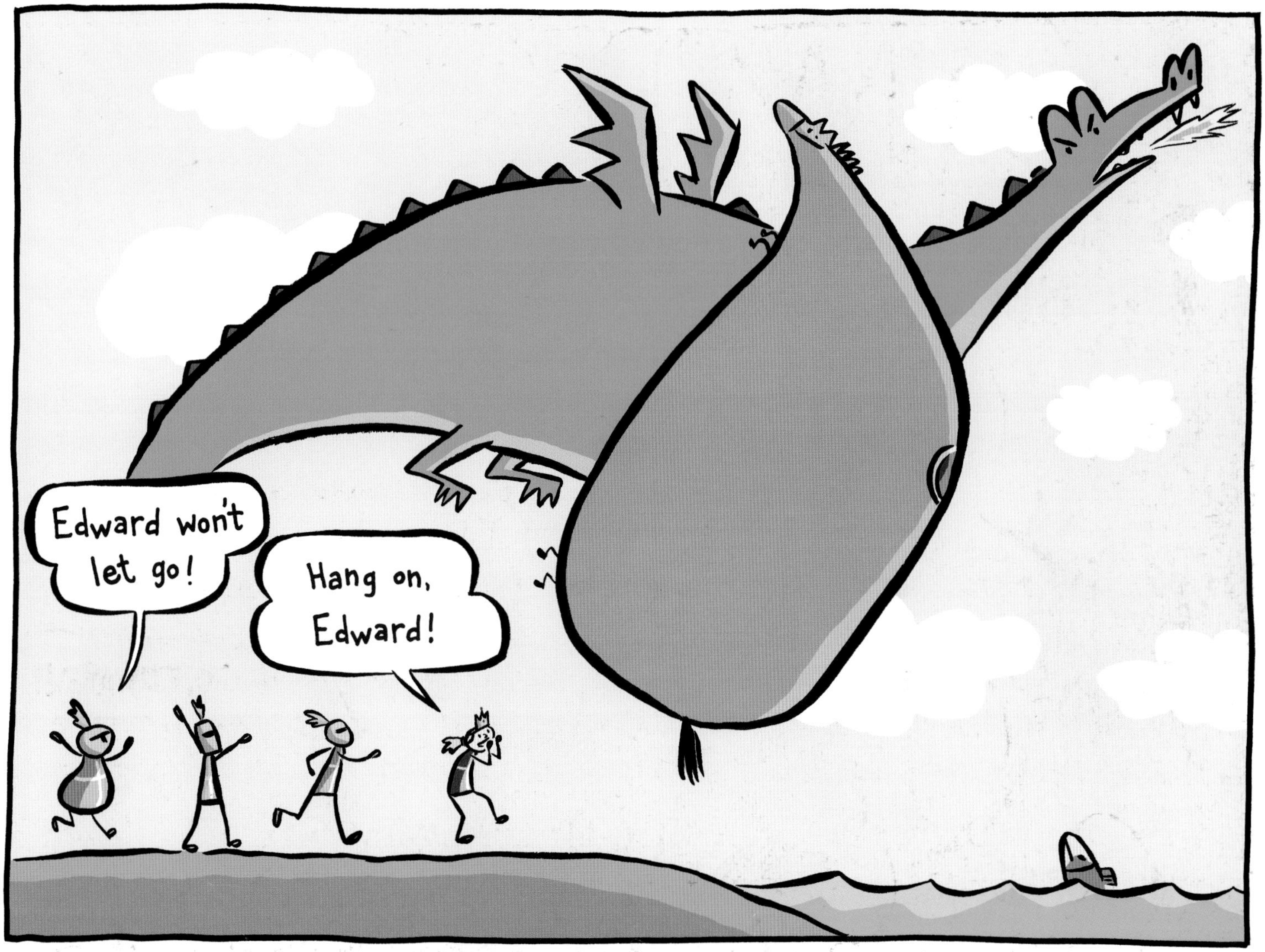
Edward won't let go!
Hang on, Edward!

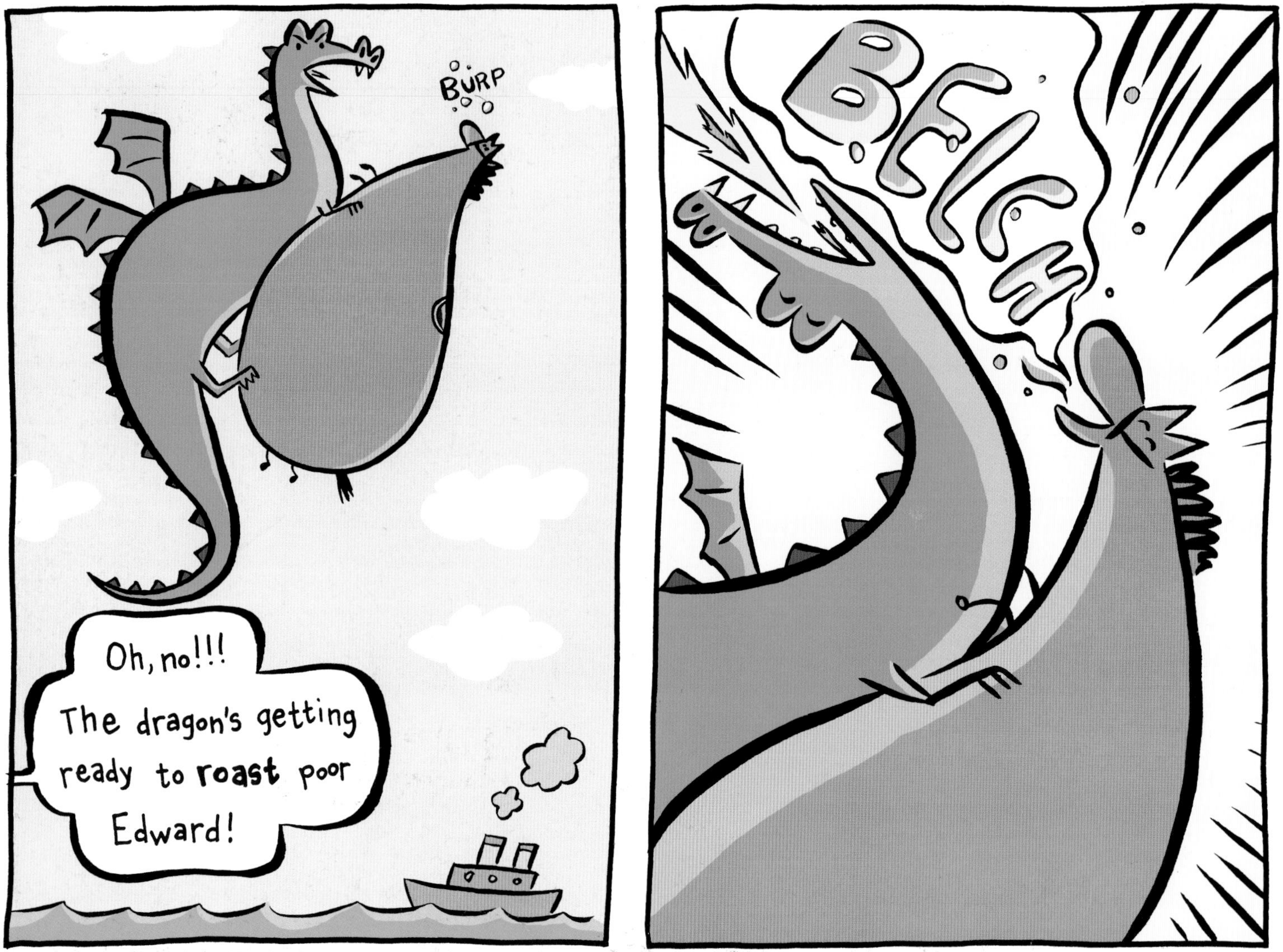
BURP
Oh, no!!! The dragon's getting ready to roast poor Edward!
BELCH

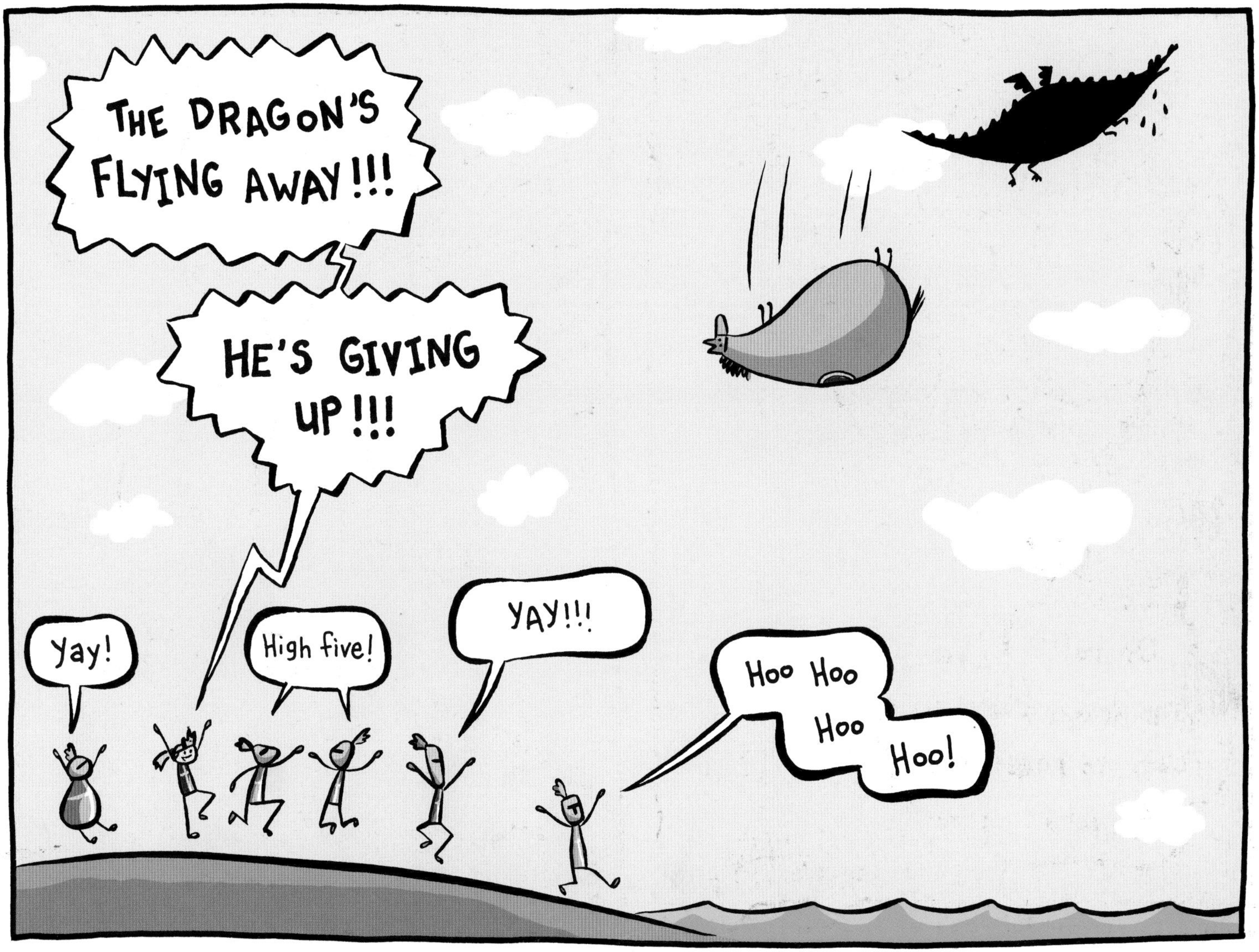
THE DRAGON'S FLYING AWAY!!!
HE'S GIVING UP!!!
Yay!
High five!
YAY!!!
Hoo Hoo Hoo Hoo!

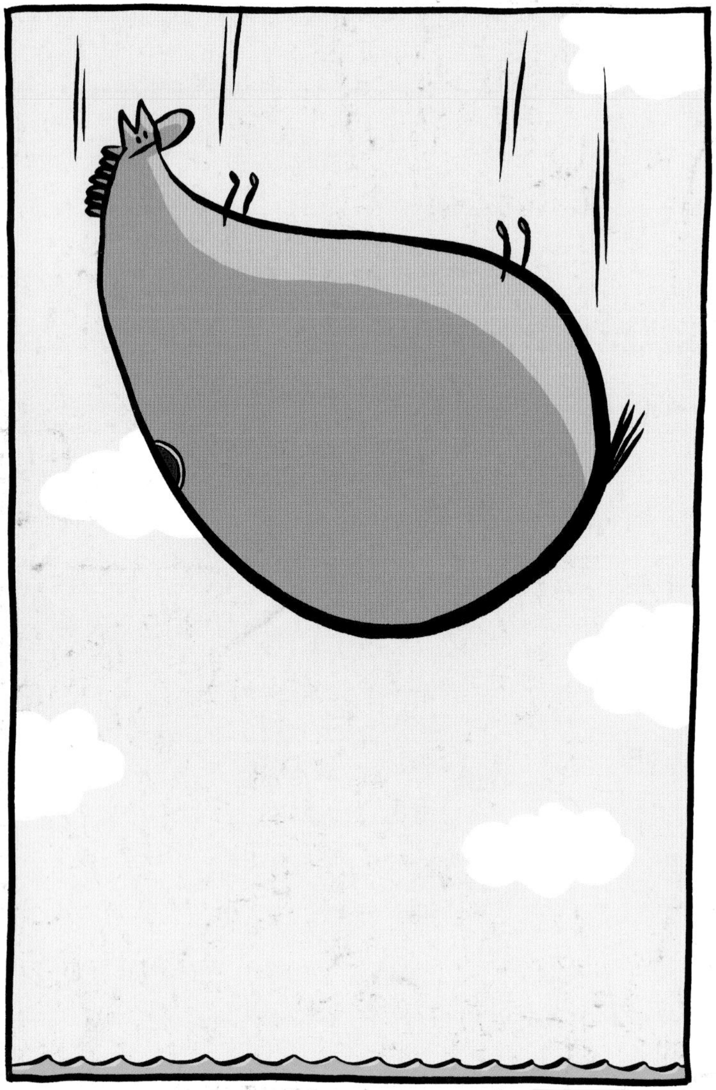

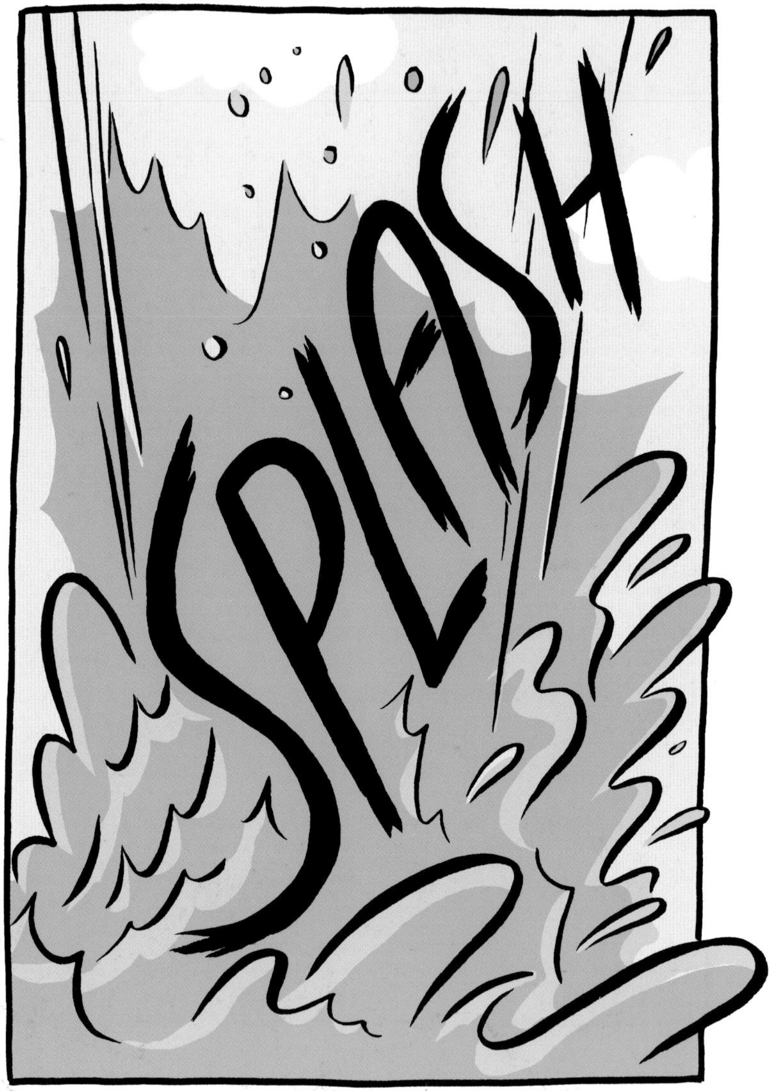
SPLASH

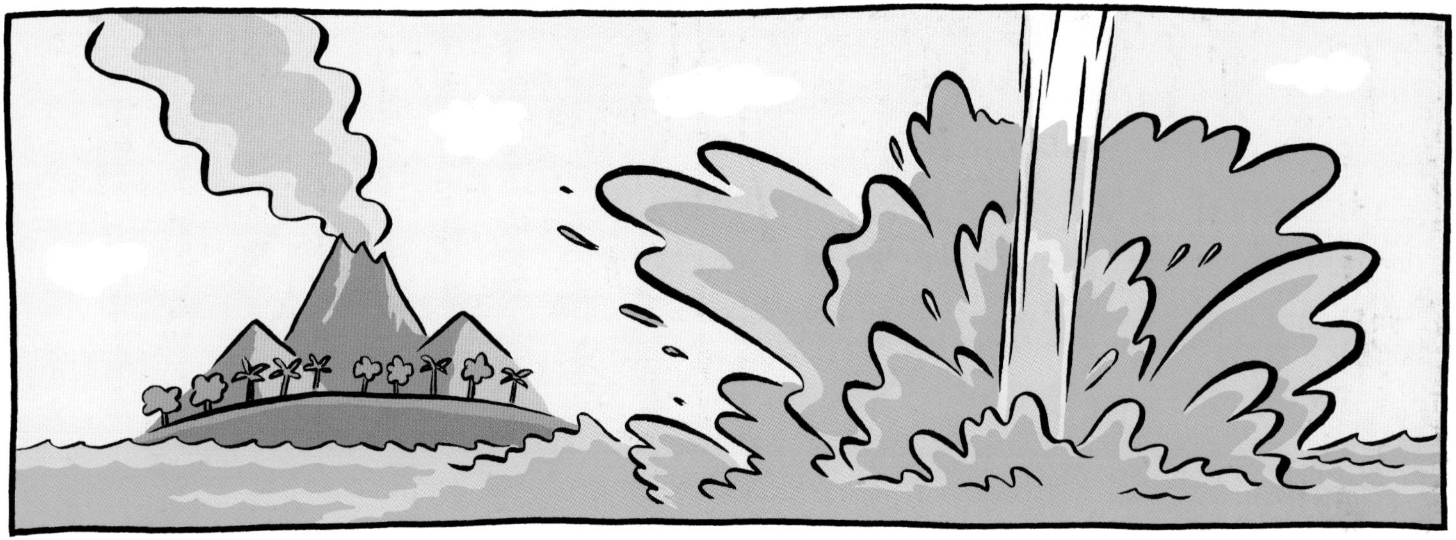

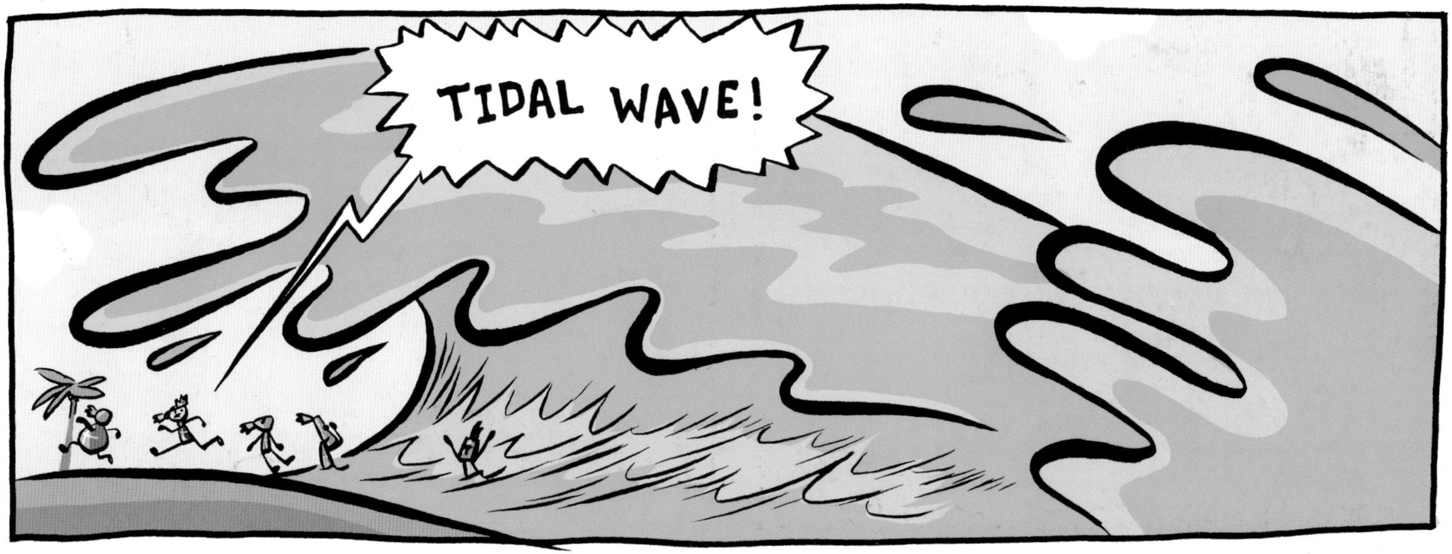
TIDAL WAVE!

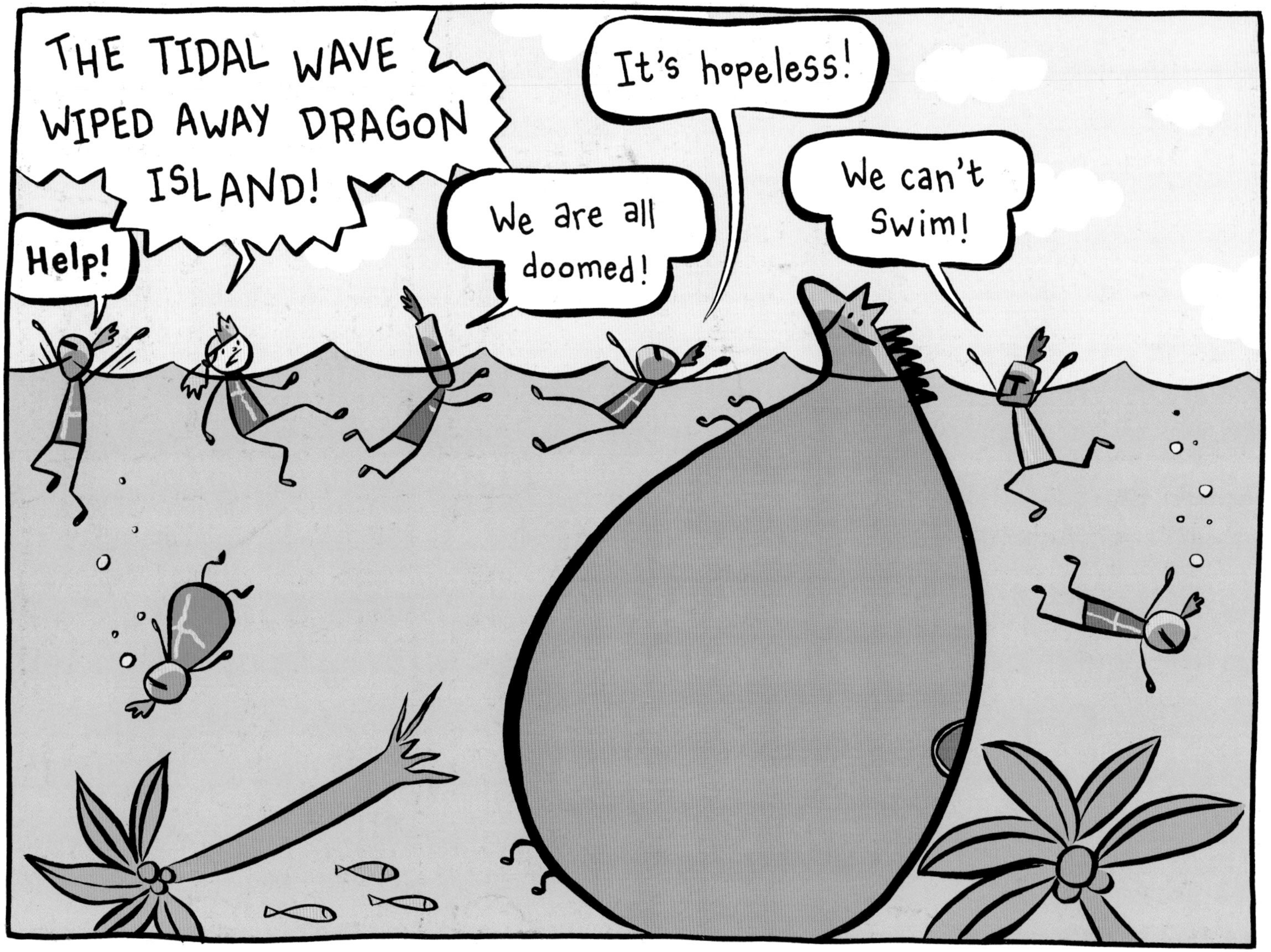
THE TIDAL WAVE WIPED AWAY DRAGON ISLAND!
Help!
We are all doomed!
It's hopeless!
We can't Swim!

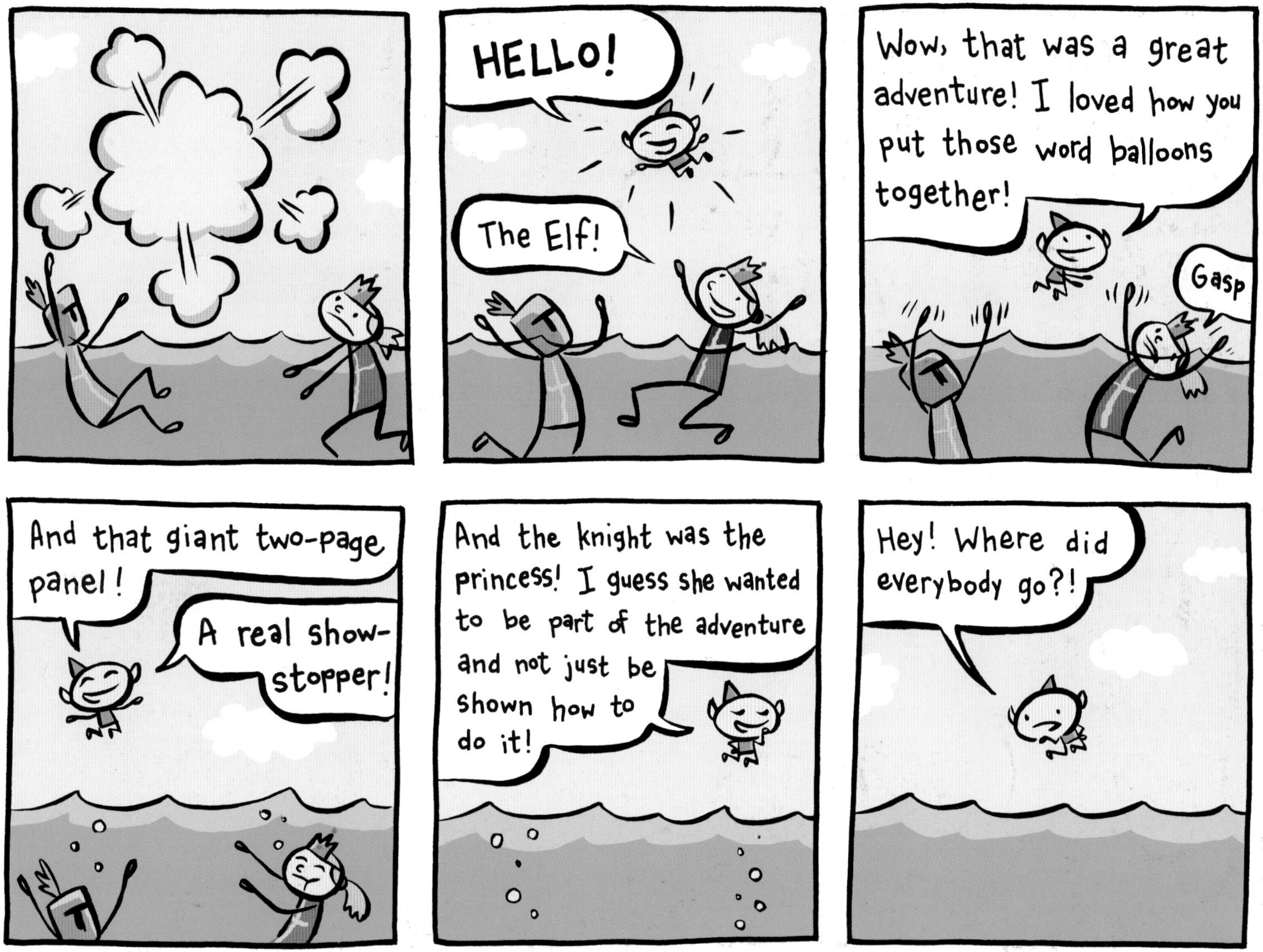
HELLO!
The Elf!
Wow, that was a great adventure! I loved how you put those word balloons together!
Gasp
And that giant two-page panel!
A real show-stopper!
And the knight was the princess! I guess she wanted to be part of the adventure and not just be shown how to do it!
Hey! Where did everybody go?!

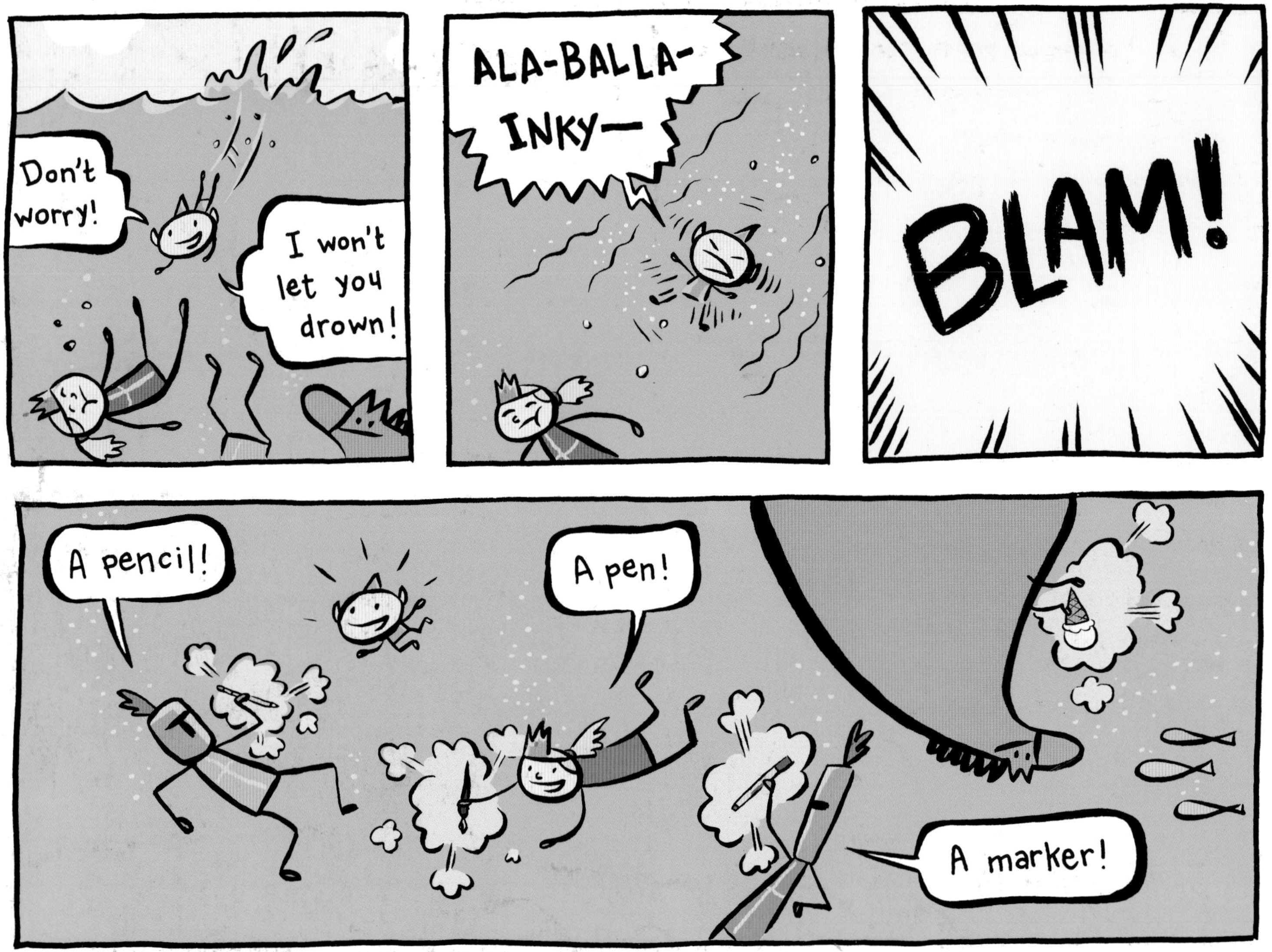
Don't worry!
I won't let you drown!
ALA-BALLA-INKY—
BLAM!
A pencil!
A pen!
A marker!

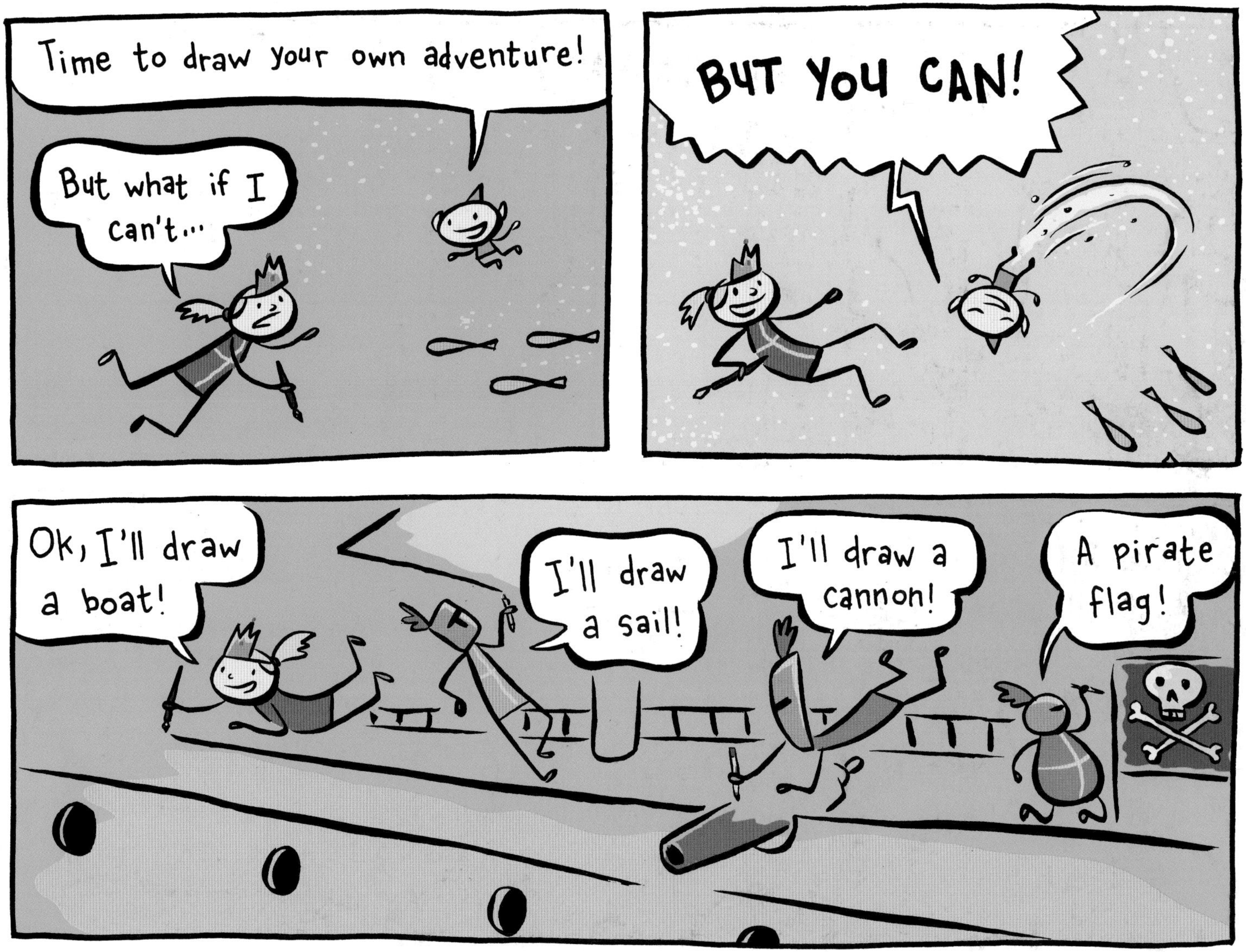
Time to draw your own adventure!
But what if I can't...
BUT YOU CAN!
Ok, I'll draw a boat!
I'll draw a sail!
I'll draw a cannon!
A pirate flag!

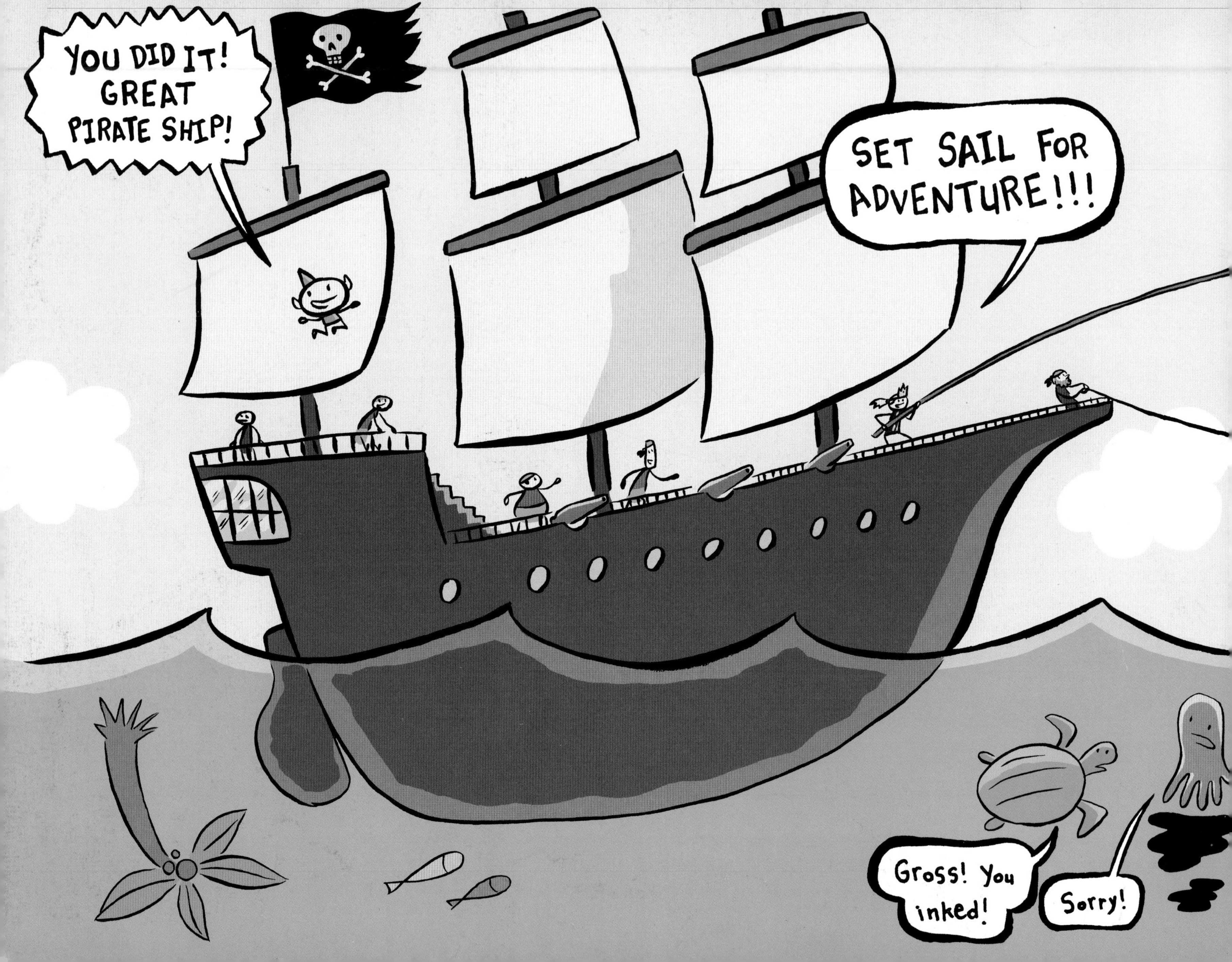
YOU DID IT! GREAT PIRATE SHIP!
SET SAIL FOR ADVENTURE!!!
Gross! You inked!
Sorry!

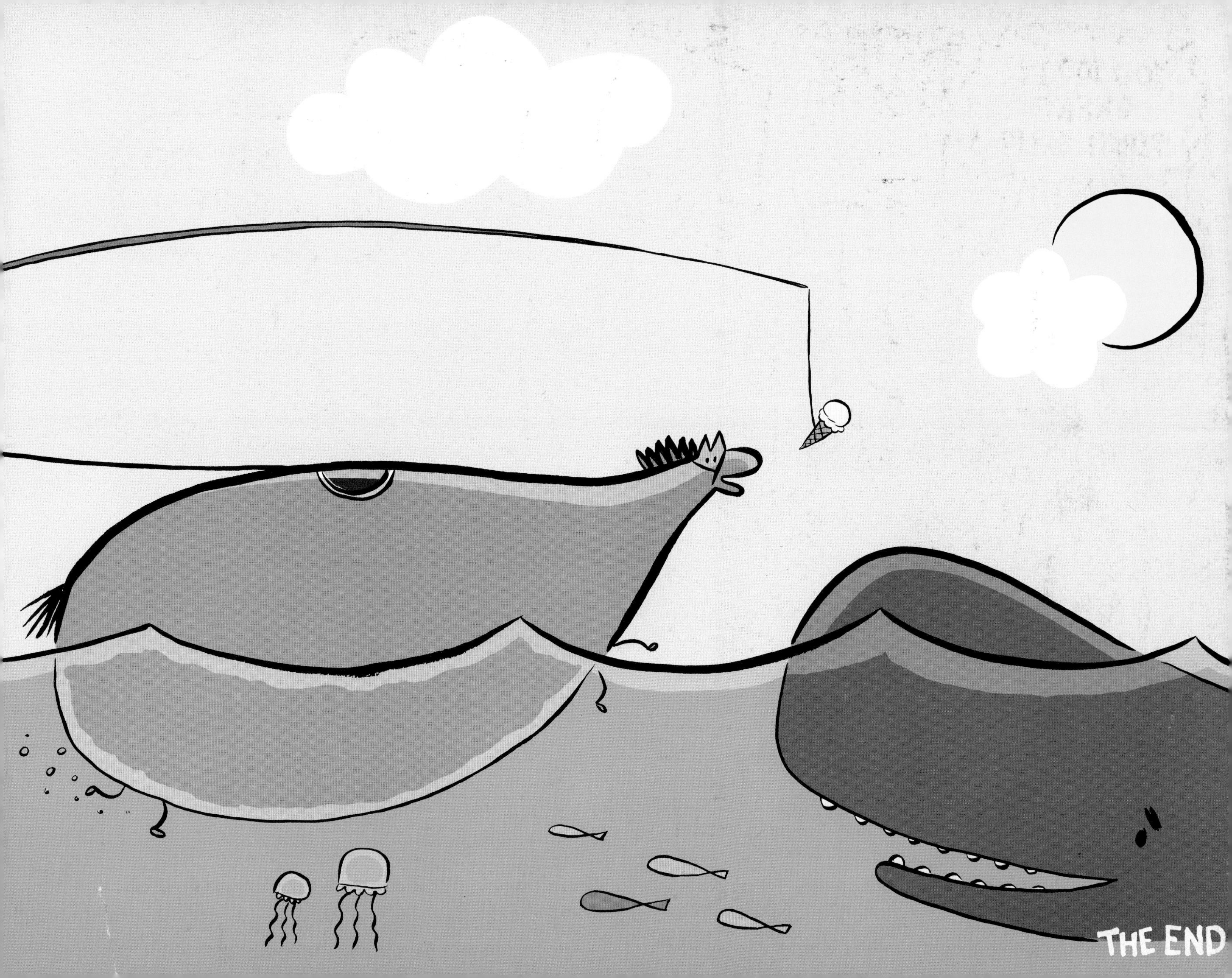
THE END

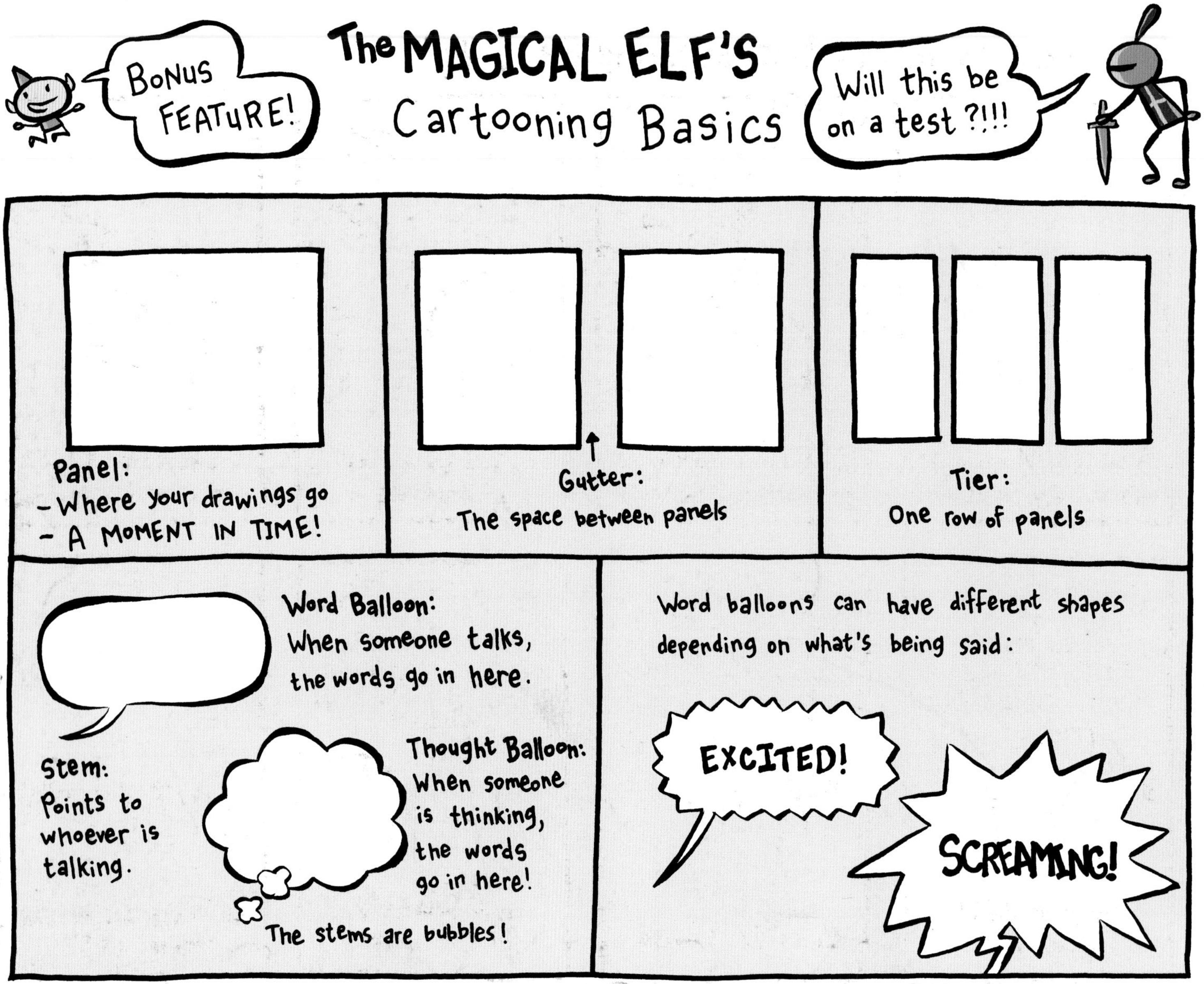
BONUS FEATURE!
The MAGICAL ELF'S
Cartooning Basics
Will this be on a test ?!!!
Panel:
- Where your drawings go
- A MOMENT IN TIME!
Gutter:
The space between panels
Tier:
One row of panels
Word Balloon:
When someone talks, the words go in here.
Stem:
Points to whoever is talking.
Thought Balloon:
When someone is thinking, the words go in here!
The stems are bubbles!
Word balloons can have different shapes depending on what's being said:
EXCITED!
SCREAMING!

Advanced cartooning tips starring **Edward!**

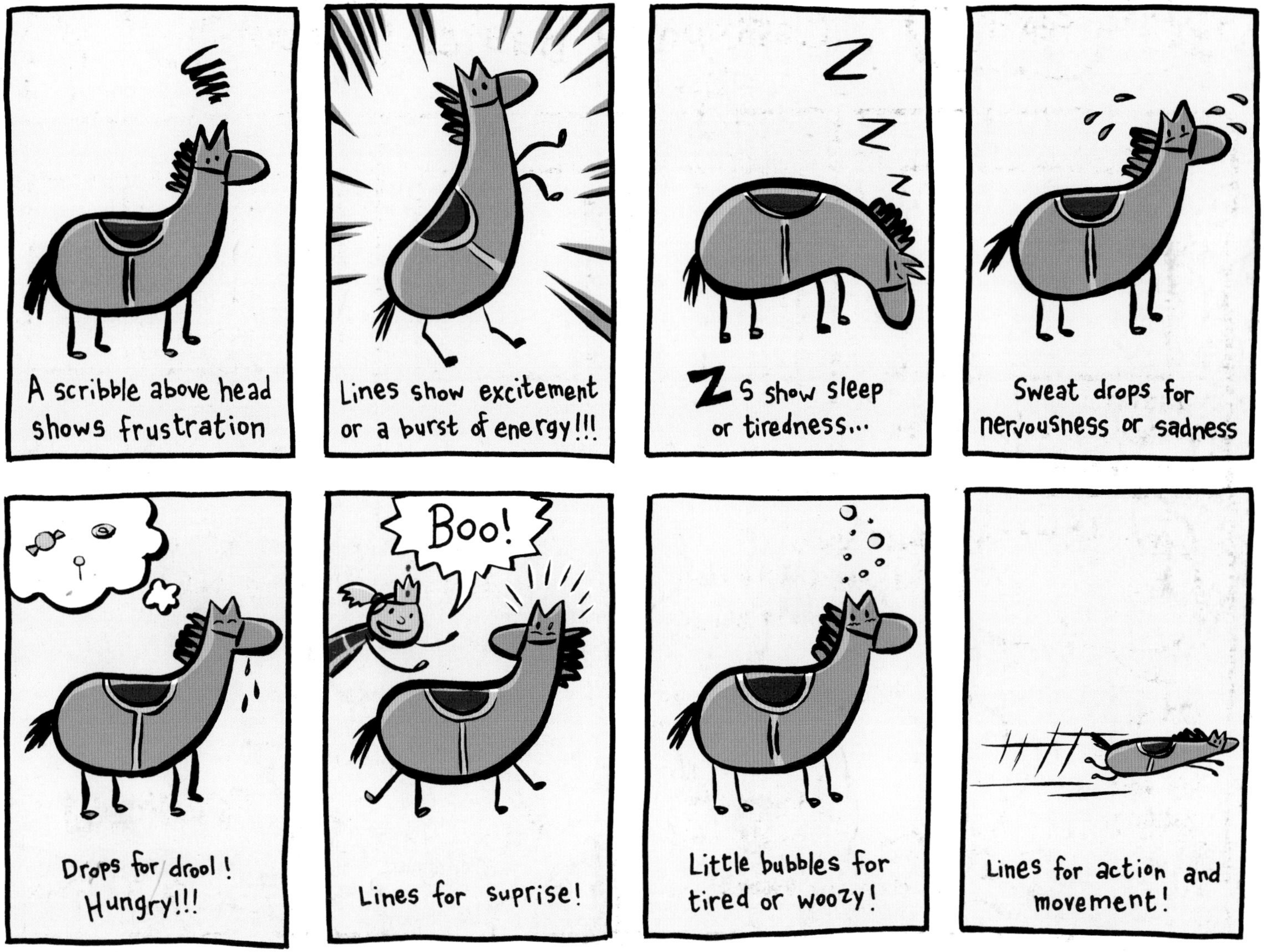
A scribble above head shows frustration
Lines show excitement or a burst of energy!!!
Z Z Z
Z s show sleep or tiredness...
Sweat drops for nervousness or sadness
Drops for drool! Hungry!!!
Boo!
Lines for suprise!
Little bubbles for tired or woozy!
Lines for action and movement!

This book grew out of an assignment given by James Sturm at the Center for Cartoon Studies in White River Junction, VT using Ed Emberly's book, **Make a World**, as inspiration. Alexis Frederick-Frost and Andrew Arnold were students in the school's very first class! Thanks, Ed Emberly!

For more information on the Center for Cartoon Studies, visit www.cartoonstudies.org

The knight

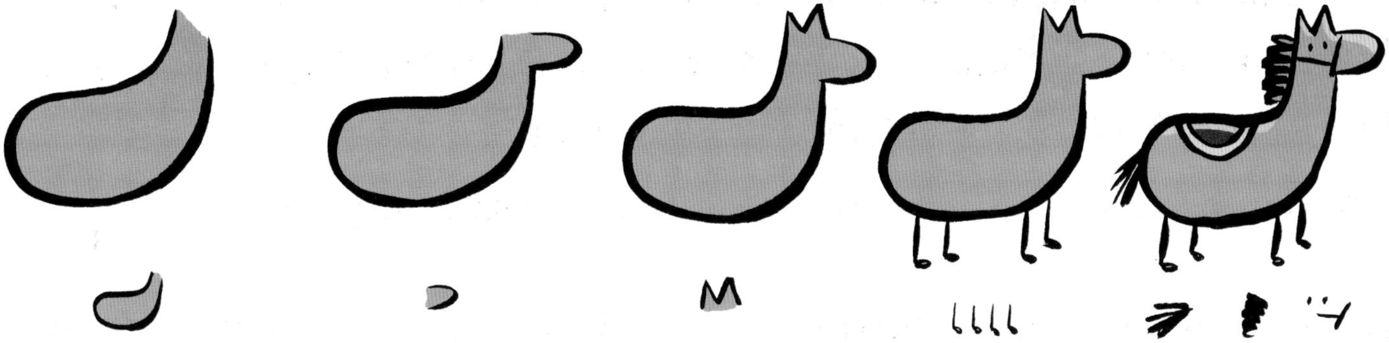

Edward

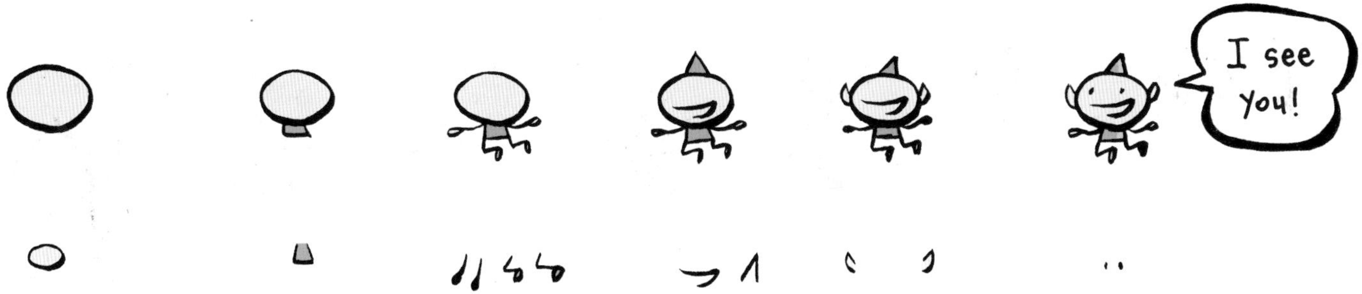
I see you!

Elf

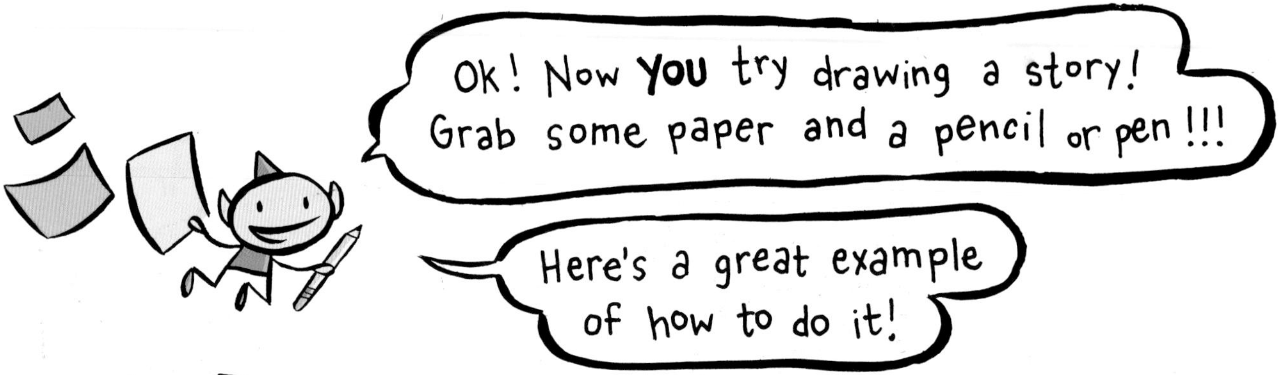
Ok! Now YOU try drawing a story! Grab some paper and a pencil or pen!!!
Here's a great example of how to do it!

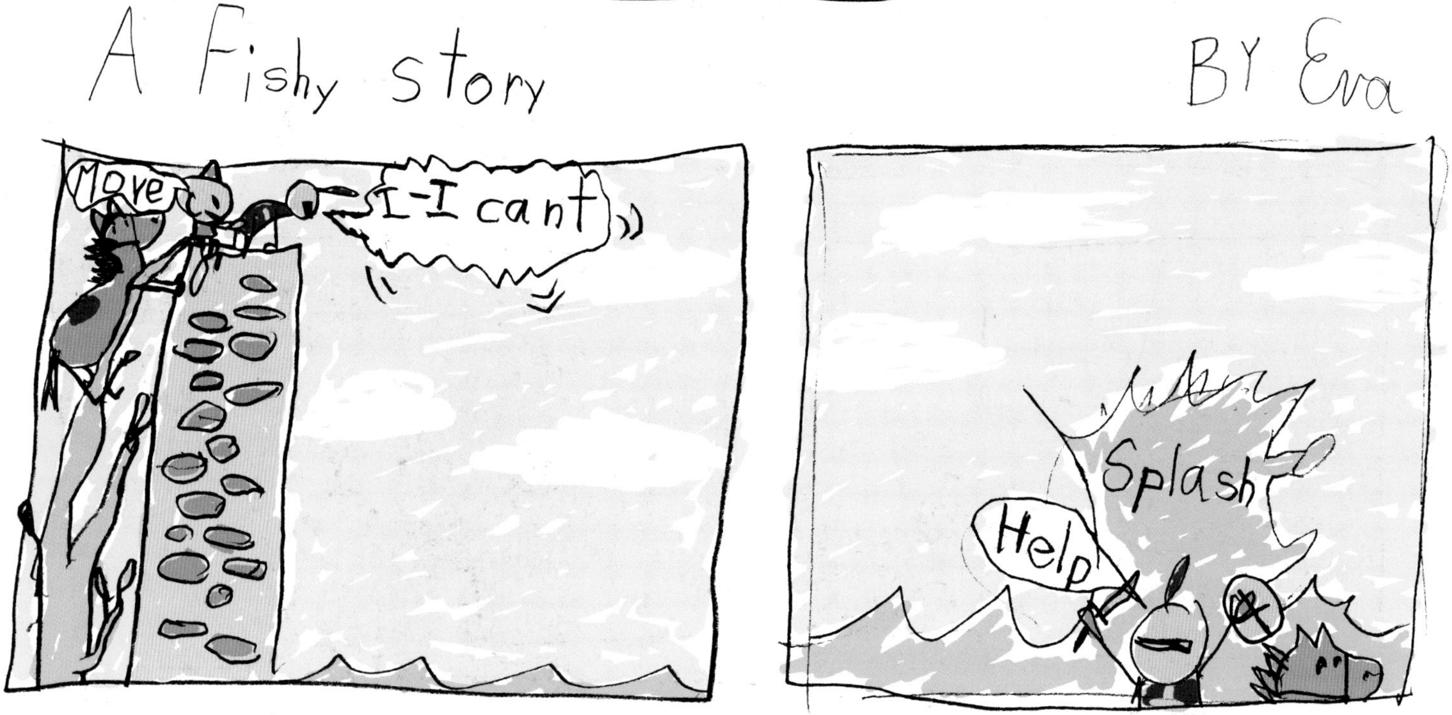
A Fishy story
BY Eva
Move
I-I cant
Splash
Help

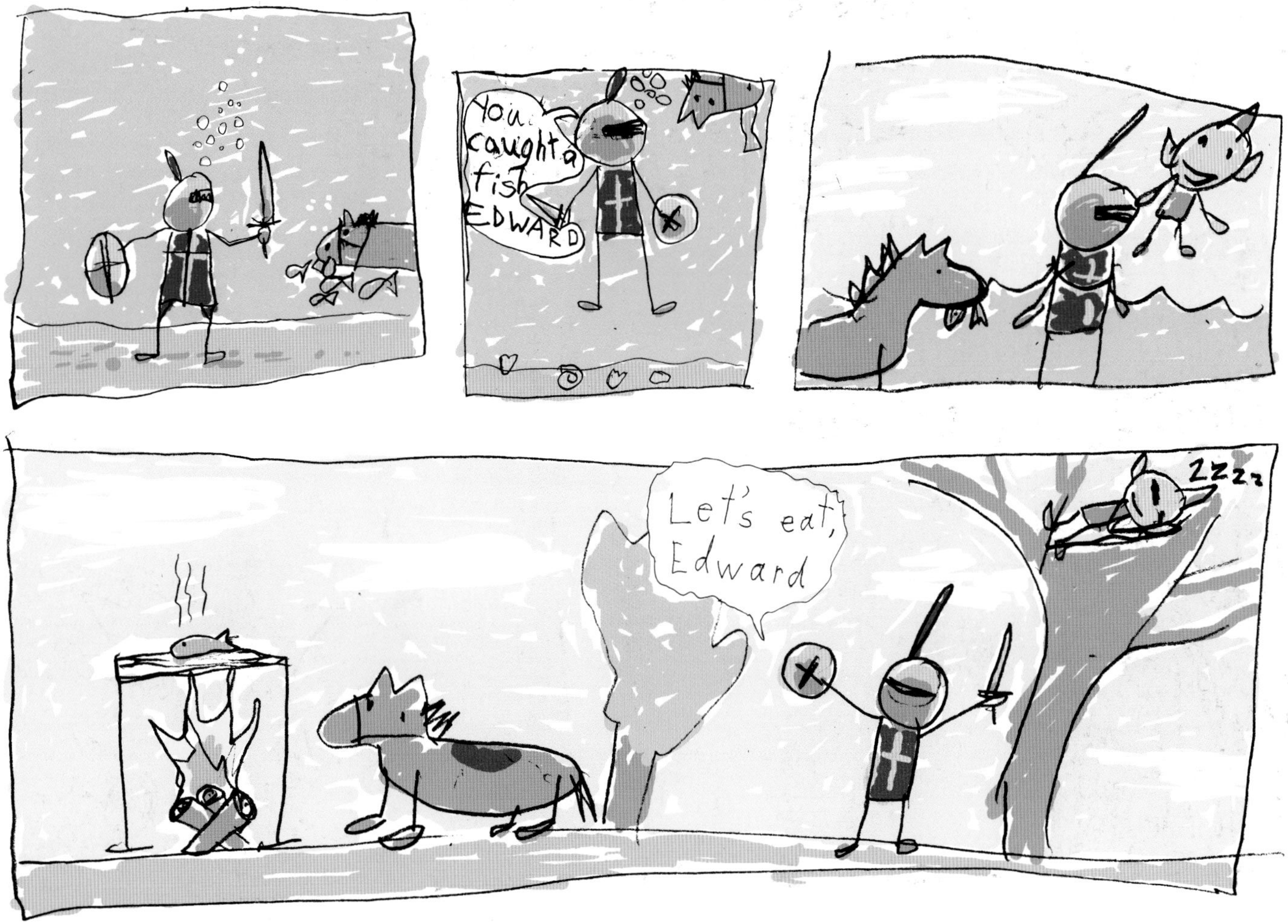
You caught a fish EDWARD
Let's eat, Edward
ZZzz

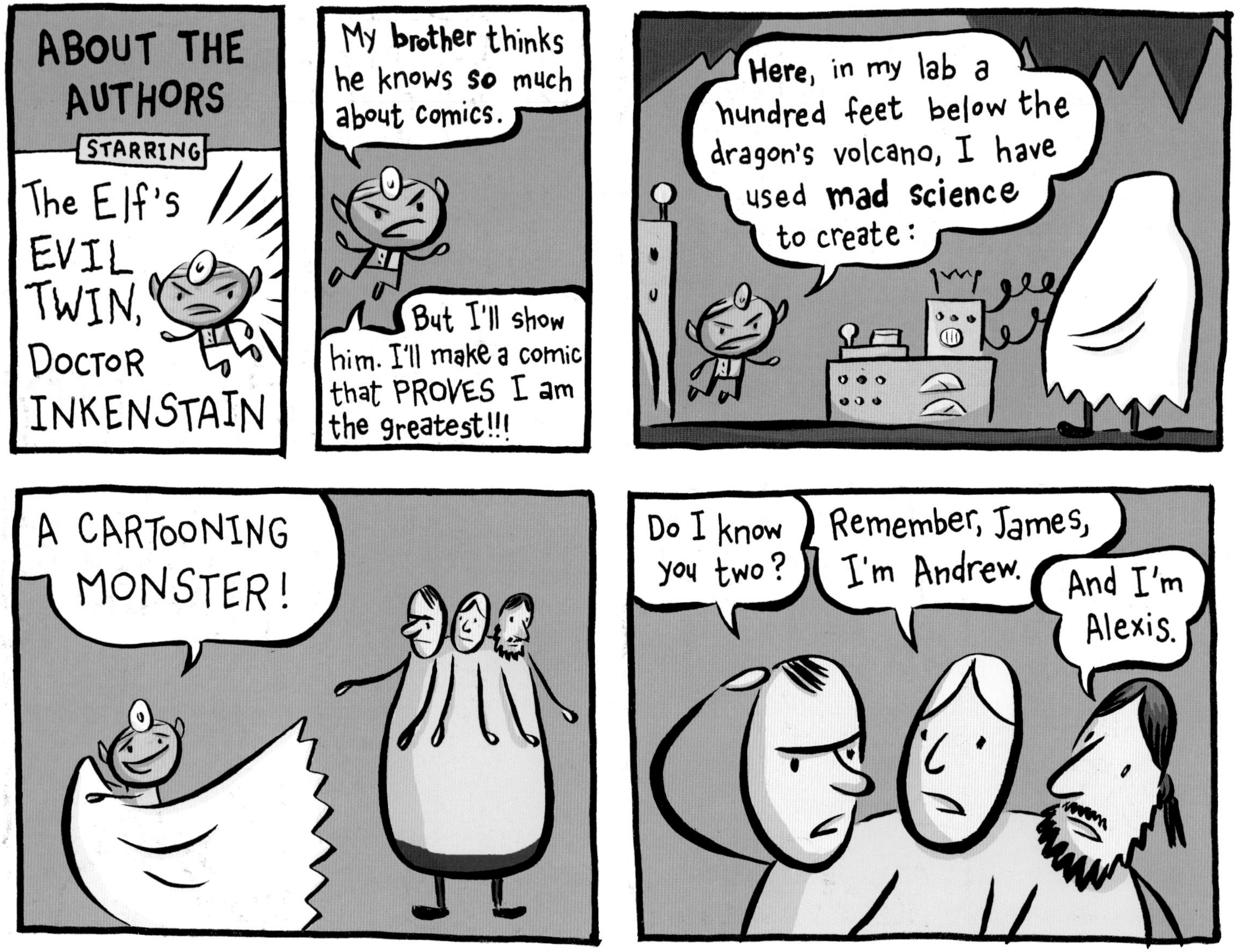
ABOUT THE AUTHORS
STARRING
The Elf's EVIL TWIN, DOCTOR INKENSTAIN
My brother thinks he knows so much about comics.
But I'll show him. I'll make a comic that PROVES I am the greatest!!!
Here, in my lab a hundred feet below the dragon's volcano, I have used mad science to create:
A CARTOONING MONSTER!
Do I know you two?
Remember, James, I'm Andrew.
And I'm Alexis.

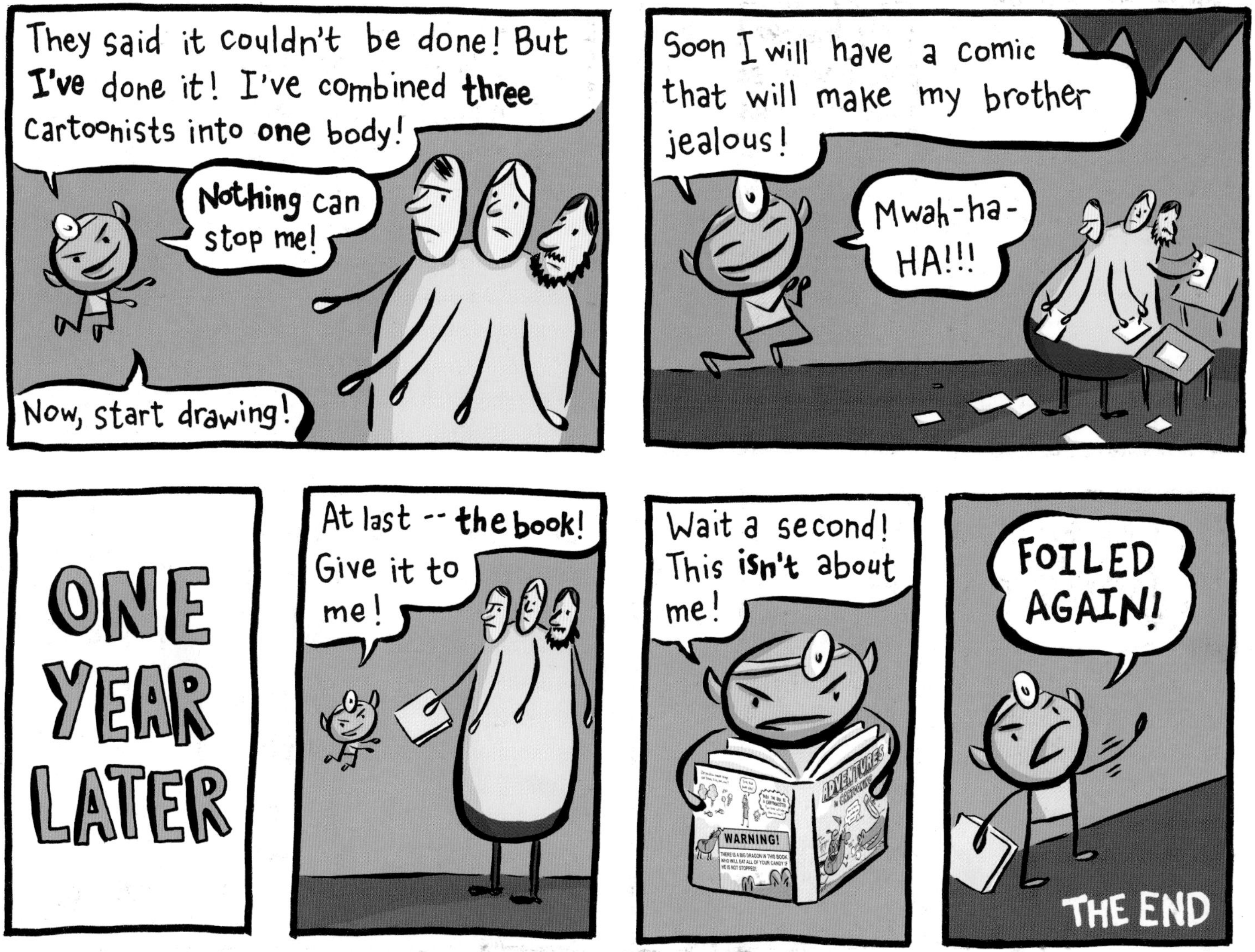
They said it couldn't be done! But I've done it! I've combined three cartoonists into one body!
Nothing can stop me!
Now, start drawing!
Soon I will have a comic that will make my brother jealous!
Mwah-ha-HA!!!
ONE YEAR LATER
At last -- the book! Give it to me!
Wait a second! This isn't about me!
WARNING!
FOILED AGAIN!
THE END

:01
First Second
New York & London

Published by First Second
First Second is an imprint of Roaring Brook Press, a division of
Holtzbrinck Publishing Holdings Limited Partnership
175 Fifth Avenue, New York, NY 10010

Distributed in Canada by H.B. Fenn and Company Ltd.
Distributed in the United Kingdom by Macmillan Children's Books,
a division of Pan Macmillan.

Cataloging-in-Publication Data is on file at the Library of Congress
ISBN: 978-1-59643-369-4

First Second Books are available for special promotions and premiums.
For details, contact: Director of Special Markets, Holtzbrinck Publishers.

FIRST EDITION
First Edition April 2009
Printed in July 2010 by South China Printing Co. Ltd.,
Dongguan City, Guangdong Province

7 9 10 8 6

BY ART WE LIVE

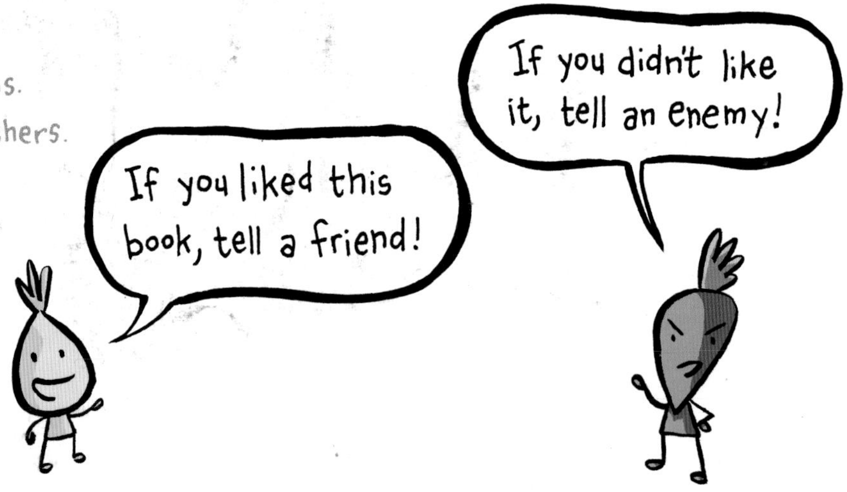
If you liked this book, tell a friend!
If you didn't like it, tell an enemy!

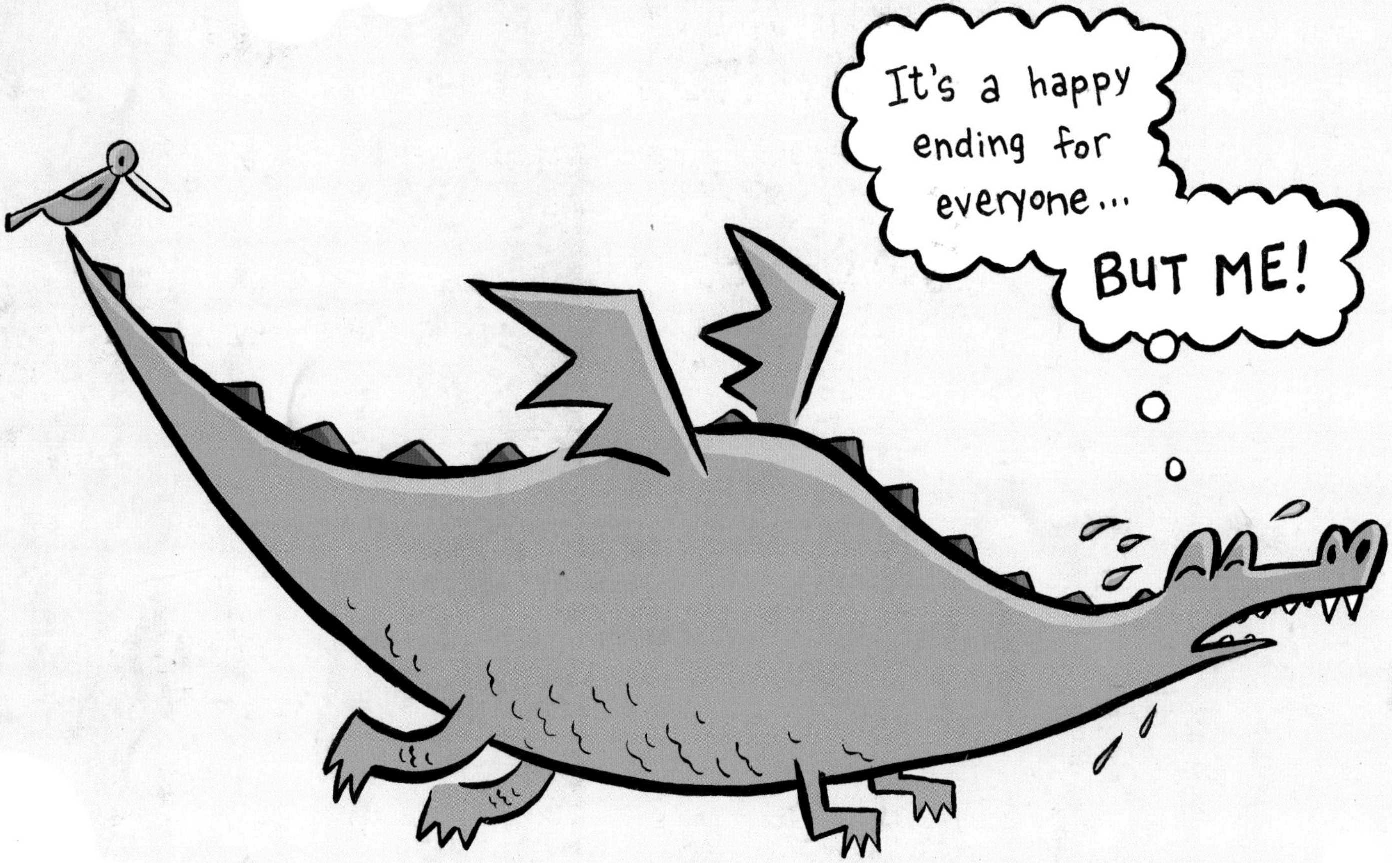
It's a happy ending for everyone...
BUT ME!

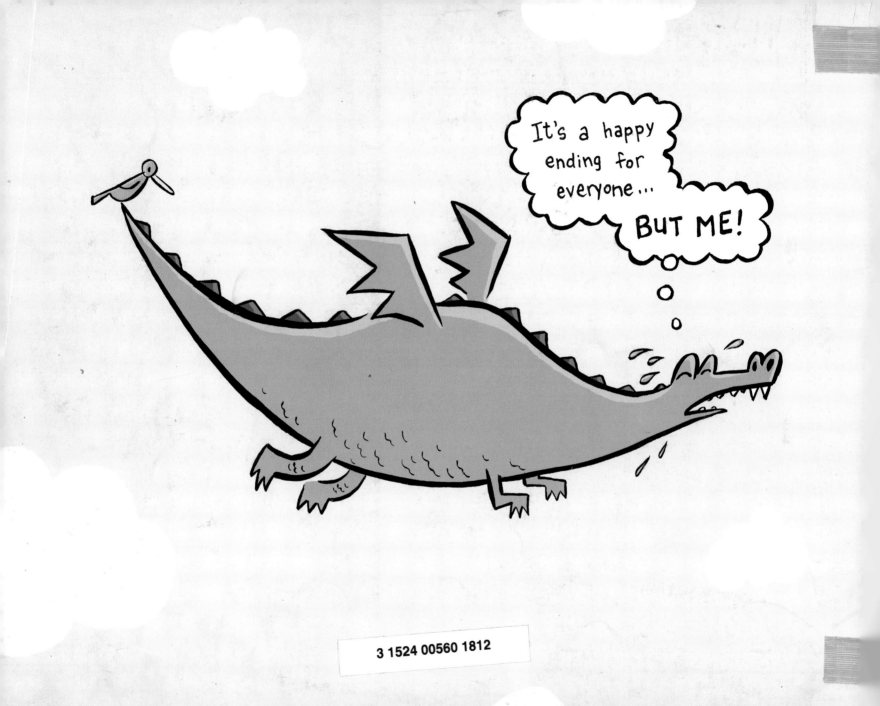

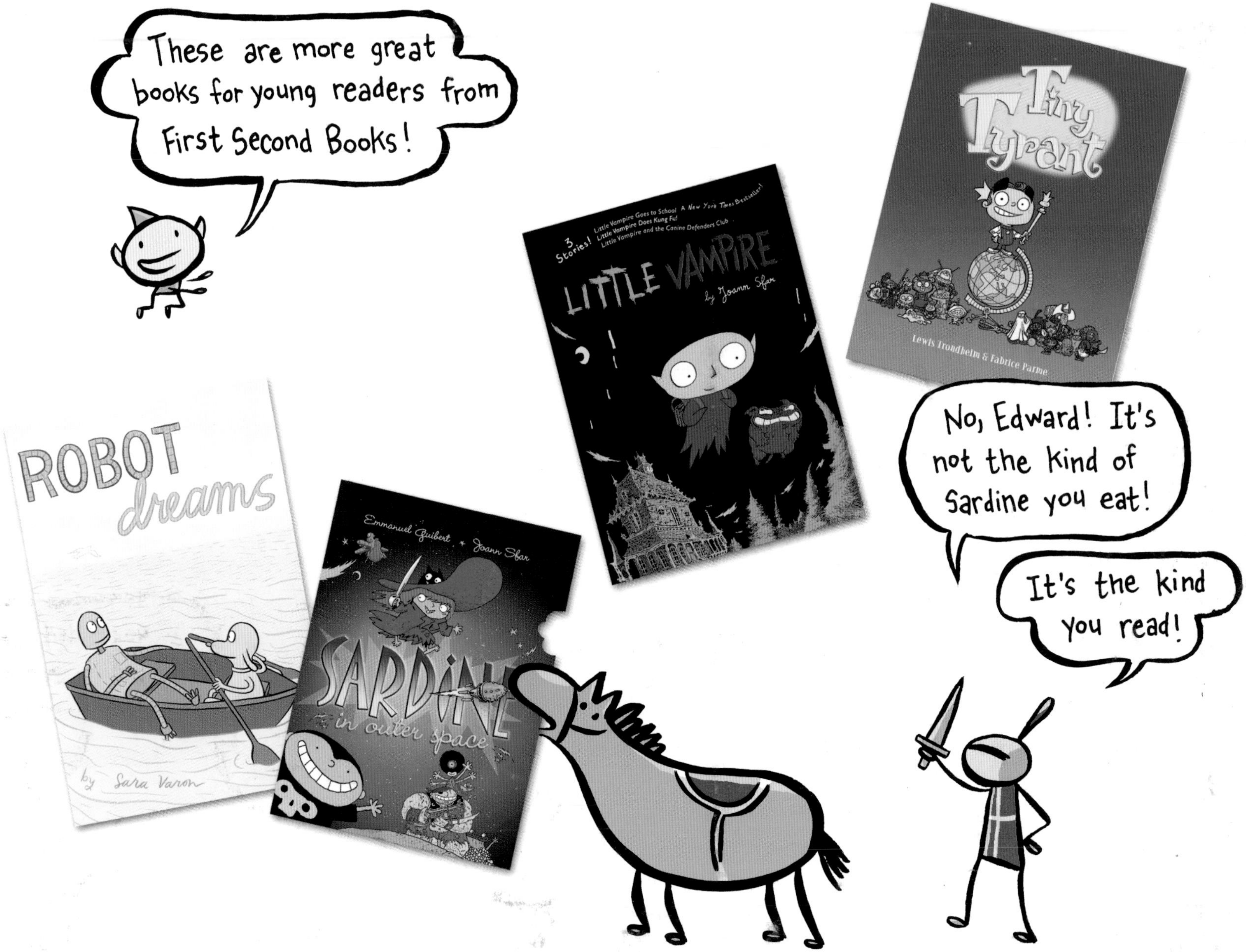
These are more great books for young readers from First Second Books!
3 Stories!
Little Vampire Goes to School
A New York Times Bestseller!
Little Vampire Does Kung Fu!
Little Vampire and the Canine Defenders Club
LITTLE VAMPIRE
by Joann Sfar
Tiny Tyrant
Lewis Trondheim & Fabrice Parme
ROBOT dreams
by Sara Varon
Emmanuel Guibert
Joann Sfar
SARDINE in outer space
No, Edward! It's not the kind of Sardine you eat!
It's the kind you read!